I0698764

Feral Winter: Book Two

MUTATE

Benjamin Rempel

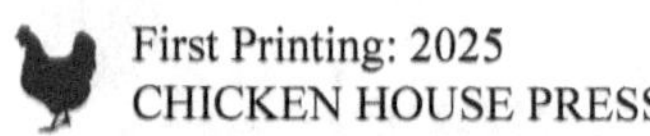

First Printing: 2025
CHICKEN HOUSE PRESS

Library and Archives Canada Cataloguing in Publication
CIP data on file with the National Library and Archives

ISBN trade paperback edition: 978-1-997584-05-6

Publishers note: Information on EEEV adapted and fictionalized from: Ontario Agency for Health Protection and Promotion. Eastern equine encephalitis: history and enhanced surveillance in Ontario. Toronto, ON: Queen's Printer for Ontario; 2014.

Author photo by Kimberly Vincent Photography

Chicken House Press
282906 Normanby/Bentinck Townline
Durham, Ontario, Canada, N0G 1R0
www.chickenhousepress.ca

We acknowledge the support of the Canada Council for the Arts.

To Amy, always
And Asia, also
And Will, of course

Other works by Benjamin Rempel

Novels:

Infect

Short Fiction:

Out From the Grey Barn
Last Shift
Small Town Monster
In Search of Damien
The Magician's Last Trick

This may get worse…

MUTATE

Benjamin Rempel

MOTEL

Chapter One

November 1995
Day 637 | Before Dawn

Evelyn Stone hurried along the dark forest floor, her boots treading over the crusted snow. Even in the black of night she seemed to know where to step, how to press down to not make a sound. Each stride was careful and true, rarely snagging or slipping, as she hustled through the dense brush and crowded clasp of trees.

Slowing to a trot, she removed her gloves, rubbing her hands together, blowing puffs of warm air on them. She wriggled her nose as a stink of icy mulch and rotted leaves rose up from the frozen earth.

Tugging at the tattered leather strap, she tightened the rifle against her spine. A bowie knife hung from her cargo pants, a flashlight shoved into a pocket. She shivered then zipped up her camouflaged jacket, the frayed wool collar scratching at her throat.

Her eyes darted between the trees. As she drew in the crisp November air, she felt her way around a fallen trunk, her fingers spidering along the wood, each touch telling a story.

Get down, the tree seemed to say. *Stay low*.

Or was that Damien's voice? *Stay low, Ev*, the voice seemed to whisper. *Danger is near.*

She crouched, alert to the sounds of the forest. A skunk digging for dinner, the sharp trill of crickets, the screech of a saw-whet owl. And then a different sound. Something large, lumbering toward her.

Slipping her hands back in her gloves, she turned and furrowed deeper into the bush away from the noise; a wiry body pulsing with fear and rage, all packed in, ready to erupt.

She snaked through the snow-dusted scrub and brushwood until she heard the angry swill of the creek. As she neared the water, the wind picked up, the winter air furious against her olive skin, seething its way through her sleek, midnight-black hair.

"Storm's coming," she whispered.

Several paces behind, a man grunted. Nearly invisible, he resembled a wraith in the darkness. "Still a few hours off," he grumbled.

A monster of a man, Xavier dwarfed his younger cousin as he came up behind her. Dressed in stained camouflaged overalls and black rubber boots, he was almost indistinguishable from the gnarled oaks and tall shadowed pines surrounding him. His black hair was cropped close to the head, his skin dry and coarse as sandpaper, his face pocked with stubble and tufts of beard along his square jaw.

With calloused hands rough from carpentry, he fidgeted with the aged rifle strap hanging from his broad chest and shoulders. The tart smell of forest oils and woodsmoke leaked from his pores as he secured the eight-inch knife to his thigh.

He studied the sky. "She's brewing, that's for sure. But still a few hours before she opens up."

They continued their cautious advance along the shore of the creek until they came to the base of a hornbeam. Evelyn flicked the flashlight on, assessed their surroundings, then cut the light.

"Tree's wide enough for both of us, lots of low branches for cover," she said, as if reciting a checklist. "Still upwind from anything approaching from the south. Seems a good spot."

"Jesus, who's teaching who?" Xavier said, eyeing the girl. "Take you on half a dozen hunts and you've got it all figured out, huh?"

Evelyn smirked. "Had a good teacher."

Xavier shrugged out of his heavy backpack of rope, water, matches, cartridges, a hatchet, a wool sweater, an extra pair of socks, needle-nose pliers, zip ties, a compass, a thermos.

Rummaging through the bag, he removed the thermos and unscrewed the top, tilting a flow of steaming coffee into the overturned lid. He removed an errant hair from the rim, blew on the liquid, then gulped half of it down. He leaned his rifle alongside the tree then sat against its trunk.

"Won't they smell that?" Evelyn asked.

Xavier took a second swig. "Worth the risk. Besides, I'm useless without it."

"Twenty-one and already addicted to coffee?"

Xavier smiled then placed the drink down, reaching deep into the snow on either side of him. He clawed underneath it, bringing it up to mix with the dirt and dead leaves, creating a cacophony of shades and textures. He spread the potluck of nature over his legs.

"To blend in with the terrain," he explained as Evelyn looked on with curious eyes.

Following his lead, she sat then covered her lower half with snow and dirt until she was more in the ground than on it. An icy dampness slithered up her body. "Now we wait?"

"Now we wait."

Evelyn nodded and they both fell into an uneasy silence.

She had grown considerably since moving into her cousins' farmhouse last summer. She stretched close to five-and-a-half feet now and her body was powerful, the result of dragging felled trees and hauling stacks of lumber about the property.

With Damien gone and her mother still missing, she took to her cousins like a duck to water, soaking in knowledge like a sponge.

Andrew showed her how to fish, the correct spinner to use, the proper weight of line, and where the bass hid amongst the rocks.

Xavier taught her how to hunt, how to approach without a sound, how to be patient for the kill. He instilled in her the importance of staying calm and steadying her breath, ensuring the shot is true.

Andrew encouraged her in her studies; Xavier protected her like a staunch guardian.

She discovered the value of hard work, attacking the day before the sun, the worth of dirt on your boots and sweat on your brow, the importance of honesty and toil and sacrifice.

She grew in other ways too, gradually understanding how she contributed best to their makeshift family. She reflected on the teachings of her mother to appreciate her reciprocal relationship with the natural world, the sacredness of it all. She thought about her relations, her role in community, her evolving part in all of it.

And as the weeks turned over, a calmness spread through her; a burgeoning confidence she now wore like a warm winter coat.

In the forest, a whip of wind caused her to shiver. She cracked her rifle open and stared down the breech, checking for bullets. Snapping it shut, she brought it to her eye, scanning the forest through the scope.

"You've checked that thing like a dozen times since we left the house," Xavier said.

"Just wanna make sure," Evelyn said.

"We got 'em all, Ev."

"How do you know?"

"Because we tracked and inoculated them for months. Andrew, me, Everett. Those other two cops—Powell and Prasad."

"But what if there's more?"

"We caught all of 'em."

"Then how about my parents? Or yours?"

"Well, that's something, I guess," Xavier said, then paused as if mulling her words over. "But we'll find them. Don't worry."

"What if we don't?"

"We will. They're just harder to find for some reason."

Evelyn moved her boot through the mix of snow and slush. "Maybe she doesn't want me anymore," she said. "Maybe she stopped looking."

"Don't say that," Xavier said. "We'll find her. Your dad too. Just need a bit more time."

"Maybe."

"I'm telling you, we'll find them, Ev. I mean, we've got to …" But his voice trailed off and his mouth turned down as if his thoughts had snagged on something dark.

Evelyn clenched her jaw and turned away, growing accustomed to Xavier's abrupt bouts of silence. She too drew quiet, deep in thought, as though both were struggling with a painful riddle too difficult to crack.

They sat for a while beneath the leafless branches of the hornbeam. Xavier sipped his drink and stared into the dark. Evelyn fiddled with the rifle across her lap.

The wind had picked up, gusting through the dry stalks of cattails lining the creek. An early snow dusted a procession of boulders along the shore, the water running out from the ash and alders. Most of the ferns and fescue were already yellowed and limp as if relenting to the advancing cold, accepting the death that was coming as the frigid winds clamoured over steep bluffs and across barren lakes.

They were over one hundred kilometres outside of Barn Wood but the trees still seemed familiar, almost like running into a forgotten acquaintance—a stranger with a hint of recognition just beneath the surface.

"It's hard being in the forest like this," Evelyn said.

Xavier turned to her. "How's that?"

"The smell of the trees brings it all back."

"Hm."

"Like I can still hear the sound of their screams. Still see them in my mind, the way they hunted us."

"I'd imagine those memories will be with us for a while."

Evelyn swallowed. "The worst part is those memories are always right here," she said, pointing to the side of her head. "Just circling, bouncing around in there with no place to go. Memories of those things. Memories of Damien."

"Yeah, me too," Xavier said. It was all he could muster, the guilt of Damien's sacrifice carving deep ruts into his being.

Evelyn ran a finger up the polished stock of the rifle. Xavier had presented her with it in September for her birthday. Not a typical gift for a 13-year-old, but a practical one nonetheless, and she had teared up when he told her it used to be Damien's. Just sanded and oiled and refinished to look like new.

"Still think about him?" Xavier said.

"All the time," Evelyn said.

"And Maddy?"

"Yeah. Her too."

"Hm."

"You realize we only knew her for a week?"

"I guess that's right. Still, you and her got pretty close, huh?"

Evelyn nodded. "She was nice to me. Protected me."

She thought back to when she and Damien had come across the feisty woman in the forest last winter. How bold and confident she was. But at the same time, how much fear was behind her eyes.

She remembered how quickly the two of them bonded, chuckling in the underground cellar, attached at the hip each time they left to scrounge for food. Maddy seemed to always watch over her—a substitute mother in the absence of her own.

She recalled how Maddy had spotted the eerie logo of a buck on the wrist of one of the infected. How she questioned everything after that, leading the group to discover the virus had been issued through the town flu clinics, and that the Medical Officer of Health, Dr. Angela Till, was behind all of it.

Maddy had followed the clues, leading them to the answers they needed. Until that last morning when the creatures ambushed her and tore flesh from bones, the woman dying in the forest a few hours later.

Amongst the trees, Evelyn sniffled and gripped her chest, a sudden wave of emotion cascading through her.

Xavier cleared his throat. "Listen, these past few months have been brutal, and no one should have to go through what we did." He paused as if to collect his thoughts. "But one good thing about it all is it brought us together."

Evelyn rubbed her thighs but remained quiet.

"I mean, less than a year ago, we didn't even know each other existed. And now, Andrew and I have you as a cousin."

Evelyn wiped her eyes and looked up. She forced a smile.

"It's a small thing, I guess," Xavier said. "But still pretty cool."

The cresting of the sun was still minutes away—the hazy blue-grey that comes just before the dawn leaks out—when Evelyn heard it. A crack of branches, a crunch of snow.

"Hear that?" Evelyn said.

But Xavier was already standing, his rifle poised between his massive paws, his head titled to one side, lasering in on the sound. His thumb nervously toyed with the safety.

"It came from the south, just beyond the creek," he whispered and began shuffling toward the sound.

Evelyn sprung up, scanning the trees. "Wait, what if it's one of *them*?"

Xavier turned to face her. He pressed his lips together then turned away again, creeping along the shore.

Evelyn raised her rifle and followed, a tremor moving through her as she tried to force down the memories of last winter. The haunting visions of when all of them—Xavier, Andrew, Rachel, Maddy, Damien, and her—were hunted night after night.

She wanted to forget the smell of them, the stench of

metal which oozed from their pores, the blood and filth they carried on them.

For months she shot awake from nightmares, the horrific scene of Maddy being savagely attacked, and then the distorted image of her brother, Damien, being shot and killed. She hadn't witnessed the shooting herself—only the memory of Rachel sprinting from Dr. Till's house, the frantic woman rushing down the white-stone walkway, holding Evelyn, tearfully recalling what had happened.

When Evelyn reached Xavier, he was easing into the shallow creek, his movements methodical, precise. She followed him in and gasped from the icy waters, the frigid sting searing her bones.

As she stepped through the current, ripples cascaded out, soundlessly crashing into an eddy. Her boots struggled to gain purchase on the marshy bottom and she held her breath as a shadow passed underneath her then surfaced a few yards behind.

"Protect us, Damien," she mumbled. "Watch over us."

They skulked along the creek bed, around a bend, and then another, until Xavier stopped. His head was cocked as if seeking out a sound. He hoisted himself from the water and onto his knee, gun steady, pointed straight ahead. He pulled off a glove with his teeth then raised a fist as Evelyn slithered out of the water behind him.

"What is it?" she asked.

Xavier squinted into the trees, beyond the rotting grey of the bark, the starved silver of the leaves. There was a crash and a snapping of twigs and Xavier held firm, peering through the skinny alders and dogwoods.

Evelyn gasped. "Is it one of them? One of those things?"

Xavier unfurled his fist, his shoulders relaxing. "It's a doe," he said. "A white-tail."

Evelyn exhaled. "Oh, thank goodness. For a minute I thought it was something else."

Xavier turned and smiled. "I got the one last week. You're up."

Evelyn slid the strap off her shoulder and levelled the rifle, the smooth walnut stock caressing her cheek. She peered through the scope, finding the animal in the sights, and clicked the safety off.

Fifty yards away, she could see the skittish doe along the bank, its ears pinned back, lapping at the icy water. She took aim.

"Right behind the lead leg," Xavier whispered.

In the muted light, Evelyn exhaled. Everything around her seemed to melt away until she only heard the sound of her breath. Inhale, exhale.

Inhale.

Exhale.

A loud clap ricocheted through the morning air as her shoulder absorbed the kickback. The animal lurched straight up and then sprinted across the narrow mouth of the creek and into the trees.

Xavier remained crouched as he focused on the noise of breaking branches and trampled brush, tracking the deer's movements by sound. Eventually, its body crashed to the snow and then everything went silent.

"She's done," he said. "The shock will overtake her soon."

He grinned at the girl, bringing the backpack over his shoulder as he stood. He ducked branches and switches as he moved swiftly through the trees. Evelyn reloaded then hurried to keep up.

When he was close, Xavier squatted amongst the ferns and cautiously approached the animal, his head on a swivel, his eyes pinging through the brush. When he reached the doe, he knelt, muttering a prayer of gratitude under his breath.

"What are you doing?" Evelyn asked.

"I've learned a few things from you as well," Xavier said.

Evelyn smiled then knelt beside the doe, running her hand along the warm, coarse hide. She drew out a small drawstring pouch from her cargo pants, loosened it, and pinched out a palmful of tobacco. She spread the offering on the ground, remembering how her mother had instructed her; an Ojibway teaching instilled in her as a child.

"Thank you," she whispered to the deer.

Xavier bent over the animal and examined the wound. "You've got a crazy shot, Ev."

"Thanks."

"Accurate as hell. Right above the front leg here, right through the lungs."

Evelyn smiled and spun the rifle over.

"Any cuts on your hands from the gun?" Xavier asked. "Any blisters?"

Evelyn surveyed her hand, moving the tips of her fingers through the centre of her palm and up to her index finger—the same inspection Xavier had conducted the first time he taught her how to shoot.

"You worried about '*keep your grip loose and you'll bag a moose*,' and all that stuff?" Evelyn asked coyly, reciting the silly rhyme her Uncle Joe would say. She motioned to the dead deer on the snow. "I think we're beyond that now."

"I suppose so," Xavier admitted.

Thunder boomed in the distance, the wind continuing to whip and swirl. Xavier looked skywards. "Storm's not far off. Let's hurry with this."

The two of them flipped the animal over. Xavier unsheathed his knife and cut a coring ring around the rear of the doe, freeing the colon. He ran the blade up through the hide toward the breastbone, slitting at the stringy membranes, careful not to pierce muscle. Carving along the ridge of the pelvis, he jammed his hand into the damp heat of the carcass, exposing the crimson-red meat underneath.

He looked up, wiping a bloodied hand across his forehead. "Remember from last time?"

Evelyn nodded. She shimmied to the head of the animal and brought her knife down and through the leathery hide and wiry hair, slitting the grey fur along the sternum and across the stomach. She gingerly punctured the abdominal lining, nudging her fingers through the incision, then cut again back towards the pelvis, scrunching her nose at the moist musk swelling out.

"That's good, Ev," Xavier said. "A clean cut."

Careful not to nick the bladder, Xavier angled his knife and sawed through both sides of the pelvic bone. Returning to the sternum, he dug the blade in, carving through the stiff gristle, prying the ribcage open, and removing the heart and gullet.

Slicing at the sinewy diaphragm, he severed the windpipe then gripped it, dragging the line of organs and entrails out from the animal—a soggy heap of mushy stew.

Evelyn stepped back and surveyed the gutted animal. She stared at it, an ache in her eyes, as if reliving a memory.

"Toss me some rope," Xavier instructed.

She reached into the bag and pulled out a short line. Xavier tied the cord around the doe's neck and cinched it. He handed the backpack and rifles to Evelyn and began pulling the deer, its legs folding behind it as he toiled through the trees and saplings.

"Ever dragged 120 pounds of dead weight?" he asked, stopping to catch his breath.

"No," Evelyn said. "That's why I bring you."

"Gee, thanks," Xavier said, wiping the sweat from the back of his neck.

They continued their slow exit from the forest, dragging the doe belly down so it could drain. When they reached the pickup, Evelyn tossed the backpack and rifles into the backseat. They each grabbed two legs and hoisted the animal into the truck bed.

As Xavier fastened the tarp around it, he motioned to the other side of the road. "Are those prints?"

Evelyn scurried over and surveyed the markings. "These are pretty big, X."

"How big?"

"Way bigger than a coyote."

Xavier finished securing the tarp and joined her. He crouched, examining the prints; a crooked line jutting out from the woods then back into the trees. "Jesus, these are massive. And fresh."

"Maybe a wolf?"

"A wolf print only has four toes plus the foot pad. This one has five."

"Cougar?"

"Their prints have four toes as well. And besides, we wouldn't get cats this far south."

Xavier drew quiet, peering down at the set of tracks. He looked up, his eyes flitting across the gritty terrain, scanning the bush.

"What are you thinking?" Evelyn asked.

"I don't know…maybe a wolverine?" he said. "Can usually see the fifth toe, along with these claw markings." He pointed to what looked like a serrated knife above each toe. "But these look even larger than that."

"Maybe it's a really *big* wolverine?"

"Maybe."

Xavier twisted his mouth. He rose from his squat then lifted his boot and shook it free. He removed his wool sock and placed his bare foot beside the print. The similarities were immediate: five toes on both with an exaggerated arch ending in a heavy heel. However, even his large foot paled in comparison to the marking on the ground.

"You think *a person* made these?" Evelyn asked.

"Not sure," Xavier said.

"But they're huge. And what about the claws? People don't have claws."

A screech ripped through the air and Evelyn's face dropped. "It's those things!"

"It can't be," Xavier said, feverishly pulling his sock and boot back on.

"They're still out there, I knew it!"

"But we got them all."

"That's the same scream Damien and I heard every night when we were in the forest!"

Evelyn sprinted for the truck but Xavier stayed in the centre of the road, straining to see through the trees.

"X, we need to go!" Evelyn yelled. She swung the passenger door open and jumped into the cab. "X!"

As if shaken from a dream, Xavier blinked then lunged for the truck. He threw the door open and climbed in.

"Okay, let's get out of here," he said, starting the engine then slamming the gas down, the tires spinning on the icy gravel.

He took the first right, peeling down the dirt road, but skidded to a stop when they came to a dead end.

"What the..." he muttered.

"Where are we?" Evelyn asked.

"Just give me a second to figure this out."

"Are we lost?"

"No, no, we're not lost. I just, ah, I just..."

"You just what?" Evelyn snapped.

"I just get turned around back here. All these county roads look the same."

He jammed the truck into drive, exiting the same way they had come. He took a sharp left and then a right, leaning forward in his seat as he tried to read a passing road sign. "What does that say? Can you read it?"

"It says Camp Clearwater," Evelyn said. "Clearwater? I know that name..."

"Good, then I think this is right," Xavier interrupted. "This road looks right."

But as he took the next left, the truck drove into another dead end of brambles and thorns.

"Dammit!" he shouted, slamming the steering wheel with the heel of his hand.

Evelyn frantically scanned the ditch and the trees beyond. "What do we do?"

"Must be the other way," Xavier mumbled, spinning the

truck around. He slammed the pedal down and drove for an-other minute. "I think we're good now. There's a bend com-ing up which eventually takes us back into Barn Wood."

A second squeal tore through the air, this one much closer than the first, and Evelyn's nails dug into Xavier's forearm. He shook her off and spun the truck around, hauling now in the opposite direction.

"Tell me you know where you're going," Evelyn said, her voice shaking.

Xavier chewed at his lip, his gaze gripped on the road. "It's this way, I'm sure of it."

He peeled around a blind corner and drove a few seconds before slamming to a stop. "What the…" he said. He rolled the window down, something in the distance vying for his at-tention. "What is that? Up that hill?"

"Who cares!" Evelyn said.

He stepped from the truck to the opposite side of the road. "It's a barn."

"So what, it's a barn," Evelyn hollered. "Let's just go!"

"But it's…it's moving." He stared a few moments longer before returning to the truck.

"X, let's get outta here!"

He said nothing as he reached into the backseat and grabbed his rifle, shoving extra rounds in the bib of his overalls.

"You heard the screams! You saw those footprints!" Evelyn said.

"But we got them all," Xavier mumbled.

"They're out there!"

"We tracked and got them all," Xavier said, as if in a trance.

"Just get in the truck!"

He turned and squinted toward the barn. "I mean, there might be…I should at least check it out."

"We need to go! We can talk about it with Rachel at home and make a plan from there."

"I'll be right back. I just…I just need to see…"

"Stop," Evelyn pleaded, her words strangled in her throat. She reached out to him, shaking as tears funnelled down her flushed cheeks. "Please stay."

But he was already gone, swiftly moving through the scarred birch and twisted oaks. And all Evelyn could do was stare after him.

She rolled the windows up and locked the cab. All at once, the sky opened and the storm broke. A heavy mix of hail and sleet came fast and hard and Evelyn lost sight of him, swallowed up by the trees, the branches bent and limp from the sudden rush of water. She reached to the backseat and grabbed her rifle.

Get down, Damien said.

She slid low in her seat and cracked the gun open, staring down the breech, checking for bullets over and over again.

Stay low, Ev, Damien said. *Danger is near.*

Chapter Two

**November 1995
Day 637 | Morning**

Andrew Stone made his way up the winding dirt driveway toward the family farmhouse. The morning was clear and bright, but he stumbled as if moving through a mist or heavy sheets of rain, only able to see a few yards ahead, unsure where his next step would land.

His head felt the same way—full of fog and water—and he struggled up the drive, muddled and confused. He moved slower than he wanted to, each step heavy and burdensome as if he were trudging through mud.

He glanced down and noticed his feet were bare and filthy with long cracked nails. He appeared confused as to why his boots were missing, lying in the snow somewhere, carelessly tossed into the bush.

A strange film circled the farmhouse, its grey brick and bay windows shrouded, as if he was viewing the house through a veil.

The birch and ironwoods standing guard in the front yard spontaneously caught fire and melted before him, then disappeared, swallowed up by the earth as though they had never been there at all.

In a daze, he approached the creek which flowed in front

of the house. He eased into the icy water, the sharp stones slicing into his heel. As the blood drooled out, the stones softened, becoming mushy and moist, and then turned to biting leeches, a slimy legion of black worms ripping flesh from his ankles and arches.

He stared down at the bloodied mess. In his muddled stupor he thought nothing of it.

He slid out of the water and stumbled through sharp hedges toward the wraparound porch, passing underneath the rusted gutters. Teetering, he lost his balance and pitched to the left, landing in the thorns and thistles. He stood and righted himself, his eyes rolled back in his head, and continued forward.

He gawked at the overturned truck in the driveway then turned to the underground cellar, sixty yards from where he stood. He turned again, lurching toward the house, gliding his hand over the cracks between the bricks, his mouth ajar in awe.

The house was familiar enough—he could feel it in his bones—but for the life of him, he couldn't remember exactly whose house it was or how he had arrived.

He nudged the front door open, his feet crunching over the slivers of glass lining the floor, the red glow of the rising sun reflecting off the pool of shards. A trail of blood seeped from his feet into the slits of the hardwood as he limped into the kitchen.

Cupboards hung from their hinges with drawers pulled out, the contents of the pantry emptied and smashed.

He dragged his body from the kitchen to the mudroom and then to the dining area, each room presenting new wonders. He would gasp and stand wide-eyed for minutes at a time until his face twisted in confusion, perplexed as to why he was there.

He surveyed the main floor, intent on locating something; but what exactly, he wasn't sure.

He made his way to the base of the stairs. Dust and massive paw prints covered the stairwell, an array of tools scattered along each step. He stepped over rakes and shovels, a cord of frayed rope, a metal mallet.

His foot caught on the last step and he tripped and fell upon a pair of shears. The serrated blade split his shoulder as it travelled up and underneath his clavicle. He staggered to his feet and stared at the shears. Confused, he reached across his body and yanked them out, the skin shredded and raw around the wound, black blood dribbling to the floor.

Dropping the bloodied garden tool, he continued down the hall toward his half-brother's room. He pushed through the door to find the familiar grey paint faded and chipped, a wind chime split in two. He stood over Xavier's twin bed, the sheets ripped, stained with vomit and bile.

He scanned the room, eyeing the assortment of hunting knives huddled on the bedside table, a framed photo of a canoe excursion teetering on the corner. A leather tool belt sat crumpled at the foot of the bed, a hammer, Philips screwdriver, and pliers jammed within. A lacrosse stick leaned against the scuffed drywall, its shaft nicked and warped, a rubber ball snared in its netting.

He shuffled to the window and stared into the yard, drool running down his chin, until a faint thump drew his attention to the closet. Lumbering over, he yanked the door open, the hinges squeaking in refusal.

The stink was immediate, the small space covered in

blood and stool and urine.

Inside, he found an Ojibway man struggling on the floor, kicking the wall as though a rhythmic spasm coursed through him. He was gaunt and bony, nearly emaciated, with wiry brown hair sprouting from his scalp and ears. His face and torso were covered in blood and a red rip ran along his lower lip, long-scarred over.

A blurred image of a buck was tattooed on his wrist. The smeared animal menacingly stared out from the man's ashen skin, the thick lips of the beast drooping and slack as if it had suffered a stroke.

The man looked no more than 20 and his head shot up at the rush of light, his copper eyes squinting. He yelped and curled in a ball and Andrew noticed a familiar bowie knife protruding from his spine.

"Jeremiah?" Andrew asked.

The man rolled toward the voice, his eyes straining to focus. "You!" he hissed.

Andrew stepped back. "Jeremiah, what is all this?"

"How could you stab your best friend?" Jeremiah said. His voice was high-pitched and when he spoke, splatters of bloody saliva sprayed upon the walls.

"What happened to you?"

"How could you kill me and still live with yourself?"

"I-I had no choice," Andrew stammered. "You attacked us. I mean, you were about to—"

"Wait for a cure! You should have waited for a cure!"

"I had no idea about a cure. I had no idea about any of that."

"Liar! You're all liars!"

"What are you talking about?"

"You and Xavier and Joe and Simon—all of you lie!"

"No," Andrew said, his breath hitching. "That's just not true…"

"You killed me! And then your brother's careless actions killed the boy."

"What boy?"

"Damien!" Jeremiah screamed, and as he did, a mouthful of wet larvae bubbled out from behind his teeth and tongue and slid down his chin.

"Those were accidents!" Andrew said. "We never meant for any of those things to happen!"

"And what of the young child in the closet?"

"We tried to save him!"

"Another death on your hands, hmm?"

"We couldn't get to him in time. We tried but we couldn't."

"Liar! All of you are liars and murderers!" Jeremiah shrieked. And then a bloodied grin unfurled across his face. "And we both know the dark secrets your step-father, Joe, holds."

Andrew gasped and stuttered backward. "Wh—what are you talking about?"

"He has blood on his hands too."

"That was a long time ago, a misunderstanding."

"Liars, all of you!"

"You don't know what you're saying."

"And you should know, my father is not pleased with you, not pleased at all."

Andrew huffed and slammed the door.

"He knows exactly what you are, what you *really* are," Jeremiah hissed from inside the closet. "And he will come for you! He is coming for you!"

Jeremiah continued to shriek, clawing at the door as Andrew fled, scurrying to his mother's and step-father's room.

As he pushed through the door, he noticed their oak dresser on its side, the lacquered wood smashed and splintered. Damp and pungent towels were crumpled in the corner, a mix of blood and mould steeping the fabric.

He listened to the tick of the bedside clock before shuffling toward the window. Noticing a draft between the glass and sill, he placed his hand over the gap, but instead of suffocating the wind, it intensified, the cold air whisking through his outstretched fingers.

Something caught his attention and he turned to find his mother hunched in the corner, her spine bent like a crooked branch. Her eyes were swollen and bloodshot as if emerging from a fight. Black blood pooled at the side of her mouth. Her soggy grey hair was matted to her forehead and she breathed with such force a grating sound came from deep within her chest.

"Mom?" Andrew asked.

Elizabeth raised her head. The sound of his voice seemed to stir something inside her.

She was wearing her favourite white dress with flowers printed on it, but it was torn and filthy, a moist splotch of red staining the front. She pushed toward him, her movements sluggish and forced. She lifted her arms, one much longer than the other, and he saw how both her hands ended in gnarled claws.

"Mom, is that you?"

Elizabeth nattered under her breath, the rubbery skin of her mottled neck swaying back and forth as if it had a life of its own. When she spoke, her voice was slurred, a high-pitched squeal. "Why haven't you found us?"

Andrew covered his ears, the harsh noise reverberating throughout the room. The bedside clock ticked louder as the wind whipped around him.

"I'm trying," he said. "I'm trying to find you."

Elizabeth shook her head, her hair blowing from the sudden gusts. Her skin was thin and translucent, knotted black veins coiling beneath it. "You've lost hope," she trilled.

"No, no, I haven't," Andrew said.

"You're not coming for us."

"I am, Mom. I just need more time."

"You're not coming."

"I'm coming for you. Both you and Joe. I am."

The wind in the room was now raging with such force that it lifted the bedside clock from the table, the deafening *tick, tick, tick,* echoing off the walls.

Elizabeth dropped her head and turned to leave. "Why can't you find us?"

"Tell me where you are and I'll come," Andrew said.

"Why haven't you found us?" she screeched before running from the room.

"I'm coming for you, Mom!" Andrew shouted after her. "I'm coming for you and Joe!"

Torrents of air pinned him against the window as if a tornado had sprung up from nothing. The clock spun furiously around the room, the ticking growing louder.

"Mom!" he yelled as the clock came to hover by his ear. He yelled her name again just as a piercing clang sounded.

He threw the quilt off and shot awake. He was shaking and breathing heavy as he frantically scanned his apartment.

He swiped across his brow, his shaggy brown hair mussed, his shirt sticky with sweat.

The phone rang a second time and he sprang for it, clumsily pawing at the receiver. "Hello?"

A soft voice came through and it caused his shoulders to relax.

"Juliana?" he said. "Hi, yes, yes, I'm fine, how are you?"

Juliana spoke on the other end.

"No, no, I'm good. Just had another…just another one of those nightmares I told you about."

He paused as Juliana's voice floated through the receiver again.

"Yeah, it's always the same."

She spoke once more.

"Yeah, of course, looking forward to it." Andrew switched the receiver to the other hand as he fumbled out of bed. "Sure thing, I'll grab you at the airport. Okay, bye—have a safe flight."

He hung up and then his legs gave out and he crashed against the wall. A shudder moved through him as visions of his mother boiled up again.

"It's been nine months," he said. He shook his head, trying to flush the nightmare from his mind. "You've been missing nine months. Where are you? Where the hell did you go, Mom?"

After a hot shower and bowl of cereal, Andrew gathered his things for class. He clunked the fourth-year epidemiology textbook into his backpack followed by his tattered journal—the pages all dog-eared and full of study notes.

He slid his latest essay inside a protective sleeve, the title in bold along the top: *The Ecology and Epidemiology of Eastern Equine Encephalitis Virus: A History of Incidence, Incubation, and Replication.*

He reached for a pen and notebook but froze as his hand hovered over a different report. This one was marked 'CONFIDENTIAL' in bold yellow lettering and had a logo of a buck stamped along the top.

Xavier had taken the folder last winter when he and Rachel raided her sister's home and found evidence of a terrifying plot—horrifying experiments conducted unknowingly on the residents of Barn Wood. Due to her involvement, Dr. Angela Till was now a convicted criminal, awaiting a re-trial on a slew of charges.

After Staff Inspector Tom Everett took a copy of the report, the police team eventually returned the original to Xavier. The stack of papers were shoved in a corner of the family farmhouse all summer until, on a whim, Andrew pitched them into his travel bag and boarded his plane for school.

Andrew scanned the first few pages of the report, reading over the details.

Copy 1 of 2: Highest security level - CONFIDENTIAL.

Natural observational study to assess the effects of pending drug, Lilasvir

Lead financier: Aaron Pak

Lead of operations: Alan Mackenzie

Hypothesis: Pharmaceutical drug, Lilasvir, to mitigate symptoms and potentially cure the Eastern Equine Encephalitis Virus (EEEV).

Study synopsis: Minute amounts of Lilasvir to be systematically added to town water sources for a period of nine to twelve months. Sample subjects to be injected with traces of EEEV during month nine to ten. Observational research to be conducted four to six months post injections to assess full effects of Lilasvir.

Location of sample population: Town of Barn Wood

Principal investigators: Dr. Simon Stone and Dr. Angela Till

He flipped through the remaining pages but already knew what was on them. It was all there: how Angela tainted Barn Wood's water with an untested drug, how it was ingested by unsuspecting residents, and then triggered nine months later by a doctored virus through the town's flu clinics.

Once proven, the drug would be packaged by BioHealth Pharmaceuticals and sold to the highest bidder; profits lining the pockets of Aaron Pak, Alan Mackenzie, and their gaggle of investors.

Instead, it poisoned an entire town, creating horrifying, unbridled monsters.

Andrew shook his head as he read the statement at the bottom of page 4: *If successful through natural experiments, the drug will have supportive data to proceed to clinical trials.*

"Looks like there's no need to proceed to clinical trials," he muttered. "*Natural experiments* get a hard fail."

He skimmed the report further, reading how the virus can cause death within one week of exposure, that it has been known to jump species, and how, in nature, the virus typically resides in horses and deer.

He ran a finger over the image of the buck. "Suppose that's what this cute logo is for," he scoffed.

The image reminded him of the marking smeared across Jeremiah's wrist when the boy ambushed the group. The virus had turned him violent and wild and Andrew plunged his knife into him before realizing who he was.

Telling Jeremiah's father was nearly just as hard. Andrew visited the old man and, through tears, recounted the events. He told Mr. Cook how the virus had overtaken Jeremiah, how he had attacked the group, and how Andrew had no choice but to put him down.

Mr. Cook didn't say much to that. Just bit the inside of his cheek until red drool began to pool at his lip. He stood like that on the porch, staring absently, as if trying to unpack a riddle. After a while, he turned, walked back into his house, and closed the door, not saying another word.

Andrew scowled at the report. He had read it so many times he had it nearly memorized. He had scoured over it for a sign, a misstep, a clue—anything that might point him toward the origins of the altered virus or the drug or how the whole thing started. Or maybe, even, the whereabouts of his mother.

The thought of her brought on a fleeting vision of when he was much younger, he and her whisking eggs and milk and flour at the kitchen counter. He would spend Sunday afternoons with her baking muffins or banana bread, his small hands struggling to pour the goopy mix into the baking trays.

Elizabeth didn't mind the mess, always smiling at him, her kind eyes devouring him. "Chocolate chips?" she'd asked playfully.

"Yeah!" Andrew would say, and then his mother would laugh—a warm bubbly sound.

He remembered when she would take him to the mall. It was a long drive, a few towns over. They would walk it several times, peering into shop windows, mesmerized by the newest gear or latest fashion.

Of course they could never buy any of it; neither her nor Joe's paycheques stretched far beyond the mortgage and groceries. But he recalled how they would always stop for a donut and hot chocolate on the drive home. That was the best part. Laughing in a warm corner of the café, bragging that he would buy her everything in that mall if ever he won the lottery.

But those memories were rare now. Instead, he had grown accustomed to the constant chill of worry, the ache of her absence gnawing at him.

"Nine months," he sighed, tossing the report back on the desk.

He adjusted his grey hoodie and dark jeans, cinching his watch tight across his wrist. He towelled off his hair one last time in front of the mirror, his woeful eyes reflecting back at him.

He grabbed his school bag and flicked the light off, locking the apartment door. But as he twisted the key, a heavy sadness fell over him, and it took nearly all his strength to compose himself and walk the short trail to campus.

Chapter Three

November 1995
Day 637 | Late Morning

Xavier bounded through the soaked sedge and poplars as he advanced toward the shaking barn. The frigid mix of rain and hail clinked upon the stones as the stabbing wind flogged him, his chin tucked low beneath his collar.

He struggled through the spindly black branches until he found a path passing under a sagging wooden arch, *Camp Clearwater* etched into the pine.

He stopped to catch his breath as features around him came into focus.

Down the left side of the path, he saw a dilapidated mess hall, a storage unit, a massive oval building with missing planks and smashed windows. Beyond that, large stones surrounded a firepit, a tiny kettle lake beside it. Along the right were rows of sleeping cabins dotting an open field, some huddled within the bordering woods.

He continued up the path until he heard a sound: a song, muffled and far away. The noise stopped and he stood motionless, scanning the area, until it came again.

He spun to locate it but then stopped, something in the trees catching his attention. He looked up and spotted a small shape, just over a foot tall; a smudge of colour against the dark sky.

Straining to see through the rain, he moved forward. As he stepped closer, he noticed there were several of them: blue and yellow silhouettes, drenched and wilted and swinging from the branches.

He gasped and reeled back. "Those are kids!" he said, turning away.

He dropped to his knees, gagging and heaving. He swiped the back of his hand across his mouth and spit the last of his breakfast upon the snow. Trembling, he pushed himself from the ground and rushed through the trees in the opposite direction until something caused him to stop.

Perhaps it was their unusual size or the curious way they were all dressed the same, but whatever it was, he turned back. As he inched closer, there was a shift in shadow, a playing of the light, and he clearly saw what swung above.

"Jesus," he exhaled. "They're just dolls."

He shook his head and stepped out from the brush, a strained smile on his face. "Just a bunch of goddamn dolls," he muttered, and soon he was chuckling to himself.

He turned and marched up the path until he came to a rickety tin storage unit, the door ripped off and lying lopsided in the snow.

He peered inside to see broken bows and pointed arrows scattered on the floor, various lengths of canoe paddles poking out from a dented rain barrel. A corroded ATV sat in the shadows, the front passenger tire flat, stringy cobwebs skulking between the seat and handlebars. A rusted key stuck out of the ignition.

In the opposite corner stood a bunch of shovels, a pickaxe, a pint of oil, a jug of CLR. He spied a stack of yellow lifejackets piled high, green and black mould biting at the straps and seeping through the nylon.

He scrunched his face at the odour, covering his nose with the crook of his arm. "Jesus Christ," he said, coughing from the stench.

He exited the tin shed and continued up the path. Beyond the camp was a steep escarpment of rocks and crags. He climbed it and when he reached the peak, he stopped and looked around. To the west, from where he had just come, the camp was now hidden, the buildings tucked behind the tall stones and dense trees. To the east stood the shaking barn alone in a field, and beyond that, a wooden cabin, tendrils of smoke curling from the chimney.

He crossed the clearing of tall blackened straw and yellow weeds, slowing to a trot as a low hum leached out from the barn. As he neared, the hum became louder, now a ghostly chorus of grunts and growls. The ground trembled as if enormous shapes were shifting beneath it.

When he reached the barn door, he stood and listened, trying to decipher who—or what—was on the other side of it. His hand brushed against the stock of his rifle and he shuddered, a rope of tension snaking across his shoulders.

He cracked the door and a musty, fungal scent rushed out from the barn's throat like a ghastly buffet of vomit and sweat and burning metal. He pulled his collar up over his nose and stepped through the door, his boots sliding along the dusty floor.

It was dark inside, the storm clouds stripping most of the light from the sky, only thin shafts squirming between the uneven planks. Several brown rats scurried along the walls, through cobwebs and their own droppings, squeaking as they darted around a corner.

A panicked thrum swelled up in him so that he needed to

brace himself against the thick beams, a feeling he didn't quite know how to navigate. He tightened his grip around his rifle and clicked off the safety, inching forward.

The buzzing of flies caught his attention and as he squinted into a darkened corner, he saw a half-eaten carcass. The massive buck had been torn in two, its insides pink and moist, white larvae bubbling about the edges of its hide. Its antlers were split, jagged ends jutting out like deadly wooden daggers. Its neck was pulled forward and underneath its own chest, painfully contorted in a most unnatural position.

Xavier studied the buck, all butchered and carved up, and an unsettled feeling came over him. It was as if he had seen this before—this slaughter, this malice. Or perhaps, he was seeing what was to come.

In the dim light, his eyes travelled up the pillars to the rafters, the timber groaning and creaking as if something heavy hung from them. He bent his gaze to the shaking floor, a methodic and thunderous thud coming from the centre of the barn.

He shuffled forward and as he twisted around a high wooden wall, the sights and smells overtook him.

There were dozens of them, sweaty hordes of blood and dirt piling on top of one another, grunting and baying and snarling. Massive beasts, naked from the waist up, scarred and mutilated, their arms nearly twice as long as any humans, with huge bare feet ending in knife-like claws. Boils pitted several of them while others were mottled with bruises, crusted scabs down their legs. One of the larger ones tossed others into the support beams and walls, the barn shaking on impact.

They resembled rabid animals, snapping at each other, vicious and unhinged. Not long ago they were young men. Now they were something else entirely.

Crouched in the shadows, Xavier observed a strange routine repeating. The creatures were indeed fighting, but not in a chaotic manner. The kicking and punching seemed controlled, almost rehearsed, like a staged fight, performing for an audience yet to arrive.

One of the beasts roared and swung his meaty fist upon a smaller, obese one. The force of it drove the fat one's tooth down and through his lip, black blood spraying to the floor.

But instead of hitting back, the heavier creature simply nodded and stepped away as though the whole sequence was expected. It reached into its mouth and tore the tooth away, then dropped it into its dirt-stained palm, a coveted pearl within a filthy cave. It grinned and then jerked around, its guilty eyes scanning the back wall as if expecting someone to enter.

Xavier swallowed his fear down and scanned the rest of the room.

Several creatures were crowded underneath a high window, one of them climbing the wall toward it, desperate to peer out. The thing was rangy and decrepit, its skin loose and flaccid, a thin web of spittle hanging from its chin. Its eyes were glassed over, wet and rheumy, and it had almost reached the sill when the others swarmed it, pulled at it until it fell to the floor. They snarled and clubbed it until it retreated, coiling in the corner like a threatened snake.

Xavier noticed another creature, alone, its skin smeared with bile and mucous. It was unnaturally tall, nearly seven-feet. A jagged scar rivered down its forearm, tufts of hair between its toes and knuckles. It was ghost-white—an albino—and it stood in one place with its head bowed.

It held something close to its chest, humming softly, when

a noise caused it to turn. Its eyes found Xavier and, in an instant, they turned hungry, as if waking from a long slumber to feast.

Xavier turned and sped toward the exit, tripping down the short hallway. He pushed the door open and leapt out, kicking it shut behind him. He stumbled before righting himself, sprinting across the clearing just as the beast crashed through the door and gave chase.

Xavier galloped down the escarpment, ducking boughs and branches, the beast keeping pace forty yards behind. Xavier moved with precision, reading the slope of the land, swiftly reaching the edge of the abandoned campground.

He flew past the sleeping cabins, the firepit, the kettle lake, then ducked into the storage unit. He slumped against a back wall, panting heavily, hidden in the shadows of old tarps and blankets.

His heart pounded as he strained to hear. The snapping of branches had gone silent, only the patter of freezing rain on the tin roof.

He crept toward the doorway when a shimmer of light caused him to pause. He returned to the back wall and stared out through a narrow slit.

Something on the other side moved. Something moist and yellow. It moved again and it was such a subtle flick that it took Xavier a moment to realize what it was: the beast's eye, locked upon his own.

"My God," Xavier gasped, and frantically turned for the door.

The beast smashed its way through the shed as Xavier sprinted down the path and into a thick grove of dogwoods. A deafening scream rang out and when he looked back, he saw the monstrous shape hurtling toward him.

His rubber boots jittered over loose shale and limestone as he navigated the steep pitch. He went head-first into the mist, the pines and alders now chocked with fog, and careened through the basin of trees.

The road began to appear below him when something swiped at his legs. He lost his footing and tripped, screaming as his knee smashed against a stone, his rifle flinging from his grasp.

He spun onto his back and all at once the creature was upon him.

It was breathing heavy, mucous dripping from its mouth and nose and the heavy stink of it caused Xavier to twist his face away. He kicked at it, squirming to get loose, but the beast held firm, its strong arms pinning him. He reached for his knife but the beast grabbed his wrist and wrenched it around as if expecting the attack.

He stared at the creature. It wasn't like the ones he and Andrew fought last winter. It was larger and stronger. But it was its eyes that made Xavier draw back in horror. Something about its eyes.

He shifted to kick the beast off but it predicted the movement and held him tight. A twisted grin tunnelled across its face. It raised its fist and came down upon Xavier's jaw. Blood fanned upon the snow and Xavier cried out just as a second fist came down, cleaving the skin open along his forehead.

It raised its fist a third time but then stopped, a strange blare echoing through the trees. Its head shot up as the truck horn boomed again and Xavier used the distraction to bring his knee into the beast's abdomen and free himself from underneath it.

He rolled over and drew his knife, driving the blade into

the beast's shoulder. It wailed and swiped again but Xavier slipped the blow and brought the knife up and through its ribs. He yanked it out as the creature stumbled forward.

Finding his rifle amongst the drenched ferns, he plunged down the hill, limping, the road within a dozen yards. He crashed through the saplings lining the shoulder. "Where the hell's the truck?" he shouted.

He hobbled a few paces then heard the honking. He turned toward it, now seeing the truck in the distance, but stopped. The creature was at the edge of the road, bent at the hip, its eyes seized on him.

Xavier looked to the pickup, sizing up the distance, then raced through the rain, the beast staggering after him. When he reached it, he threw the driver's-side door open.

Evelyn laid off the horn and swatted at him, her eyes red and wet. "Why did you leave me?" she shouted.

Xavier hopped onto the running board, tossing the rifle into the backseat.

"I told you not to leave!" Evelyn said.

"We gotta go," Xavier said, straining to catch his breath.

Evelyn shimmied into the passenger seat. "What happened? Are you okay?"

"We gotta go."

"I heard you scream so I started honking and—"

"There's more of them!" Xavier said, turning the key, the engine bursting to life. "Lots more! And they're bigger and faster and—"

A horrible thud came down upon the truck bed. Xavier whipped around to see the creature moving up the wet metal grooves, lurching toward them. It picked up the tarp-wrapped deer and pitched it across the road.

"Time to go!" Xavier said, yanking the gearshift into drive.

He spun the truck around and pinned the gas pedal, the creature losing balance, bouncing off the wheel well. But it soon righted itself and smashed through the cab window, shards of glass piercing Evelyn's skin as she shrieked in pain. The clawed hand searched feverishly along the rear seats, grabbing onto the backpack and then Xavier's rifle.

"It's got your gun!" Evelyn shouted.

Xavier slammed the brakes then accelerated again. The creature lost its footing, crashing through the tailgate and onto the road.

Xavier spun the steering wheel, the tires chittering over the packed snow and dirt until they faced the beast. He looked at Evelyn, her eyes wide with terror. "Hold tight," he said.

He slammed the gas once again, driving hard into the creature. It careened off the hood then rolled into the shallow ditch. Xavier righted the truck then sped further down the road, swerving around the rocks and ruts.

"Everyone said we got 'em," he muttered.

"What was that thing?" Evelyn screeched.

"Everyone said we got 'em, everyone said we got 'em all," Xavier said, panic clutching his words. He checked his side mirror, the creature motionless in the ditch.

"How are they still out there?"

"I don't know but those things are back. Piles of 'em."

"But how?"

"I don't know but we gotta tell Everett. We gotta tell Everett."

The truck was nearly out of sight when a spasm travelled through the creature, its body jerking awake. It wobbled upright, then limped from the ditch to stand in the middle of the road. It snarled, glaring at the red taillights.

But then an awkward smirk crossed its face. It stared at the truck, squinting at the licence plate, mouthing the numbers and letters as if committing them to memory.

Chapter Four

November 1995
Day 637 | Noon

Rachel Till stood in the freezing rain facing the twelve-foot fence. She shook as she breathed in and out.

In.

Out.

No matter how many times she stood outside the prison, it always forced her to take pause, as if somehow this might be her last moment of freedom. She surveyed the barbed-wire lining the top of the fence. It reminded her of claws, all gnarled and coiled and razor-sharp, bent low as if ready to strike.

Brayfield Penitentiary was nearly two hours from Barn Wood and its clunky, square shape towered high upon an isolated hill. The structure stood cold and menacing, as if the architect meant for it to be as uninviting as possible; a grotesque concrete block dwarfing the bare trees and dead plants surrounding it.

"It's a totally different world over there," she had told Xavier months earlier after visiting Angela the first time. "Like all light and air has been sucked out of it. Feels alien, like a different planet."

Xavier blew on his coffee, the two of them sharing a

booth at Brenda's Bistro. "I hate that place," he said. He took a sip then set the mug down. "Won't ever go back."

Rachel sat up straight, startled. "Go back?"

Xavier averted his gaze, his cheeks growing dark, as if a secret had been let loose. "It's nothing."

"What happened?"

Xavier drew out a long exhale. "When I was young, we were out shopping and this guy started yelling at my mom and I. For no reason, really. Then he came at us. But my dad was also there and he wasn't having any of it."

"My word," Rachel said.

"I mean, Dad was just defending us, but…"

"But what?"

"Well, he already had a record from a bar fight when he was younger so that's not how it played out."

"I'm sorry. I had no idea."

"Anyway, my mom brought Andrew and I to the prison to see him. I think it was more of a warning than anything else, something to try and scare us into behaving."

Rachel shuddered. "That place would set anyone straight. It's downright creepy."

"When they brought him out to see us, you could see he wasn't in a good state, like he had been roughed up some."

"By who?"

Xavier shrugged. "The guards? Other inmates? Who knows? Had this deep gash above his eye and he could hardly walk on his own, like the guard had to prop him up the whole time."

"Jesus."

"He yelled at my mom, asking how could she bring Andrew and I to see him in a place like that, how we shouldn't

see him all beat up like that. She started crying and then Andrew started crying. But I just stood there watching it all."

"Then what happened?"

"They hauled him off, forced him back through the door.
Who knows what they did to him then."

Rachel reached across the table and grabbed Xavier's
hands in hers.

"Anyway, he was only in for about a week or so before the
lawyer assigned to us got it all sorted," Xavier said.

"Still, sounds like it shouldn't have happened in the first
place," Rachel said.

"You know, I still remember the sounds. All those voices
coming at you at once, the echoes. Some voices even seemed
to come from inside the walls, like trapped ghosts or something."

Rachel pressed her lips together and nodded. She
squeezed his hands.

"All the shouting and banging and seeing my dad like
that," Xavier said. "It was overwhelming." He pulled his hand
away and gulped down the last of the bitter coffee. "I made
up my mind that day I'm never going back there," he added.
"Something evil is in that place."

"That must've been so hard," Rachel said. "With you being so young and all."

"We all learn the world is cruel, Rach," he said, staring at
the dregs at the bottom of his mug. "Some just learn it earlier
than others."

Outside the prison gates, Rachel drew up the hood of her
raincoat. She rubbed her hands together to ward off the cold
as she trudged through the puddles, the fog starting to lift beneath the overcast sky. She passed a couple guards chatting

quietly and then pushed through the heavy metal door, her rubber boots squeaking down the narrow hallway.

She walked around a prisoner mopping the floor, cursing under his breath, a hefty guard standing watch over him. She wiped the sharp sting of bleach from her nose and approached the cut-out window. She lowered her hood, strands of brown hair matted against her dark skin, and gently tapped the glass.

An officer seated at a computer looked up. Annoyed, she straightened her glasses and spoke through the thick pane. "Reason for visit?"

"Um, y-yes," Rachel stammered. "Here to see Dr. Angela Till."

The clerk's glossy nails clacked along the keyboard. "Relationship?"

"Sister," Rachel said, clearing the nerves from her voice. "She's my sister."

"Your sister's popular," the clerk said, scanning the computer monitor. "You're the third visitor this week."

"Oh? Who were the others?"

"We normally don't give out that information."

"It's no bother, I was just curious."

The clerk hesitated. "Seeing as you're next of kin and all...let's see here." She moved the mouse around the screen. "Three days ago, it was a Mr. Brad Moseby. Says here he's a journalist with some paper called *The Chronicle*."

"Oh, that's the local paper we get up in Barn Wood."

"Never heard of it."

Rachel shrugged and the clerk continued. "And the other visitor was a Mr. Aaron Pak," she said.

"Aaron Pak?" Rachel mumbled. "I feel like I know that name..."

"Well, I won't be much help to ya. It was my day off when he came through so someone else would have processed him." The clerk shifted in her seat and snatched a lanyard, the word VISITOR printed in bold lettering across a laminated card affixed to it. She slid the glass open and handed it to Rachel. "Wear this at all times."

"Y-yes, of course. I remember."

"Stu, we got one here for pat-down," the clerk hollered to a guard at the other end of the hallway. A burly man ambled over.

"Umm, aren't there rules about men patting down women?" Rachel asked. "Last time, I had a woman."

"This ain't the airport, dear," the clerk sneered. "You get whoever we have. Consider us short-staffed."

"Sure, but I'd feel far more comfortable if a woman was able to—"

"Listen, you got a problem with our protocols, you're free to call the mayor. But you ain't gettin' through that door without a proper security check."

Rachel eventually nodded. She stood rigid, her hands clasped in front, wringing them nervously as the officer clumsily felt around her torso, legs, and arms. When he finished, he nodded to the clerk.

"Officer Vedan here will escort you to the visitor's section," the clerk said then snapped the glass pane shut, busying herself on the computer.

The guard pointed over her shoulder in the opposite direction. "This way," he huffed, shuffling down the hallway, Rachel on his heels.

He shoved the key in the first door then led her deep into the building, unlocking then relocking each door as they went through. Minutes passed with a series of doors slamming and locks bolting as they wormed their way along several corridors and into the belly of the prison. A shudder travelled through her as it became less clear whether she was gaining access or gradually being locked in.

They finally arrived at a heavy steel door. Officer Vedan turned his key and shoved his shoulder against the thick metal. It creaked open.

Several tables and chairs congregated at the centre of the dimly-lit room. The pocked ceiling measured at least twelve feet high, with several thin windows sitting just beneath the air ducts, slivers of natural light struggling to shine in.

Officer Vedan plodded across the room. "You can sit here," he said, pointing to a metal chair bolted to the floor in front of a metal table, also bolted in place. "Visits are twenty minutes max. She'll be brought out shortly."

"Yes, I've been here before," Rachel said.

"No exchanging anything and no touching," the guard said.

Rachel nodded and eased into the seat. She had heard the instructions half a dozen times, but each visit they still seemed to haunt her.

No touching.

Two inseparable sisters. Little girls who grew up holding hands and wrestling and swatting each other. Paddy-cake, secret handshakes, braiding each other's hair. Always touching. In high school, there was hugging and high-fiving and crying on the other's shoulder as each moved through bad acne, braces, cheating boyfriends, and the unfair journey through teenage years.

When they were adults, the touching would end, a chasm

gradually forming between them, and then the death of their mother wedging them further apart.

But still, *no touching?*

The order seemed unnecessarily cruel, like Rachel was being punished for the crimes of her sister.

The door on the opposite side creaked open and a guard entered, followed closely by a tall, Black woman in an orange jumpsuit, her head held high, her wrists cuffed in front. Seeing Rachel, the woman smiled curtly and followed the guard to the table.

"Can I take these off?" the guard asked, gesturing toward the handcuffs. "Or will there be trouble again?"

"Oh, I'm full of trouble," Angela said, a smirk swelling across her face.

The guard stood expressionless, his arms crossed over his beefy chest.

Angela went still and averted her gaze. "But not this time, Officer," she added. "I'll be on my best behaviour. Scout's honour."

The guard rolled his eyes and unlocked the handcuffs. Angela exhaled, rubbing the skin along her wrists. She nodded her thanks and the guard clunked away.

"You were never in Scouts," Rachel whispered.

"You know that and I know that, but Officer Meathead over there doesn't know that," Angela said, her smirk returning.

She swiped her brown bangs off her forehead, her once healthy, long hair now cut short. It was rattier than Rachel remembered, dry with frayed ends, the shine leaked out of it after seven months behind bars.

Gone too was the expensive jewelry, the make-up, and the

flashy heels. Her nails were chipped and cracked, her skin raw and flaking. Normally well kept with an athletic build, Angela was plain-looking and reed-thin, a shadow of her former self; as if she had been trampled on and hollowed out.

Only her eyes remained the same—alive and intense—mischief and callousness behind them.

"I suppose it's silly to ask, but how have you been?" Rachel said.

Angela sighed. "Not much changes in this place. I'm the same as the last time you were here."

"Has anyone else come to visit?"

Angela sat up straight. "Who?" she blurted out. "Who in the world would come see me? Both Mom and Dad are dead. You're the only one left."

"I just thought maybe one of your colleagues or something," Rachel said, remembering the names from the visitor's registry.

"Colleagues? Hell, they've been out to get me since this whole thing started. Nobody's on my side."

"I don't think there are sides, Angela. There's right and wrong, but no one's taking *sides*."

Angela huffed but said nothing.

"Regardless, I'm here, aren't I?" Rachel said.

"You're here while at the same time dating the guy who put me here," Angela said.

"He didn't put you here," Rachel shot back. "You got yourself arrested."

"Because of him."

"No, because you poisoned an entire town!"

"As I've told you before, it was all to find a cure. Besides, you make me sound like such a horrible person. *Poisoned an entire town.*"

"That's what happened, isn't it?"

"That wasn't the goal, wasn't the intention."

"Every resident of Barn Wood was experimented on and then turned into crazy lunatics."

"It wasn't *my* fault. It was that Dr. Simon Stone idiot. A fool who prepared the virus and the vaccine all wrong."

"Oh, please, spare me the blame game."

"Facts are facts."

"You played your part in all of it and we both know it. Your name is all over those reports found in your house."

Angela coughed into her hand, her frail frame bending with the movement. She wiped the white mucus from her lips. "The whole thing was mired in poor communication and mis-calculations," she said. "If we were able to do it again, we'd get it right."

Rachel drew back. "Do it again? You created a nightmare that people are still recovering from, may never recover from!"

"We just wanted a fool-proof way to test the drug. We were so close to finding a cure. It's all so frustrating."

"Frustrating for who? You?" Rachel said. "Neither Xavier or Evelyn have found their parents. And don't get me started on the two friends I had to bury because of your so-called *mis-calculations*."

"Oh, please. You knew them for what, a week?"

Rachel jabbed a finger through the air. "They. Were. My. Friends!" she said through clenched teeth.

"Okay, okay, let's stop talking about this. We argued about it last time. All it does is rile you up."

"I think I have the right to be riled up given all the hurt you've caused."

Officer Vedan stepped out from the shadows. "Lower

your voices, both of you," he barked. "Or I'll end this session early."

Angela smiled nervously and nodded.

Rachel closed her eyes, trying to calm her breathing. She turned to Angela and shook her head. "Still no regrets, huh? No remorse?"

"For what?" Angela snorted. "I'm a scientist who was trying to cure a disease."

"That's not how everyone else sees it."

Angela bristled. "Well, that's no surprise! The court of public opinion has already decided I'm the villain thanks to that twit, Brad Moseby. He spins quite the yarn about me in his pathetic column."

"Is he wrong?"

"That twerp has had it out for me ever since he ran into me at that motel a year and a half ago. Always trying to make a story out of nothing!"

"Nothing?"

"Do you know he even tried to come and talk to me here? In prison? Confronting me with all these asinine accusations."

"I thought you said no one else has visited you?"

"That little rat doesn't count," Angela sneered. "As soon as he opened his mouth I demanded to be brought back to my cell. I'd rather sit in there than listen to him ramble on about his conspiracy theories."

Rachel cleared her throat and stood. "I should go," she said. "As usual, this seems to have been a waste of time."

Angela reached out but quickly drew back, giving a sideways glance to the guard. "No, please, don't go," she said. "Please sit. We can talk about other things."

Rachel swallowed and then lowered into the chair.

"Tell me about this guy you're seeing," Angela said. "You'll remember, I only met him the one time." She smiled wryly and Rachel wriggled in her seat, trying to push away the memory of when Angela caught her and Xavier in her home.

"It's nothing, really," Rachel said.

"Nothing? It's been months, hasn't it?"

"I guess. Since September."

"You sounded much more confident about him last time you were here. What's changed?"

"I think the intensity of everything going on when we first met. Being hunted by those things, him saving me in the woods."

"Yes?"

"Well, I think all that fear and emotion…it just propelled me to him, drew us together."

"And now?"

"Well…it's complicated. I mean, the circumstances surrounding it are complicated."

"Do you live with him?"

"Off and on. But his younger cousin lives there as well, so…" Rachel trailed off, averting her gaze.

"So?"

"I guess he and I are slowing it down a bit. Just seeing if something's actually there, if any of it is real."

Angela nodded. "Well, believe it or not, I'm happy for you. Growing up, you were always awkward with the fellas, so I'm glad this one's showing promise."

Rachel scoffed. "I don't remember you exactly being a superstar with the guys."

"True. But men never really interested me. I always preferred a feminine touch."

Officer Vedan stepped forward. "Time's up, ladies."

He heaved Angela up from the chair then cuffed her. She turned to Rachel, her face wilted, all emotion drained from it. "I guess 'til next time," she said.

Rachel gave a gentle wave, but Angela didn't see it as Officer Vedan spun her roughly around, her shoes squeaking as he dragged her to the door, handing her over to a second guard. He motioned to Rachel who followed him to the exit. He unlocked and relocked the maze of doors until they were both standing outside the check-in desk.

"Have a good visit at Club Pen?" the clerk asked with a snigger.

Rachel bit her lip but said nothing. She pulled off the lanyard and remitted the visitor badge.

"We'll see you next time," the officer said. "Drive safe. The weather's miserable out there."

Rachel stepped outside into the freezing rain as the heavy door slammed shut. She glanced again at the barbed-wire snaking along the top of the fence before hustling across the parking lot and ducking into her car. She shivered as she turned the key, the damp cold of the prison difficult to shake, the sinisterness of the building rooting down into her.

But as she pulled out of the parking lot, she thought of the protective nature of Xavier and the innocence of Evelyn, and she felt lighter. She was returning to a confusing home, yes, but one of warmth and welcome, and a smile teased at her lips the rest of the drive back to Barn Wood.

Chapter Five

November 1995
Day 638 | Morning

Xavier brought the hammer down, securing the shingles in place. He repeated the action, gripping the tool, nails clenched between his teeth. He scurried along the ridge of the aged-farmhouse, close to the flashing, steady as a bobcat.

When he was done, he leaned into the hips of the roof admiring his handiwork. "That should hold," he said.

Holstering his hammer, he gazed across the backyard. The snow had come hard and early this year. Only mid-November and already it was heavy on the boughs of the elms and spruce, white hillocks piled at their trunks. The wooden fence along the border was cracked and splintered with much of the lawn covered in white, the occasional tufts of dead brown grass peeking through.

He surveyed the dense forest beyond the backyard, thick bare limbs and wilted ferns stretching in all directions as if threatening to suffocate the small town. Once a hopeful place for hunting—alive with spry deer and nimble rabbit—the woods now sat dark and foreboding, smeared over with memories of blood and fear and death.

His attention turned to the cellar—a refuge where he, Andrew, and a group of strangers sheltered from feral monsters last winter—now emptied, locked, and boarded up.

His gaze stumbled over the stone marker and small pile of rocks atop Damien's grave. A weathered tobacco pouch was tied to a wooden stake, bobbing in the sharp wind. He bit his lip and turned away.

He rubbed his knuckles across the purple and yellow of his jaw where the beast had come down on it yesterday. He fingered the taped gauze along his forehead, the gash cleaned and bandaged by Rachel after he had burst through the front door, frantic and half-mad, hollering that the beasts were back, howling that he needed to call Everett.

He kicked at the new shingles one last time, testing their hold. He adjusted the cuffs of his filthy plaid jacket and began gathering his tools, listening to wood being chopped close to the house.

He shuffled toward the ladder when the crunch of tires caused him to turn. He watched as the police cruiser made its way up the driveway, stopping a dozen yards from the house.

Staff Inspector Tom Everett swung the door open and heaved his portly frame from the vinyl seat, his black boots slipping on the snow and gravel. His navy-blue police shirt was wrinkled and stained, and despite the cold November wind, his pasty skin was blotched with sweat. He waved up to the roof. "We gonna conduct our meeting up there?"

"Yesterday's storm shook a few shingles loose," Xavier hollered down. "Think I've got them all tacked down again."

"Better you than me up there," Everett said. He patted his paunch and laughed. "I'm not quite as *athletic* as I used to be."

Xavier smirked. "Just finishing up. I'll be down in a few."

"Take your time on that ladder, huh? After what you told me over the phone, you and I are gonna be working real close again. The last thing I need is you getting injured."

He shuffled toward the wrap-around porch just as Rachel came through the screen door. She was tall and lean, wearing black jeans with a grey shawl. Her skin glistened in the morning sun. She carried two cups of coffee and she smiled as Everett made his way up the front steps.

"Well, what a nice thing to see you here," Everett said.

"Hello Staff Inspector, it's great to see you again," Rachel said. She handed him a mug then brushed her hair out from her eyes. "Although, each time you come it seems to follow bad news."

"Nature of the job, I guess," Everett huffed. "But never you mind with all this formal *Staff Inspector* stuff. Tom will do just fine."

Rachel smiled and gestured for him to sit on the cedar bench hemmed into the corner of the porch.

Everett sat, groaning as his knees creaked, then blew on the coffee, steam curling up into his friendly eyes. He took a long drink. "Thanks for this," he said, raising the mug. "I can use all the caffeine I can get. Haven't slept since he called."

"Yeah, he's pretty worked up. Don't think he slept much either," Rachel said.

"He gonna be okay?"

"Not sure. I've never seen him this worried before."

"He really thinks there's more of them, huh?"

"Oh, you'll believe it too when you talk to him. It's been pretty tense around here since they got back yesterday."

"They? Andrew's home?"

"No. He took Evelyn with him."

"Evelyn? She was with him when he saw those things?"

Rachel nodded. "They were supposed to hunt deer.

Ended up hunting something else."

Everett shook his head. "Goodness, that girl's been through so much. Had to grow up quick, didn't she?"

"She's doing okay."

"Not a typical year for a 13-year-old."

"She's tougher than you think."

"Well, I suppose that's true."

"But, Tom, listen," Rachel started, leaning closer. "X says these new ones, the ones from yesterday…they're not like the ones from last winter."

"How so?"

"He says these ones are stronger."

"Is that right?"

"Smarter, even."

Everett exhaled, pressing his knuckles into his temples. He glanced upon the front yard, a flash of sorrow across his face. "Funny what we're made to talk about these days, huh?"

He shifted along the bench, adjusting his trousers, attacking an itch along the inseam. Repositioning the police radio on his belt, he tested it for volume, then turned back to Rachel. He forced a wooden smile.

"How are you otherwise?" he asked. "Everything else okay?"

"You mean besides being hunted by infected monsters, that my sister's in prison, and that I'm falling for someone seven years younger than me?" Rachel said.

"I-I didn't mean to pry," Everett stammered. "I was just tryin' to make small talk is all, just tryin' to—"

"I'm joking, Tom," Rachel interrupted, stifling a coy smile. "I'm just playing with you."

"Ah, okay," Everett said, shifting awkwardly in his seat.

"To answer your question, things are okay," Rachel said. "Slowly returning to normal."

"That's a…that's a good thing."

"Yeah, we're starting to have a bit of stability around here. A routine of sorts."

"That's good to hear. You stay in touch with your sister?"

"I try."

"Her court hearing was scheduled for September, if I recall. How'd that go?"

"She'll be re-tried in a few months, so for now they've moved her from the local station to the main prison."

"Ah, okay."

"I was there yesterday, actually. Try to get out there every few weeks."

"How's that going?"

"I was furious about it at first. But I'm learning to be calmer with her."

"Hm."

"And she's slowly becoming more self-aware of the role she's played in all this."

"You think it's genuine?"

"Hard to tell."

"She did produce a temporary antidote," Everett admitted. "So, at least a part of her knew she needed to do something to help."

"That's true. Some days she expresses remorse and other times she's just as defiant as she's always been."

"Might take a while. My interactions with her were always…*challenging*."

"I get that. She's still bitter at everyone involved in the experiments—the investors, that Alan Mackenzie guy,

Evelyn's dad."

"Aren't we all."

"But she's also still angry our mom died, angry about our childhood, stuff like that. It's like she can't let the past go."

Everett nodded and slurped his coffee.

"She's angry about a lot of things, I guess," Rachel added. "But gradually her perspective is shifting, I think."

"Sounds like progress," Everett said.

"Slow, but progress, nonetheless. The prison physician has her back on medication, which is good."

"I didn't realize she was on meds."

"She's always suffered from…I mean, she's always dealt with mental health issues. So, at least now her and I can have a civil conversation when I visit."

"Mm-hmm. And Evelyn?"

"She's doing better. Started school in September, seems to enjoy it."

"That's good to hear."

"Still wakes up with nightmares, but they're fewer now. Still mourns her brother, of course."

"To be expected," Everett said, his bushy brows sinking toward his sad eyes. "That type of wound takes a long time to heal. If ever."

"We keep her busy to help keep her mind off of it," Rachel said. "She helps out with the chores and X has taken her on a few hunts."

"You don't go with them?"

"You couldn't drag me out there again. I used to love the forest, but now…"

"Yeah, I get that," Everett said, eyeing the dark trees surrounding the house. "So, Evelyn's staying here?"

"Yeah, she's good here."

"I mean, I guess until we get a location on her parents."

"She's fine here," Rachel said sternly. "Doing just fine. She belongs here."

"Right, right," Everett said. He averted his gaze and pressed his lips together as if mulling over a problem. Then: "And how about the big man? I mean, besides his scare yesterday."

"Well, you know how he is: grumpy, with a short temper."

"Ha! Don't I know it. He, Andrew, and I hunted those crazy things for months last year and not once did I see him smile."

"It's rare, I'll give you that," Rachel snickered. "But he smiles more now. I think Evelyn has a lot to do with that."

"And you, I'd imagine."

Rachel turned away, a soft blush darkening her cheeks. "There's a security with him, you know?" she said. "Something I didn't grow up with."

Everett nodded.

"And a rawness," she added. "Like he wouldn't think twice to get his knuckles bloodied for me. It's scary, but also... safe, if that makes sense."

"Mm-hmm."

"Anyway, he should be down shortly. He's always fixing or tinkering with something."

"No problem. Is Evelyn around?"

"She's around back. Stays as busy as he does, always finding something to fix. Or break."

Everett smiled and gestured toward the backyard. "You mind?"

"Not at all, I'm sure she'd love to see you."

Everett stood and drank the last of his coffee.

"I'll get you a refill for when you get back," Rachel said.

"Many thanks," he said, handing her his mug.

He stepped off the porch and lumbered around the side of the house until he spotted her. She was chopping wood, pulling the axe high above her head then splitting the log cleanly as the edge came down. Flecks of dirt hid under her chipped nails, bark and dust buried within her braids. She swung once more before she saw him.

"Mr. Everett," she said with a soft smile.

"Well, look at you," Everett chuckled. "You must be half a foot taller since I saw you last."

Evelyn dragged the crook of her arm across her brow.

"And my goodness, I couldn't swing an axe like that at your age," Everett added. "Look how strong you've become!"

"They're back, Mr. Everett," Evelyn said. "Those things are back!"

Everett swallowed. "Yes, Xavier told me last night over the phone."

"They're bigger. And stronger."

"That's what he said."

"One of them chased us," Evelyn said, and as she shifted her jacket collar slipped, revealing abrasions along her neck and shoulder.

Everett pointed at the wounds. "Those from yesterday?"

"Yeah. That thing smashed the window and got glass on me. Rachel cleaned me up last night."

"My word." Everett shook his head. "How are you otherwise? Rachel tells me you're doing well here, doing well at school?"

"Yeah."

"Things back to normal?"

"Mostly, I guess," Evelyn said, her eyes pausing on Damien's grave.

"And what've we got here?" Everett asked. He moseyed over to a leaning oak with three concentric circles carved into its trunk, the smallest one no larger than a dime. A knife stuck out of the innermost circle.

"X has been teaching me how to throw a knife," Evelyn said.

"So, this poor tree's the target?"

"Yeah. Been practicing every day for like three months now."

Everett eyed the knife. "Seems you got the hang of it."

Evelyn nodded, awkwardly dragging her boot across the snowy ground. "Any word on my parents?"

Everett hesitated. "I'm sorry, dear, nothing yet," he said. "Sometimes these missing person cases are tough to crack."

"Okay," she said then tossed the axe to the ground.

"As you can imagine, there are a lot of families still separated," Everett added. "But we're doing our best to track down who's still out there. And soon, all of them that's missing will start coming out of the woodwork, you'll see."

Evelyn nodded. "So, I guess you're here because of yesterday?"

Everett fiddled with his watch and ground his teeth. He gestured to the front of the house. "What do ya say we discuss all that with the other two?"

"Yeah, okay."

They ambled around the side of the house to find Xavier and Rachel seated on the front porch. Rachel was speaking softly, her head buried in the crook of Xavier's neck. Xavier stood when he saw Everett.

"There he is," Everett boomed. His hand all but disappeared within Xavier's as the men shook hands. Everett gazed at the house. "Looks like you fixed it up since I last saw it, since those things tore at it."

"It's on its way," Xavier said as he picked at the dressing affixed to his forehead.

"Well, it looks great."

"Lots to do still. Keeps me out of trouble, I suppose."

"Apparently not! From what you told me yesterday it seems trouble has found you yet again."

Rachel handed Everett a fresh cup of coffee. He thanked her then turned back to Xavier. "What's with the bandage and bruised jaw?" he asked. "You get those yesterday as well?"

Xavier nodded but said nothing, just wiped at his brow and chugged water from a glass container. He shoved his hands in his pockets and took a few steps from the porch, his mouth set, turning something over in his mind.

He squinted upon the fields, dotted with slush and snow and debris. Mere weeks ago, there stood acres of tall golden stalks. Now the ground was littered with mushy brown stubs, the wheat hacked and scythed out of it just before the frost set in. As he stared upon the fields it became difficult to distinguish him from the land, both dour and desolate and bleak.

He buttoned his jacket to his throat as if anticipating colder weather. Or perhaps, something else was coming.

He paced in front of the porch as if struggling over what to say. "You told us they were all captured, right?" he said finally, a bite to his words.

"That's right," Everett said.

"Then why the hell did we come across a hive of 'em?"

Everett's smile slipped. "Whoa, slow down, let's talk this

through. The last I heard, all these damn creatures were taken care of." He took a deep breath. "First, let's establish where this was. Where were you when you came across this…this *hive,* as you call it?"

"I'm not entirely sure. About two hours from here."

"Have you been there before?"

"Yeah, Andrew and I hunted there years ago. But I got turned around. The roads wash out back there and you just have to know your way around—which I don't."

"You remember anything specific about the area?"

"It was close to a camp. Camp…camp…I forget the name of it. Some kid's camp."

"Clearwater," Evelyn piped in. "The road sign said Camp Clearwater."

"Yeah, that was it," Xavier said. "The camp though—it's abandoned."

"How do you know?" Everett asked.

"Most of the cabins were in shambles, nothing really there but old sports equipment."

"Abandoned campground, huh?" Everett said. "I recall we had reports of this over the summer. Just never had enough officers to go and check it out. We were stretched so thin."

"But the place where I saw those things—it wasn't right in the camp," Xavier said. "It was a few hundred yards beyond it. In an old barn."

Everett placed his mug on the railing and took out a pad and pen, scratching notes onto the page. "Okay," he said. "So, the barn is not on camp property, but you can see it from the camp?"

"Barely. It's up on an escarpment, away in the distance."

"Still, if we can find the camp again then we can likely find—"

"But Tom, listen," Xavier interrupted. "The barn was shaking."

"Shaking? How so?"

"They shook the walls—like a massive party going on inside."

"Did you approach?"

Xavier nodded.

"Of course you approached, don't know why I even asked," Everett muttered, shaking his head. "Okay, so you approached. And?"

"There were loads of 'em. Creatures like we saw last winter but…different."

"Different how?"

"Larger and definitely stronger. But smarter too."

Everett cocked his head.

"I don't know how to describe it," Xavier said. "They were just more…aware. Like they knew what they were meant to do, like why they were there. I'm probably not making sense."

"No, no, this is good, this is all useful information." Everett jotted a few additional points in his notepad. "Can you describe them?"

"The ones we fought last winter, well, they were creepy and frightening, sure. But they were just people."

"Those weren't people," Rachel said.

"What I mean is, you could tell they *used* to be people. Like they were normal height, normal size." Xavier paused, struggling to collect his thoughts. "I guess the best way to describe it is last winter I never came across one I didn't think I could fight off. But the ones yesterday…" His words trailed off. Rachel came to stand beside him and placed a hand on his back.

"They were evolved," he said finally. "A stronger, smarter version."

"Like a mutation?" Everett asked.

"I don't know. Maybe. But it was the first time I was truly afraid of them. Like if one attacked, I might not be able to fight it off."

"But you told me on the phone that you *were* attacked."

"Yeah, one chased me down. Evelyn honked the horn to distract it and that's the only reason I got out of there alive."

Rachel gasped. "You didn't tell me that part!" she said, gripping his hand in hers.

"I got lucky."

Everett turned to Evelyn. "Did you see it?"

Evelyn bit her lip and nodded.

"Was it as big as he says?" Everett asked.

"Bigger," Evelyn said.

"Tom, it tossed a hundred-pound doe out the back of the truck like it was a bag of groceries," Xavier said.

Everett adjusted his uniform and pulled at his collar. He closed his notepad and shoved it back in his jacket pocket. After a long silence, he cleared his throat. "If what you say is true, then we'll need to convene a team to go out again."

"It's true," Evelyn said. "All of it."

"I thought we got them all, thought we were done with all this," Everett said. He shook his head, a look of dread falling across his face. "I'll try to assemble a team, but you need to know that last time headquarters didn't take this seriously."

"You need to get as many cops up there as you can," Xavier said.

"I'll call Constables Prasad and Powell. You remember them from last time, right?"

Xavier nodded.

"And I'll try to reign in a few others," Everett added. "But we could use your help again. And your brother's. There's no one on my squad that can track like the two of you."

"How soon can we start?" Xavier asked.

"Give me a couple days. I should have a team assembled and briefed by then. Still, we could use more resources. Do you have any friends that might be up for this?"

"Ev will come."

"Oh no, no, this isn't a task for a child," Everett said, his eyes catching on the girl. "Especially one in such a…such a fragile state."

Evelyn scowled at Everett, searching him silently.

"She's different now," Xavier offered.

"Let's see what I can muster up over the next few days," Everett said, breaking from Evelyn's glare. He turned to face Xavier. "Besides, one thing I've learned is never try to reason with you Stones."

He picked up the mug from the railing and looked into it. There was no steam coming from it, the coffee now gone cold. He drank the last of it down anyway then returned the mug to Rachel. "Thanks again for the caffeine," he mused. "Seems I've got a lot of late nights ahead of me."

Rachel gave a tense smile as Xavier stepped forward.

"Tom, you need to appreciate what I've told you," Xavier said, his words cold and sober. "These things are calculated, they stalk and move like predators. They're pure hunters."

Everett nodded then lumbered toward the police cruiser, his eyes suddenly tired, his shoulders hunched as if laden with a weight he hadn't arrived with. "I thought we were done with all this," he muttered.

He sank into the driver's seat and turned the engine over. As he reversed out of the driveway, he scanned the surrounding scrub, twisting back and forth as though expecting a dark shape to conjure up right then and there, out from the black brush and bare trees.

Chapter Six

November 1995
Day 638 | Evening

Andrew gulped down the glass of ice-water. As he did, an ice cube came loose, sloshing the liquid over the rim of the glass and down the front of his wrinkled shirt.

"Ha! That's what you get for always sticking with water," Juliana Shift squealed. Some of the restaurant patrons turned at the noise. "See, you should have wine like me," she added gleefully. "No ice cubes to worry about!"

Andrew smiled and dabbed the wet stain with a napkin. Juliana had landed that morning and had brought such a shock of happiness that all of Andrew's worries seemed to wither away.

"You probably think I'm a klutz," he said.

"Sure, but a *cute* klutz," Juliana said. "And a klutz that saved my life!"

Andrew grinned. "At least I have that going for me."

He gestured at the half-eaten piece of cheesecake on the table. Juliana smiled and dug her fork in, her red lips devouring the sweet dessert. It was the perfect end to a shared entrée of fajitas and fried rice.

"Can you believe I'm here?" she asked.

"Hasn't really sunk in yet," Andrew said.

"I mean, we've hung out like what, three, maybe four times since that flight back in April?"

"I thought you'd never get on a plane again after that."

"Me too!"

"Didn't take much to get you here though."

"I know! A couple of dates and I just drop everything to fly here. I mean, who does that?"

"The power I yield," Andrew teased.

Juliana shook her head and swirled her wine. She secured a loose strand of red hair, the faint smell of lavender drifting off her.

Andrew took in her curious green eyes, the polished earrings shadowing each lobe, her slender shoulders hidden within the fitted grey sweater. The silver pendant she seemed to always wear dangled just above her full chest. When she spoke, her face glowed with excitement, her hands in constant motion.

"Now that I'm here, are you going to tour me around the city?" she asked. "Take me to your classes?"

"Oh geez. A tour of the city we can manage, but I'm definitely not taking you to my classes," Andrew said.

"Well, that's fine, I never really went to class anyways."

"Of course you went to class—you're a big-time lawyer!"

"Oh, please, I'm hardly *big-time*. I went to class when I needed to, enough to get by, and let's just leave it at that."

She glanced around as the seats began to fill, the nattering from other tables trickling through the quaint diner. She adjusted the cork coaster, her wine glass perched high upon it.

"How's your brother?" she asked.

"He's okay," Andrew said.

"You guys talking again?"

"Sure. I mean, it's not like when we were kids but…"

"No, I guess it wouldn't be."

"It is what it is."

"But he's your brother. I just wish it could be, I don't know, like it could be fixed or something."

"We're good. I mean, as good as we're gonna be. We don't talk a lot, but he'll occasionally call with updates."

"Updates on what?"

"Just if he's heard anything about our parents, if the cops have any new leads, stuff like that."

Juliana pressed her lips together then reached for her glass. "Is he still not sure what to make of me?"

"Nah, he's fine," Andrew said.

"He's pretty stand-off-ish."

"Stand-off-ish? That's a blessing! Normally he's down-right hostile."

Juliana smiled. "Seriously though, what does he think of me?"

"Oh, I wouldn't worry about him. Our own mother doesn't know what to make of him."

"Does he think it's strange I'm a bit older than you?"

"Doubt it."

"Why do you say that?"

"He and Rachel are a thing and she's older than he is."

"Oh, right."

"Even my mom has a few years on my step-father. Must be hereditary—all the Stone men like older women."

"Older women?" Juliana shrieked. "Careful or I might just get back on that plane!"

Andrew laughed and took another swill of water. He placed the glass down and ran a finger along the rim. He pushed his sleeves up his forearms.

"But seriously, your brother's okay with me?" Juliana asked. "With you and I?"

"He's always been…distant," Andrew said. "He'll come around."

"I hope so."

"Besides, Evelyn likes you!"

"Yeah, she's sweet. And crazy how you found out you're cousins!"

"*Crazy* is definitely the right word. Last winter was crazy."

"I know! I still can't believe half the stuff you've told me."

"Oh?"

"Are you kidding me? Tainted drugs and viruses, lunatics chasing you through a forest, you hiding in a cellar for a week? I mean, should I even believe you?"

Andrew arched his eyebrows. "When you say it like that it doesn't make much sense, does it?"

"But everything's back to normal?"

"I wouldn't say *normal*. A lot of townsfolk are still missing."

"I just meant as normal as they can be."

Andrew shrugged. "It's a lot for a sleepy town."

"I never heard of any of it until you called me in the summer," Juliana said.

"It was strange how people outside of Barn Wood hardly knew anything about it. I don't think any of the major newspapers covered it."

"You'd think lunatics bent on murder would be top fodder for a newspaper!"

"This local columnist, Brad Moseby, wrote about it in our local paper. Tried to even get interviews with X and I. But besides him, I guess it wasn't big enough news. Or someone didn't want it to be."

"What does that mean?"

Andrew folded his hands on the table. "Honestly, I've stopped trying to figure it all out. To me, it's just an awful story, a horrible dream I'm trying to forget."

Juliana nodded then took the last bite of cake, sliding the empty plate away. She tried to stifle a yawn but it came forth nonetheless.

"Want to get out of here?" Andrew asked. "You're probably drained from the flight."

"Yeah, I'm afraid I won't be much of a party animal tonight," Juliana said. "Just get me a pillow and a warm blanket and I'll be in heaven."

Andrew waved the server over and signalled for the cheque. After settling the bill, they stepped into the street. They meandered along the sidewalk, the street lamps glowing down upon them. The November air was cold and damp and Andrew reached for Juliana's hand, her warm fingers lacing between his.

When they arrived at his apartment, he shoved the key in and pushed the door open. Juliana stopped under the doorframe, surveying the small space.

"It's not much, but it will get me through the year," Andrew said.

There was a grey two-seater couch in front of an oak table with a TV perched on top, a rabbit-ear antennae sprouting from the black box. A desk with assorted papers was pushed into the corner, a lamp teetering on the edge.

A galley kitchen with a small breakfast nook bordered the main room with a bathroom and bedroom at the end of a short hall. Several pairs of shoes were lined up neatly on a mat. A broom and dustpan leaned against the door of the front closet.

"Not bad," Juliana mused. "Better than I thought, to be honest with you."

"What were you expecting? Rats?" Andrew said.

"Some guys are just messy, that's all. Like my ex-fiancé. Messy…and a horrible kisser."

"Well, at least I've got him beat at cleanliness."

"Oh, you've got him beat at more than that," Juliana said. She rose on her tiptoes and kissed him.

He smiled then cleared his throat. "You want something to drink?"

"A cup of tea would be nice if you have some."

"Coming right up."

Andrew skittered into the kitchen and filled the kettle. There was a clunk of mugs and then shuffling as he rummaged through a drawer. "Oh, and please make yourself at home," he called out.

Juliana rolled her suitcase into the corner and leaned it against the desk. A wall calendar hung over it, 'November 1995', displayed in bold lettering. A few exam dates were circled in black, a red heart on today's date accompanied with the note: *Juliana's flight!*

She smiled then took in the stack of documents and dog-eared textbooks. She read one of the titles out loud. "Foundations of Epidemiology: A complete history of case-control studies of infectious diseases, mortality and risk adjustments, and emerging healthcare interventions." She turned toward the kitchen. "Please tell me you have no idea what this book is about?"

"On the contrary," Andrew said, peeking around the corner. "I read it over the weekend."

"Good grief."

"And I loved it."

"Dammit, that's what I was afraid of. I'm dating a nerd."

"Yes, but a handsome nerd," Andrew said, before disappearing into the kitchen again.

She shook her head and smiled as her hand glided along the desk. It moved across a flyer for an upcoming lecture, a movie ticket stub, an electricity bill, a page of calculations, a scatter of pencils.

She spotted a thin black folder. She tilted it open and her attention caught on a report, her eyes growing wide at the 'CONFIDENTIAL' heading printed in bold yellow lettering along the top. She flipped through the pages then returned to the cover, pausing on a name near the top. "I know him."

Andrew walked into the room holding two steaming mugs of earl grey. He handed one to Juliana. "Did you say something?"

"What, um, what is all this?" Juliana asked.

Andrew eyed the report. "Well, I've told you a fair bit about last winter, right?"

"Way more than I wanted to know."

"Right. And did I tell you about Rachel and Angela?"

"Sure, Rachel's dating your brother and Angela's her sister, the masochist."

Andrew made a face. "That's an oversimplification, but sure, let's go with that for now."

"What about them?"

"This report was found in Angela's house. It explains what she was involved in—the making of a drug, the search for a cure. It's basically all we know about the origins of the virus that spread through Barn Wood."

Juliana shook her head. "See this guy here," she said, pointing near the top of the page. "I know him."

"Alan Mackenzie?" Andrew said. "But he's the lead of operations."

"I've met him before."

"Really? We don't know anything about him. Even the cops can't find him."

"Well, he wasn't always that way."

"What do you mean?"

"You remember how I used to practice pharmaceutical law?"

"Of course, you told me when we met on the plane."

"Well, this guy was the financier for a brand we were representing."

Andrew glanced at the documents. "BioHealth Pharmaceuticals?"

"No, it wasn't that one," Juliana said. "But still, I remember this Mackenzie guy. He controlled the purse strings. And the things the company was doing…"

"Oh?"

"They tried to keep it secret but my team came across some documents just before I left the firm."

"What'd they say?"

Juliana lowered her voice, even though it was just her and Andrew in the apartment. "The company used to test on apes, doing all sorts of cruel things to them."

"You read that?"

"It was all there. Laboratories full of animals, these guys drugging and doing tests on them."

"Are you serious?"

Juliana nervously wrung her hands. "But it didn't stop there."

"How so?"

"The documents described that when the investors didn't achieve the results they wanted with apes, they began testing on humans."

"This sounds familiar."

"Sometimes they would hold them for weeks, testing different pharma products on them."

"Jesus Christ. And you remember this Mackenzie guy?"

"Vividly. Always gave me the creeps. He'd speak in this soft tone, like trying to convince you he was harmless. But I could see right through him."

"How?"

"Being a lawyer, you meet a lot of liars. And being a woman, you meet a lot of creeps."

"Hm."

"They always stand out," Juliana said. "And he stood out in the worst way."

"Oh."

Juliana pointed to a small footer on the document. "What's this 'one of twelve' mean?" She thumbed through the rest of the document. "There's only seven pages so it can't be the page numbers."

Andrew leaned in. "I've never noticed that before. I'm not sure what that could mean."

A loud ring cut through the air and it took Andrew a moment to realize it was the phone.

"Excuse me," he said, slipping into the kitchen to grab it. Before he picked up the receiver, he hollered over his shoulder: "Remember to drink your tea before it gets cold!"

Juliana blew on the liquid and took a long sip, the heat from it soothing her throat and tired mind. She smiled, listening to Andrew's deep voice drifting in from the other room. After several minutes, he hung up and joined her again, his troubled eyes locked on hers.

"What is it?" she asked.

"That was Xavier," Andrew said. "It's happening again."

"What's happening?"

"The whole thing. It's happening again."

"What do you mean?"

"I need to go back. They want me to go back." He paced the room, cracking each of his knuckles.

"Who?"

"Everett, X, all of them. He said those things are back."

"What things?"

"They need me to hunt again."

"Hunt? Hunt what?" Juliana put her mug down and grabbed Andrew by the shoulders. "Slow down, you're not making any sense."

"Juliana—those crazy things are back!"

"In Barn Wood?"

"X said they're back!"

"Okay, okay. But why do *you* need to go?"

"Everett—he's the top cop I told you about. He wants me to help track again."

"Listen, I understand you want to help, but why *you*?"

"It has to be me, needs to be me."

"I'm sure there are others who can help. You're a six-hour flight away for Christ's sake!"

"I know, I know. But I've just never heard him like that before."

"Who?"

"X. I've never heard him talk like that. Sound that…that *panicked* before."

"It's probably just shock."

"It's more than that. Like he senses something…something dark, something that's coming."

"Andrew, listen to me," Juliana said. "I just got here. Literally flew in today to spend time with you."

Andrew stopped pacing and averted his eyes. "I know, I'm sorry," he said. "None of this is fair."

"Besides, if you go back home, what about your school? You're going to skip the rest of the term to go hunt a bunch of maniacs?"

"I'll be able to catch up. But this? I need to go back."

Juliana exhaled. She moved across the room and sat on the couch. Her forehead was creased and she rubbed her hands together as if concocting a ploy.

"Alright, you need to go back, I get it," she said finally. "And I'm not going to tell you what to do. But can we at least go on a date—I mean, *one real date*—while I'm here?"

Andrew bit his lip and moved across the room to join her.

"I took a week off work, flew all this way, and now I can't even go on a date," Juliana said. "Just one date with the cute nerd I came all this way to see?"

Andrew plopped down on the couch beside her. She ran her fingernails along his arm. He turned and smiled. "Totally fair," he said. "Tomorrow is all yours. Whatever you want to do, we'll do."

"Sight-seeing?"

"Yep."

"Picnic in the park?"

"Of course."

"Dinner by the water?"

"All of it. We won't worry about any of this other stuff, okay?"

"No talk of monsters or rogue scientists or nasty viruses?"

Andrew chuckled. "None of it. Just you and me. I promise."

She shifted in her seat and placed a hand on the back of his neck. She leaned in and kissed him.

"Listen, I know you're a big-time hero in Barn Wood," she said cheekily. "But here you're just Andrew. And that's all I want. Just you. Just for a little bit."

She burrowed into him and her breathing began to calm; her shoulders now relaxed. She yawned.

"You're tired," Andrew said. "Jet lag probably catching up with you."

Juliana stood. "I've still got a bit of energy yet," she said. She smiled then grabbed his hand, pulling him up from the couch. She led him into the bedroom at the end of the hall, her smell of lavender following them in as she turned and closed the door.

Chapter Seven

November 1995
Day 638 | Evening

Alan Mackenzie huffed and snorted as he struggled to break free from the tiny closet. He sat awkwardly but repositioned his heavy frame, attempting to push up from the ground. His hands were bound at the wrist—a tangled mess of rope and wire—and his arms were pulled up over his head, securely fastened to a metal bar halfway up the wall.

Furious, he blustered and shook. "Simon!" he wheezed, his throat parched. "Simon, you let me out of here! Have you lost your damn mind?"

His left eye was swollen and purple bruises pulsed along his neck. Claw marks pierced his cheek and throat like dozens of knife nicks. A soppy mix of sweat and blood pooled along the creases of his forehead. It rivered through his dark stubble and off his chin, staining the front of his wrinkled shirt.

"Simon!" he yelled again, yanking the rope, flailing his weight against the Bowline knot.

He tired before any progress had been made, his barrel chest heaving up and down. His head dropped as globs of blood and pus oozed down his wrists, the metal wire tunnelling under the skin. His legs dragged along the filthy concrete floor, dust and dead spiders clinging to his navy-blue slacks.

Oddly, he smiled. Chuckled, even. "Well, Alan, is this how you thought your weekend would go?"

He laughed again—a sad, strained sound—and then sat still for some time, staring longingly at the thin beam of light coming in from under the door.

He could see his sport coat crumpled in the corner of the closet along with his scuffed loafers. A faint glint reflected off his cufflinks, also tossed to the rear. The cold from the concrete floor seeped into his bones and more than once he shifted his gaze to find a fat brown rat gnawing on his leg.

He was nearly certain he had been locked in the closet for two days. But as he nodded off so many times, he wasn't entirely sure anymore. The smell of him suggested a lot longer and he grimaced at the musty odour coming from his pits and crotch. Maybe two days, he thought. Maybe more.

He tried to concentrate, to gather his thoughts. But even when he focused, it was still a blur of how it all happened.

His driver, Milton, had pulled into the long, secluded driveway, the rickety cabin set back fifty yards from the county road. Milton had cautiously approached the front door and knocked.

"No answer, sir," he grumbled, returning to the black Mercedes.

"Oh, for Christ's sake!" Alan exclaimed, swinging the car door open. He shuffled out from the heated interior and into the November chill. "There's smoke coming from the chimney! Someone has to be home!"

"Sure this is the right address?"

"That's what I have written down. I've only met the guy once or twice and it was always at the Main Street Inn. Not sure why he wants to meet way out here."

Milton scanned the dense brush bordering the property. A detached garage lurked around the side of the cabin, rusted tools spilling out from it, a dented black truck parked in front.

Milton adjusted his driving gloves. "It's just that, well… this place gives me the creeps."

"That's why I brought you," Alan huffed. "To deal with all the creeps."

He marched up the front steps and raised his fist to the door, but then stopped. There was movement within the maples off the side of the porch, something behind the thick trunks and crowded boughs. Something large.

Even the last of the leaves seemed to tremble at the shape, desperately clinging to their stems before winter took hold, before they all wilted and crumbled to the ground to rot.

Alan squinted into the copse and shuddered, a feeling of ants teeming over his skin. Reflecting on the moment later, he might have thought this feeling was a premonition of sorts, a warning of what was to come.

Instead, he turned to Milton. "In all seriousness, do watch out. Mr. Pak vouched for this guy, but the few times I've met him he was a little skittish. Comes off as…unpredictable."

Milton stood erect and nodded, his lanky frame dwarfing the sedan beside him. He smoothed his goatee with one gloved hand, the other patting the side of his hip, a flash of metal beneath his coat.

Alan turned and hammered his fist several times against the wooden door. With no answer, he knocked again until he heard the sound of locks clicking and then a set of beady eyes glaring through the opening. Seeing Alan, the man on the other side of the door gave a most unsettling grin.

Everything after that seemed to happen so quickly, as if

Alan was rushing toward a nightmare.

Dr. Simon Stone had excitedly ushered him inside where they travelled down a set of stairs and through a dark maze of tunnels—several metres below ground—until they came to a thick metal door.

Upon opening it, all of Alan's reservations about the impish scientist were validated.

Before him was a massive glass dome which Simon giddily explained was used to test different iterations of a doctored drug. Developing such a concoction was something he was always meant to do, he declared. And as Alan listened, he learned that Simon was testing the drug on captured townsfolk—residents somehow still infected with the EEEV vaccine administered through the flu clinics last November.

Alan watched in horror as Simon cured one of the creatures then immediately offered them up as bait. An albino beast charged, tearing the boy's limbs from his torso, devouring him while he lay awake, gurgling out his last breath.

The logistics of Simon's plan were muddied, perhaps only making sense to a mad man. But from what Alan could gather, Simon was poisoning a number of water sources, tainting them with both the original drug and a doctored version of it. As he moved from one town to the next, he used the creatures for protection; a loosely-controlled pack of savage bodyguards.

Once the concoction was in the water and the virus activated, Simon would use the threat of a pandemic to elicit panic and chaos; some act of twisted righteousness and revenge.

Livid, Alan had thrown Simon up against the oval dome, pinning him to the glass. But several of the creatures had already been let loose and they crept from the corner of the room, pushing Alan to the floor and attacking him until Simon called for them to stop. He bound Alan's wrists and the beasts dragged him to a small room, securing him within the closet.

Alan sat there now. He motioned to yell but decided against it. His voice was nearly gone from hollering throughout the night. It was all to no avail. He hadn't seen or heard from the wild-eyed scientist since being restrained. He adjusted himself, attempting to rub sweat from his eyes with the crook of his arm.

"Was it worth it, Alan? Would you say you've done well for yourself?" he mumbled. He shook his head. "I suppose this is karma. Spend a career partnering with loose cannons and low-lifes and this is what you'll get…"

He trailed off, his muddled mind searching for apt words. "Hire a sociopath to carry out your science and then get attacked by the very things he creates. So yeah, I guess that's karma."

Alan hung his head as the hours ticked by, listening to the growls of his stomach, a constant reminder of no food or water since he arrived. He breathed in the dank scent of the closet. He heard a faint shushing as his socked-feet jittered across the floor. But when he stopped the movement, the sound continued.

He raised his head, confused.

He repeated the movement, dragging his sock along the floor, then stopped. And there it was again. The same sound, a foot dragging along the floor. But this time he was certain it was coming from the other side of the wall.

His eyes lit up. "Milton?" he said, his voice hoarse and strained. "Milton, is that you?"

His question was met with silence so he rubbed his foot along the floor again, this time quicker and with more force.

After a moment, the sound was repeated.

Excited, he writhed and wriggled. "Milton! Were you captured too?"

He pounded his foot on the ground. He stopped and then heard the same sound in return, someone stomping in the next room over.

"Milton, I hear you," he yelped. "Can you hear me?"

He paused but heard nothing.

"Have they tapped your mouth shut?" Alan asked. "Milton, stomp your foot again if you can hear me."

Alan went quiet until a gravelly voice spoke through the wall. "Help," the voice seemed to say but Alan drew back at the strange sound. The words were slurred and muffled, almost uncertain; like someone's first attempt in a foreign language.

"Milton?"

"Not Milton," the voice said, still trying to work its way around the shape of certain words.

Alan swallowed. "Then who are you?"

Alan listened for a long time. And then the muffled voice spoke again: "No."

Alan scrunched up his face. "No? What do you mean, no?"

"Not no."

"Not, no? You don't want to tell me who you are?"

"Not Milton. No," the voice said.

Alan heard a crash from the other room followed by the thunder of boots and bare feet slapping across the floor. There was a shriek and an explosion of noise, as if someone was being violently thrown around the room. The crashing continued for nearly a minute before it slowed, replaced with groaning and panting.

Alan pressed his ear close to the wall, his eyes wide with fear. He heard the sound of metal clinking and then the moist squelch of liquid.

"Okay, hit record on that thing," a nasally voice cawed and Alan immediately recognized it as Simon's. "I need this footage for research."

There was a shuffling of feet followed by a clicking sound and then Simon's voice again. "Alright, now that you've settled down, it's time for your medicine," he said.

There was a deafening crack followed by an ear-piercing shrill as the commotion in the room intensified, the sounds of mammoth-sized bodies colliding against the floor and walls. The growling and baying continued until Alan heard a sucking sound, a soggy gurgle, like a stick being pulled from the mud.

"Enough!" Simon yelled.

The noise quieted.

"You know the drill! You've trusted me this long, why pull up short now?" he added.

It was silent for some time before a whimper came through the wall. Alan wasn't entirely sure, but the noise sounded like weeping.

"I hate to see you like this, I really do," Simon said, although the words lacked emotion. "I'll give you the permanent antidote soon enough. Your wife too. But for now, I need you…well, I need you under control."

There was a horrible scream, the sound nearly shaking the walls, and then footsteps retreating from the room.

"He's losing patience," Simon said nervously. "Leave the camera, we'll get it later. We can only do this so many times before he—"

The door slammed. Alan strained to listen through the wall. He could hear pacing and grunting until the sound of heavy feet softened. He heard something thump and then slide down the wall. He cleared his throat. "Hello? Are you still there?"

There was no response so Alan tapped his foot against the wall, hoping the signal would be repeated.

"Are you okay?" he asked. "What are they doing to you?"

He exhaled and sat quiet, listening, but not another sound was made. One hour passed and then another. Alan began to nod off, hunger and exhaustion pulling him under.

He spent a third night right there, locked in a closet in the basement of Simon's cabin. Exactly how many more, he couldn't be sure.

Chapter Eight

November 1995
Day 640 | Morning

Evelyn sat at the edge of the bed, a whetstone in one hand, a bowie knife in the other. She gripped the spine of the knife, digging the blade in at an angle, moving the tip and heel across the stone.

She made several passes until she felt a burr along the edge. She wiped her thumb across it—rough in one direction, smooth in the other.

Pleased with her work, she flipped the knife over and repeated the process with an even, steady motion; the rhythmic movement almost meditative. When she was done, she brought the knife to the light, turning it over, inspecting the metal.

She stood and moved to the desk, taking a piece of paper and slicing it down the middle. It cut with ease, a perfect line. She eyed the desk then drove the knife into it, the blade carving a deep rut into the wood.

She smiled. "That'll work."

She sheathed the knife then began tossing items into a canvas backpack: a cord of rope, a water bottle, sealed crackers, several granola bars, a stick of deodorant, cartridges, a hatchet, a billfold. She went through her dresser drawers and added a thin pair of gloves, wool socks, several undershirts, an extra pair of cargo pants, a fleece sweater, a toque.

She placed her foot on the bed and tied a bright red and yellow strand around her ankle, one just like her mother wore, as a pang of emptiness twisted inside her. Nine months since she had heard her voice. Nine months since she had smelled the smoky sweat of her skin or felt her tender touch.

Scanning the room a final time, she snatched her rifle from the end of the bed before her eyes caught on a photo of her mother. Short and round with her arms folded across her chest, the image showed the woman standing beside the family's peacock-blue sedan. With a tangle of brown and grey hair, she stood scowling and squinting, as if disapproving of something in the distance.

She was stern when she needed to be—a fierce, measured woman—and Evelyn grew up to be careful around her. When she believed strongly in something, her ardent stare would make anyone nervous. But she was loyal and selfless and it was easy to see where Damien got his protective nature from.

Evelyn had taken the framed memory from her house last summer. The cops had told her not to trespass, warned her that her father was considered dangerous, a person of interest. He was implicated in the documents found in Angela's study so they believed he might return at any given time to collect something from the house, something of value.

As such, the police kept constant watch over the house. They surrounded it with yellow tape and treated it as an active crime scene.

Yet, with Evelyn's parents still missing, Xavier had questions. So, every few weeks, he would sneak onto the property at night, eluding the constables, and rummage inside for anything the detectives may have missed. Evelyn often went with him, silently amassing her belongings one trip at a time.

She had taken the picture of her mother along with one of Damien. Over several visits, she had carried away nearly all her clothes, an extra pair of shoes, her mother's tobacco pouch, a bottle of perfume, her favourite jam, a cooler, Damien's comic book collection, her father's hatchet.

Each visit they came up empty for any clues but still left with an impressive haul, Evelyn's backpack overflowing as she and Xavier slipped out the back window undetected, disappearing into the long grass bordering the yard.

She stared at the picture of her mother, her hand moving over the glass, as if to feel the softness of her hair or warmth of her skin. She retuned the frame to the desk and then reached for the second one: a close-up of her and Damien from behind, leaping off the dock, the sun glistening off their wet skin.

She smiled at the memory, one of many jumping into the cold lake at the small cabin they visited each June. She could almost feel the shock of water as they plunged in, Evelyn gasping for air as she shot out of the water, Damien laughing his kind laugh then reaching out to make sure she was okay.

Afterwards, they would sun themselves on the smooth boulders bordering the lake, warmed from the midday heat, their tired bodies fit and dark and healthy.

She brought the image closer, her eyes roaming over Damien's bare back, a smatter of freckles lined perfectly down his spine, his swim trunks a bright orange against his brown skin.

A tear dropped onto the glass. Rubbing her eyes with the back of her hand, Evelyn bit down on her lip, trying to keep emotions at bay as she returned the frame to the desk.

Her nose wriggled at a clammy scent. She raised her arm to sniff at her pits and her face scrunched up. She walked down the hall to the small bathroom. She turned the shower tap on then shimmied out of her shirt and bra and threw them to the floor. When the water had warmed, she stepped in and drew the curtain, scrubbing her sweaty skin and oily hair.

When she was done, she towelled off and combed her hair before realizing she was using Rachel's brush. She smirked, sheepishly returning it to the counter.

More of Rachel's belongings had crept into the house week over week. Some of her clothes were brought over in September. A desk lamp, an umbrella, a fleece throw, and several paperbacks had seeped in by mid-October. By early November, a few of her favourite paintings hung in Xavier's bedroom, her slippers peeking out from beneath his bed.

Evelyn pulled at the bathroom mirror, a row of built-in shelves behind it, to see Rachel's toothbrush on the bottom shelf.

"Guess it's official," she mumbled.

She stuttered down the hall to her bedroom and laid out an outfit. She dropped the towel to the floor, revealing several pinprick scabs down her back, then panicked when she heard the door open. She spun and saw Xavier standing under the archway.

"X!" she hollered.

Xavier's cheeks went red as he stood frozen to the spot.

"Get out!"

"Shit," he muttered, turning and closing the door.

"A little privacy would be great!" Evelyn yelled through the door.

"I-I'm sorry, Ev. I just needed to tell you—"

"Just give me a minute!"

She slipped on a pair of cargo pants and bra, then pulled over a black t-shirt. She bent and pulled on a pair of wool socks, a toe poking through a hole in one of them. She snatched a fleece sweater from the drawer. "Okay, I'm good," she said, her voice beginning to calm. "You can come in now."

Xavier creaked the door open, his face still a dark tinge. "Sorry, Ev," he mumbled. "Guess I'm still not used to women being in the house."

"Just knock next time," Evelyn said, avoiding his eyes.

"Yeah, I will. For sure."

"What's so important that you need to barge in?"

"Ah, Everett is here now. And he brought about half a dozen cops with him."

Evelyn snapped her wristwatch on and patted her hair dry with the towel. "Okay, I'm almost done packing. I'll be down shortly."

"Okay, sure…"

His eyes awkwardly flitted around the room, unsure where to land, like a fussy hummingbird debating which flower to settle on. "Who's that picture of?" he asked, moving toward the desk.

"That's Damien and me at our cabin. Maybe three, four years ago."

Xavier picked up the frame and peered down at the photograph, his eyes moving over the glossy print.

Evelyn's brow narrowed, a sudden restlessness about her. "Actually, come to think of it, I'm pretty sure your father took that photo," she said.

"Really?"

"Yeah, he would come to see us the last few weeks of June to hunt and…well, I guess you know all that now, don't you?"

Xavier nodded. He stared at the photo as if trying to summon the secrets within it. It had only been a few months since he, Andrew, and Evelyn discovered they were cousins, the shock of the news strengthening their bond, bringing them closer together. But this same news also raised a host of uncomfortable questions: mainly why neither family told one about the other.

"I guess there might be a lot of those types of things," Evelyn added. "Like times Uncle Joe was with us and you had no idea where he was."

"Yeah, maybe," Xavier said.

"I have fond memories with him, but knew nothing about you or Andrew. Knew nothing about his life, really."

"Weird to think about, huh?"

"Yeah. Weird."

"I guess all we can do is keep talking about it, right? I'll keep telling you about my parents and you keep telling me about yours. And maybe, I don't know…maybe it'll kinda make up for lost time."

Evelyn forced a smile as Xavier returned the photo to the desk. He placed it down carefully as if it now held more value.

"You guys enjoyed the cabin?" he asked.

"Yeah, it was the only chance we spent any real time together as a family," Evelyn said. "My father was always busy with work and stuff."

"Right."

"But even at the cabin he was…distant. He was there, but not."

"Hm."

"And me and Damien—" But she stopped short, something in the name causing her to halt.

Xavier swallowed. "Still tough to talk about him, huh?"

"You know, it's odd the things I remember. Like small things that trigger something."

"How so?"

"Like if someone sounds like him or is the same height as him or has the same dark hair…I mean, the memories just flood back in."

"Yeah, I get that."

"But odd things too. Like the squeak of a door. Or heat from a fire. Or the smell of pesto."

"Pesto?"

"Strange, right? I get a whiff of pesto and it's like I can see him right there in the kitchen, piling the green goopy stuff on top of his pasta. And always with that stupid grin of his."

Xavier smirked.

"Yeah, just like that one," she teased.

"Gee, thanks."

"But even with all those memories, the only thing I really want is him. His laugh, the kind way about him. That's all I want and it's the only thing I can't have."

"Yeah, I know," Xavier said. "If I could do anything to change that day…" He shook his head and averted his gaze, as if knowing how weak and useless his words were. He nibbled at his lip before pointing at a third photo.

"That was a great weekend, huh?" he said, the print showing he and Evelyn, bright-eyed with silly toothy grins, struggling to hold a nineteen-pound steelhead on the stern of a trawler. "I mean, most of it."

"My first fishing trip with you and Andrew, just before he

left for school," she said.

"I have the same picture. Andrew must've printed two copies."

"Damien would have loved that trip…"

Xavier nodded. "Listen, we should probably head downstairs."

"Yeah," Evelyn said, wiping the corners of her eyes.

"I'd imagine Rachel can only serve so much coffee to these guys before they get antsy."

"Sure, just give me a couple minutes to finish up."

Xavier moved under the doorframe but then stopped. "Oh, Ev?"

"Yeah?"

"Those markings down your back. I saw them when you lived with Rachel and I've been wondering…"

"They're nothing! You see, this is why a little privacy would be great!"

She slammed the door, leaving Xavier silent on the other side of it. His face crumpled as his eyes cast to the worn hardwood. "Shit," he said, then trudged his heavy frame down the stairs.

In the bedroom, Evelyn paced and huffed, trying to rid her body of the sudden rush of anger. She slipped into the fleece sweater, secured her knife to her waist, and pulled the drawstrings of the backpack tight.

She turned to leave when she hesitated, her gaze catching on the picture of her and Damien. She grabbed the photo then untied the backpack, shoving it in. After closing it shut again, she heaved the bag to her shoulder, snatched her rifle, then flicked the light off, limping down the hall.

"There she is!" Everett boomed as she made her way

down the stairs and into the living room.

"Hi, Mr. Everett, it's good to see you again." She reached up to give him a hug.

Including Everett, there were eight police officers milling about the living room, some seated on the couch, others murmuring and slurping coffee by the large bay windows. A pair of constables stood along the far wall marvelling at a painting of a woodland stag as if they had never seen such a thing.

"Is your leg okay?" Everett asked. "Looks like you're favouring it."

Evelyn shrugged. "It's fine. Must've just overworked it in the yard."

"I'm sure there's no shortage of chores around here."

"X keeps me pretty busy. Says it keeps my mind off things."

"Can't argue with that," Everett said, his kind eyes roaming over the child. He motioned to her backpack. "What's with the bag?"

"X said I was coming to the—"

"Anyone need a top up?" Rachel sang. She glided into the room, carafe in hand, the bitter-sweet aroma of freshly-brewed coffee following her in.

Several officers sauntered over, mugs outstretched, surnames stitched into their uniforms: Jackson. Caldwell. Singh.

A fourth officer, Constable Dunvey, heaved himself from the couch and waddled over, glowing with glee as the black liquid splashed into his mug. He scratched at his crotch and unsuccessfully swallowed a burp. "Sorry about that," he grinned sheepishly. "There's those scrambled eggs coming up."

"Jesus, we can't take you anywhere," Caldwell scolded.

She stood proud with intense eyes, her frayed brown hair tied back, several strands escaping from beneath her cap. Her arms were inked in tattoos. She turned to Rachel. "Sorry about that. He's fun at parties but short on manners."

"And just plain short," Jackson added. The skinny officer wore a pressed blue shirt and a tidy russet beard.

"Oh, please, like you're such a towering presence," Dunvey shot back.

"Dunvey, you're so short you need them special orthotics," Singh piped in.

"You mean lifts?" Jackson asked.

"Yeah, that's them. Lifts!"

"Nah, he don't need 'em."

"Why's that?"

"Probably already got 'em!"

"Ah, shut up," Dunvey said. "You've got what, maybe three inches on me?"

"Man-oh-man, this guy is short *and* blind!"

"Three? He's got like six inches on you," Singh said. "At least."

"No matter. I could still wrestle him to the floor if I needed to," Dunvey said.

"Oh, this I gotta see."

"Let's do it then," Jackson challenged.

"You really want some of this?" Dunvey said, puffing out his chest.

"Sure do!"

"In front of all these nice folks?"

"You're low enough to the ground already, won't take much to pin ya."

"Nah, not today. On account of the eggs and all." He

gave a sly smile and his eyes softened as if the whole thing had been a ruse. He plopped down on the couch, drinking his coffee, Jackson and Singh tittering behind him.

Caldwell turned to Rachel. "Sorry again," she said. "These clowns do this sort of thing all the time. Don't mean nothin' by it."

Rachel smiled just as a handsome officer ambled over to her. He was tall and muscular, the name Munroe tacked across his chest. His hair was cut close and gelled to the scalp, a cigarette tucked behind his ear.

Rachel angled forward to top up his mug. He snapped his gum and mouthed the words *thank you,* a faint smell of mint and cigarettes as he turned and walked away.

There was a loud thud as Xavier stepped into the room, dropping a heavy duffle bag to the floor, an echo of something metal within it. He nodded at the gathered officers and two of them scurried over to shake his hand.

"Mr. Stone, I'm Officer Powell," a short Black woman said, reaching out to shake his hand. She motioned to the slim colleague at her side. "And this is Constable Prasad. We met you last spring when we were first dealing with these things."

"Yes, I remember," Xavier said. He shook their hands, dwarfing each in his shadow. "Thanks for coming."

"Hell, we just follow him," Prasad said, motioning toward Everett. "Wherever he goes, we go."

"Your brother was with us too, wasn't he?" Powell asked.

"Yes," Xavier said.

"What was his name again?"

"Andrew."

"Right. Is he here?"

"He's overseas at school. But Everett told me to get him so

he's making arrangements to fly in any day now."

"Geez, the Staff Inspector has *international* influence," Prasad joked. "He's even more important than he says he is."

Xavier smiled. "In the spring, we were teamed up with a third officer. The two of you and…"

"Lawson," Powell said, her smile slipping. "Constable Lawson."

"That's right. How's he doing? Is he coming with us?"

"Not this time."

"He's still shaken up from the last time we went out, when we found that boy in the closet," Prasad said. "He sat this one out."

Xavier nodded, recalling how the stout officer had come across the dead child and then was attacked by a creature. They inoculated him before he had fully turned, but he was traumatized from the event, not quite the same in the months after.

Prasad leaned into Xavier, his mouth close to his ear. "These creatures, these new ones you saw—are they as bad as Everett says? Worse than last time?"

Xavier motioned to speak but Everett cleared his throat and the chatter stopped. Everett clunked his mug on a side table then moved to the centre of the room. He appeared restless, his eyes troubled. He removed his hat and held it by the brim, a shiny bald spot at the crown of his head.

"Just a few items to note before we hit the road," he said, his words coming quickly. He put his hat back on then reached into his shirt pocket for his notepad. He flipped it open. "As you've been briefed already, there have been recent sightings of these…these *virus-infected folks*, which some of you helped locate and inoculate this past summer."

He nodded in Powell and Prasad's direction and then continued: "We're still unsure why or how these new ones have surfaced, but Xavier tells me there are dozens of 'em living in the forest a little ways from here."

"So, the antidote wore off?" Caldwell asked.

"Well, we don't know that for sure."

"But those things are back," Prasad interrupted. "So, obviously it didn't work."

"Our forensics team is looking into it."

"What does that mean? *Looking into it?*" Dunvey asked.

"It means they're taking blood samples from the ones we've already inoculated to see what they can learn, if there's a way to reverse these…these recent changes."

"But we always knew the antidote was temporary," Rachel said. "My sister told us."

"I suppose the upper brass felt it was permanent enough when things started to return to normal."

"So, what's the plan for today?" Munroe asked. "Go in guns blazing!"

Jackson stifled a laugh as Dunvey jokingly motioned for his gun.

"No, we're not going in with intent to kill," Everett said, raising his palms to calm the chatter.

"Then what are we going in with?" Powell asked.

"We still have a version of the antidote Dr. Angela Till surrendered to us. It's not perfect, but it's the best we have for now."

"So, it's a track and capture assignment?" Powell asked.

"We'll go in slow to gather intel and will only issue the antidote if it's safe to do so."

"So, track and capture," Powell snorted.

Everett turned to her. "I suppose so," he relented. "*Track and capture* is the gist of it."

"Where were they last seen?" Caldwell asked.

"A good two-hour's drive from here, deep in the woods," Xavier said.

Powell took out her notebook and began scribbling furiously as if she had just arrived at a crime scene. "Any identifying structures out that way?" she asked. "Anything of interest?"

"There was an abandoned campground and a run-down barn."

"The camp and barn—are these accessible by car?" Singh asked, adjusting his blue turban.

"We can get most of the way by backroads, but the last push will be on foot."

"Anything else we should know going in?" Powell asked.

"Just that the campground seemed empty for the most part," Xavier said. "Those things were all up in the barn."

"Just hanging out up at the barn, huh?" Munroe said. "Learning to square dance or something?"

Xavier glared at him and Munroe stared back, snapping his gum.

Powell closed her notebook. "Okay, I think we've got enough to go on. When do we leave?"

Xavier broke from Munroe's stare. "I guess when the others arrive."

Everett nervously rubbed his hands together. "This is it."

Xavier surveyed the room. "Only us?"

"I'm afraid so."

"We're going up against dozens of those monsters and all we have is who's in this room?"

"I'm sorry, Xavier, but this just isn't a priority for my

supervisor. He thinks this should have been wrapped up months ago."

"But there's still so many missing. Isn't that a priority?"

"Other units are getting calls. He's just fed up with it all."

"I'm fed up with it too but it still doesn't change the fact that those things are back."

"My supervisor—he just wants it to go away—"

"To hell with your supervisor!" Xavier said. "Send thirty more officers and an emergency response team and this can all go away!"

Everett hung his head. "No one else is coming."

"Tom, with these numbers we'll be lucky to walk out of there alive!"

"Look, he's breathing down my neck," Everett said. "Rumours are swirling, travelling through other towns."

"I don't care about other towns! I care about this one!"

"He's getting grilled by the Chief. We just need to end it. Us in this room—we need to somehow shut this down."

"Jesus Christ!" Xavier paced the room, sweat forming along his brow.

"I'm sorry, Xavier, I truly am. But this is the situation we're in. This is what we have to work with."

Xavier surveyed the room. "Nine versus, I don't know, fifty?"

"Well, your brother makes ten when he gets here."

"Sure, and Ev makes eleven. But we're still outnumbered."

"Sorry, did you say Evelyn?"

"Yeah."

"She's not coming."

"Are you kidding me? At this point we need every gun we can muster."

"I'm afraid that can't happen."

"We talked about this last time you were here."

"Well, I've thought about it some more and the answer is no."

"Her parents are still out there. Her brother died trying to stop these things."

"I just can't allow it," Everett said, his voice rising. "It's against all protocols. Besides, she's not trained for this sort of thing—"

Evelyn snatched the knife from her belt and whipped it at the painting across the room. The blade thumped into the canvas, the knife rattling inches from Constable Jackson's head.

The officer reached for his weapon, but Xavier and Evelyn already had their rifles trained on him, their steely eyes mirror images, unmoored and a little unhinged.

Stunned, the other officers raised their weapons, their eyes springing about the room.

"Stop it, all of you!" Everett shouted. His chest was heaving, white spittle flinging from his mouth. "Stand down, that's an order! We're not having a goddamn stand-off just before we leave!"

One by one, the officers lowered their weapons. Eventually, Evelyn and Xavier did as well.

Everett was as animated as anyone had ever seen. Perhaps it was the stress of it all—gruelling months spent tracking and inoculating vile creatures, losing some of his best officers to them, his supervisor's arrogant approach—it all seemed to spew its way out of him as he spun around the room.

"We're all on the same team here," he shouted, sweat staining the pits of his collared shirt. "We just need to establish a few ground rules, that's all."

He marched toward the painting and studied the knife, dead centre in the print. He sucked at his teeth. He reached up and yanked it from the canvas, running his finger across its edge. He walked over and presented it to Evelyn.

"I believe this belongs to you, Ms. Stone," he said.

Evelyn snatched the knife, glaring at him.

He chewed at his cheek, his eyes returning to the slit in the painting. He cupped his chin in his hand. "I suppose you're no longer the frightened child I met last winter," he mumbled, as if working out a problem.

He pinched the bridge of his nose. He shook his head, as if searching for a different answer than the one forming. He turned to Evelyn. "Alright, you can come," he said, the familiar kindness seeping back into his voice. "But when we're out there, I'm in charge. Not you. Not Xavier. Every decision goes through me, understood?"

Evelyn nodded and turned away, a slight smirk tickling the edges of her mouth. Powell smiled as well, winking at the girl.

Everett returned to the centre of the room and clapped once to get the group's attention. "Okay, now that we're all friends again, let's go over some details," he said. "As Xavier said, we can get most of the way by vehicle. After that, prepare yourselves for some time in the woods—sounds like there's a fair bit of hiking involved."

"How long will we be out there?" Caldwell asked.

"As long as we need to be," Everett said. "Pack for an overnight, just in case."

She nodded and began rummaging through her duffel bag, checking her supplies as the other officers followed her lead.

"The weather's getting colder so pack accordingly," Everett added. "Gather what you need. We move out in fifteen."

"I thought we were waiting for Andrew?" Xavier asked.

"Well, I suppose we could. When does his flight get in?"

"I thought those things were super dangerous," Munroe said. "What if they come here, start attacking the town?"

"Still, it would be better with Andrew."

"You telling me one guy is gonna make a difference?" Munroe said. "We're already locked and loaded. Let's just go now!"

Everett turned to Xavier. "I suppose he could just meet us there? Probably won't hurt to get a jump on things."

Xavier made a noise in his throat then turned and began rummaging through his bag. When everyone had finished readying their gear, Everett stepped forward. He made eye contact with each of them.

"Don't fool yourselves, this won't be like last time," he said, a sudden heaviness to his words. "If what Xavier says is true then these things are stronger, meaner, and smarter than anything we've encountered in the past." He ran a hand down the front of his shirt, smoothing the wrinkles. "Just so we're clear, this assignment will be different than the others."

Powell swallowed. "Meaning?"

Everett removed his hat and ran a hand through his thinning hair. His gaze was cast to the floor, a weariness settling in. "Meaning this mission could get…" He started then stopped. "What I mean to say is, watch out for each other. This could…this could all get very unpleasant."

Chapter Nine

November 1995
Day 640 | Afternoon

Two SUVs followed two patrol cars along the snow-dusted backroads out of Barn Wood. A small procession of lights and sounds until Everett radioed for everyone to cut the sirens; no need to advertise their approach.

In the second SUV, Xavier looked out the passenger window at the gathering dark clouds, the thunderheads threatening again. He squinted upon the mounds of snow and mush piled high in the ditch and then to the dense stand of trees beyond it.

A shudder moved through him. Even after all these months, he was still on edge each time he left the house, expecting the bush around him to explode with a horde of feral maniacs.

As the vehicles continued down the gravel stretch, he surveyed the farmhouses set back from the road. Many of the properties had porch lights on with Christmas bulbs strung up and hedges wrapped in burlap. There was a toboggan in one of the driveways, a man tinkering with his truck in another. A wisp of smoke from a chimney. Signs of life.

But others had nothing, the houses dark, noiseless shapes, the slow creep of disrepair unfolding upon them. He took note of these ones. The overflowing eaves, the slanting gutters. The front windows smeared and soiled, the unplowed driveways, the roadside mailboxes swollen with bills and flyers. A bird feeder emptied of seed, a cord of firewood stacked beside a lean-to, untouched.

The land exposed the same absence. Bales to be twined, a spade or set of tools discarded along the fence line. There were acres of unharvested crops, tills and tractors abandoned in the fields.

Some residents tricked themselves into believing their neighbours had sold the house, up and moved someplace better. Or maybe they were on an extended holiday and would return any day now.

But the grief Xavier wore suggested otherwise. He knew what a dark home meant. And as sure as the winters were cold, those folks weren't coming back.

They drove on past a run-down convenience store as flurries whipped across the windshield. Several kilometres later, a two-story building appeared, *Creekside Motel* sprayed on the sign out front.

Xavier removed his bowie knife from its sheath. He pulled out a thick thread of twine from his backpack and laid it over the blade. The knife nicked through easily.

"Should work," he muttered to himself.

In the driver seat, Officer Munroe worked a toothpick between his teeth. When he finished, he flicked the splinter to the wet floor mats.

"Mind passing me a cigarette and lighter, big man?" he said. "Should be in the front pocket of my bag."

Xavier reached in and shook a cigarette loose from the carton. He handed it to the officer then flicked the lighter until Munroe inhaled, the tip of the cigarette glowing red. The officer exhaled, smoke funnelling from his nose.

Xavier waved the fumes away and turned his attention back to his knife. He ran his finger down the side of it, assessing its sharpness.

"You know, I didn't even bring mine," Munroe said.

"What's that?" Xavier said.

"My knife. Not planning on lettin' 'em get that close."

"Is that right?"

"I'm only gonna see those creeps through my scope." He chuckled, but his laugh was hollow, something fake about the sound. He took several hauls off the cigarette, the black and orange embers creeping down toward his dirt-stained fingernails.

Xavier looked at him sideways. "You ever faced them before?"

"Nah, I was just hired a few months ago. But Prasad says they aren't that bad. Said he faced tonnes of them the last time around."

"These ones are different."

Munroe shrugged. "Prasad says you and Everett are making them out to be more than they are."

"Is that so?"

"Says you're just trying to scare us so we take the whole thing seriously."

"Then maybe you should take it seriously."

"I was top of my class in marksmanship in police college," Munroe said, taking one last drag then flicking the cigarette out the window. "I'll be fine."

Listening to Munroe, Xavier was flooded with horrific memories. Last winter, fleeing to the forest; then, just a few days ago, chased from the barn. If not for his knife, any one of those attacks would have cost him his life.

He sheathed the blade and shook his head. He turned to stare out the window again, studying the fields as they whipped by, dead yellow stalks bent with a white frost. Eventually, the snow stopped and the clouds lifted, a bit of sunshine peeking through.

In the rear seat, Evelyn was nodding off. The sun through the glass landed warm on her face, the rhythmic sway of the car lulling her to sleep. The shadows along the road shortened as the sun gradually ticked lower in the sky until she awoke with a start, swinging violently at the air.

Constable Jackson was seated beside her. He shirked away, evading her flailing arms.

"Ev!" Xavier hollered.

She continued to claw at the air, her eyes wide and wild as if in a possessed rage.

"Evelyn!"

She went rigid then shook her head, the nightmare draining from her mind. She turned to Jackson. "Sorry," she blurted out. "I'm so sorry. I get these visions and—"

"Was it Damien?" Xavier asked.

"No. This time it was Maddy."

"Hm."

Evelyn reached out and touched Xavier's shoulder. "Was she really as brave as I remember her?"

"Maddy? Hell yeah, she was full of grit. Fought to the very end."

"That's what I thought. And remember we met her husband and son last summer?"

"Mm-hmm."

"What were their names again?"

"Oh geez, I don't remember. Taylor? Or Travis, something like that."

"Yeah, Travis, that was it. And the boy was Jacob. He was nice. I mean, it was nice to meet him, given he's Maddy's family and all."

"Sure."

"Are they still around? Like in town, I mean?"

"Dunno. But I think the husband said they had stayed up north during the initial outbreak."

"Yeah, 'cause Maddy told them they had to go," Evelyn chuckled.

"Maybe they're still up that way," Xavier said.

"Maybe. Or maybe they're back in town—"

The car radio crackled to life. "We're coming up to the insertion point in five klicks," Everett said. "Prepare yourselves, weapons at the ready. Our first goal is to gather intel, but if things go sideways…"

The radio went quiet. After an uneasy silence, his voice came through again. "We have no idea if these things are still at this location or where they are. Or if they might be watching us," he added, almost as an afterthought. "Be sharp. Keep your wits about you, and we'll all be laughing about this tomorrow."

The first patrol car signalled and then slowed, coming to a stop on the gravel shoulder. The other vehicles followed in sequence, the doors swinging open, the officers lumbering out.

Each of them inspected their gear, examining their scopes and magazines, then hoisted the heavy bags over their shoulders. Singh and Jackson each held a Maglite. Powell carried a stainless-steel briefcase. They formed a loose circle around Everett.

"We go in from here," Everett said, pointing toward a narrow path through the trees. He motioned toward the briefcase. "Powell will be in charge of the antidote, but only if we need it."

"And if we need it?" Prasad asked.

"Then we'll use it. But again, our assignment is to gather information and radio back to headquarters."

"And then what?" Munroe said. "We just wait around until the geniuses up at headquarters tell us what to do?"

Everett rolled his eyes. "They'll communicate how to proceed, yes."

Everett zipped up his parka and exhaled, his breath a white cloud of steam in the winter air. He reached for his gun and checked for bullets before holstering it again. "Okay, Xavier, over to you," he muttered, turning his attention to the darkened trees.

Xavier swung the strap of his rifle over his shoulder and cleared his throat. "So, if memory serves me, it's a bit of a hike to get to the campground from here."

"There's gotta be an easier way in than this," Caldwell said.

"How do you mean?"

"It's a children's camp. It's not like '*Hey kids, welcome to camp. Now go hike a kilometre to your cabin.*'"

"Good point," Xavier said, studying the sharp incline leading into the thick brush.

"My camp was like that," Dunvey said. "Had to hike for a while to get there."

"Man, what are you talking about?" Jackson said.

"Yeah, my parents would drop my sister and I at the end of a laneway and we'd hike ourselves in."

"Are you being serious right now?"

"We'd be fine. We'd have our bag and pillow and everything. Would just take us a while to get to the front gates."

"I hate to break it to you, dipshit, but your parents didn't send you to camp," Jackson said. "They just left you at the side of the road and *told you* it was camp."

Singh howled as Dunvey turned and spat on the ground. "Oh shut up, will ya?" he said.

"Pipe down, you two," Caldwell said. She turned to face Xavier. "So, is there a driveway or something around the other side of this?"

"Didn't exactly have time to fully assess everything last time," Xavier said.

"So, we go in from here?"

"I think that's our best bet. I know my way from here."

Dunvey sized up the steep bank. "I think I feel those eggs coming up again."

Xavier looked to the sky, the sun continuing its sluggish descent. He stepped into the woods, the forest cloaked in afternoon shadow, a look of uneasiness stretched across his face. One by one, the others followed, cautiously moving around the thick trunks and bare branches as they trudged up the hill through the snow and slush.

After some time, Evelyn pulled Xavier aside. "You okay?"

"Sure. Why?" Xavier said.

"You look nervous."

"Most of these guys are too green for this."

"What's that mean?"

"It means they haven't seen much action. Not like this, anyways."

"But they're cops. They're trained, right?"

"Not for this."

"Not for what?"

Xavier looked around. "It's different in the woods. And it's getting dark. If you don't know the land like we do, then… well…"

"You worried?"

He looked back at the group. "I just wish Andrew was here, that's all," he said. "We'd all be a lot safer if he was here."

"He'll be here soon, right?" Evelyn said.

"I hope so," he said then stepped back into the trees, swiping a branch from his path. Evelyn ducked it easily, reflexes like a lynx.

The group plodded on, snow and dead leaves caked onto their boots, occasionally slipping on stones and tree roots. It was well after the dinner hour when they reached the entrance of the campground, the faded *Camp Clearwater* sign etched into the archway above them. Everett gathered the group and motioned for Xavier to speak.

"We're close to where I first saw them," he said. "Up over that escarpment, in an old barn."

"What the hell are those?" Dunvey yelled, pointing high into the trees.

Everyone in the group turned, weapons raised.

Xavier peered into the brush before shaking his head. He lowered his rifle. "Ah, right," he said. "Forgot about the dolls."

"Dolls?" Dunvey said.

"Yeah, they're just dolls."

"You sure? 'Cause from here they look like…"

"I'm sure," Xavier said. "Ran into them my first time through."

"What the hell are dolls doing up there?" Prasad said, his revolver still pointed into the trees. Singh switched on his Maglite, half a dozen yellow and blue shapes dangling listlessly from the tree limbs.

"I mean, why are they just hanging there like that?" Prasad added.

"Any other creepy shit you failed to tell us about?" Munroe said, his voice on edge.

"Okay, okay," Everett said, his breathing heavy. "Let's all calm down. We'll just keep a closer look out from here on in, that's all."

"But why are they there?" Prasad muttered. "I mean, like, who put them there?"

"Let's refocus, okay?" Everett said. "Now, Xavier, when you saw those creatures, were any of them in this campground?"

Xavier scanned the area, pausing on the rickety storage unit where he had been cornered, the beast smashing its way through to get at him. "Yeah, there was one."

"Okay, so here's what we're gonna do," Everett said, turning to the group. "We're gonna conduct a search down here first—through all these cabins and buildings and such. Make sure none of those things are still here. After we've cleared the buildings, we'll make a plan to approach the barn."

"But it's already getting dark," Singh said.

"Yeah, it'll be pitch black by the time we get up there," Prasad added.

"If we already know those things are up there, then let's just go now," Munroe said.

"And risk some of them sneaking up from behind?" Everett snapped.

"That's what the Maglite's are for."

"I won't risk the safety of my officers—"

"But we're just wasting time down here!"

"We clear this area first, just like any other assignment!" Everett boomed. "And if you don't like that order, you can head back down and mull it over in the truck!"

Munroe didn't move, holding Everett's stare. He pressed a knuckle against one nostril and fired a spray of snot to the ground. "Whatever," he muttered and stepped away.

"Split into pairs, we'll get it done quicker," Everett huffed, making a face at the rookie cop. "Meet back here in one hour. Understood?"

Everyone in the group nodded, and after a brief discussion, separated into pairs, fanning out and dispersing across the grounds.

Dunvey and Jackson searched the sleeping cabins. One would peek around the doorframe then creep inside, the other following close behind. Jackson lifted each mattress from its wooden slats as Dunvey stood with his revolver raised, a tremor moving through him each time one was flipped.

"Jesus, it's creepy in here," he whispered.

After the final mattress was turned over, something scurried along the back wall. They whipped around with weapons pointed into the corner until a fat raccoon wedged herself out from behind a bed frame, her angry yellow eyes glaring at them.

"My word, I thought that was something else," Dunvey said. He exhaled, dragging the cuff of his uniform across his sweaty forehead.

"You and me both," Jackson said.

"I'm so worked up about these things I can't think straight."

"You ever seen one?"

"Just from the surveillance photos."

"Yeah, me too."

"Powell and Prasad worked the last assignment, must have tracked and inoculated hundreds of those things."

"You serious?"

"They've probably seen enough for the both of us."

"Let's keep it that way," Jackson said and they both skittered out the door toward the other cabins.

Down the path, Singh and Caldwell crunched over the snow and dirt until they reached what appeared to be a gymnasium. Caldwell jerked the handle, the rusted hinges whining as the heavy metal door creaked open.

They stepped inside to find a multi-purpose court. A ripped volleyball net was crumpled in the corner, a pair of bent basketball rims at each end of the floor. Many of the benches were broken with lewd graffiti covering the back wall. Spiders and earwigs crawled in the musty corners.

"This place has seen better days," Singh said.

"You're tellin' me," Caldwell said. "Looks like this place hasn't been used in years. Stinks too."

They slid across the dusty hardwood until Singh gasped. "What's that?"

He pointed to the far side of the gym underneath one of the windows. Darkened by shadow, there was a thick lump in the corner, about the size of a dog, with brown and black hair all over it.

He flicked the Maglite on and as he stepped closer, he could hear the buzz of flies about it, the shape giving off a stench of wet musk. Caldwell held her breath as they crept closer.

"It's just a raccoon," Singh blurted out. But as he bent low to the ground, a look of confusion crossed his face. "It's trapped in a…in a…I don't know what that is." His brow furrowed as he took in the device wrapped around the animal's leg. He angled the beam deeper into the corner. "Fiona, you ever seen something like this?"

Caldwell shook her head. "Looks like some sort of homemade trap."

"Barbaric for a trap, don't you think?"

Caldwell stooped and surveyed the knot of wires and rope. The wire dug into the animal's torso, the rope securing it flat to the ground. "Looks medieval, don't it?"

"Never seen anything like it."

"Not exactly a humane way to catch these things, is it?"

Singh exhaled. "Yeah, but if all we find in here is a dead raccoon, I'd say we're pretty lucky."

In the mess hall, Prasad and Munroe dragged the wooden chairs out from the long tables then bent and peered underneath.

"Is that all of 'em?" Prasad asked when they had shone a light under the last table.

"That's it," Munroe said. "Let's check the kitchen."

He shouldered into the swinging doors and entered the kitchen, yanking open the walk-in fridges, checking behind the aisles of ceramic mixing bowls and metal serving spoons.

"Here kitty kitty," Munroe joked, clicking his tongue. "Come out and play."

He tilted each oven door open, then checked between the racks of baking trolleys, stained trays piled high upon them. He ambled to the back and creaked open the massive deep freezers, several unlabelled boxes coated in a thick layer of ice.

He rummaged through the pantry but nothing fresh was to be found, only canned goods and a few bags of rice. Dozens of salt and pepper shakers sat idle on the top shelf.

"This is a waste of time," he said.

"Mm-hmm," Prasad said, inspecting a jug of dish detergent, the solution cloudy and murky.

"No one's been in here for months, maybe years."

"Looks that way."

"Can you believe Everett's making us check all this?"

"I mean, he typically knows what he's doing. At least the first time around he did."

"All this is doing is wasting daylight!"

Munroe grabbed the metal handle of the industrial dishwasher and lifted the heavy door. It clanged open but was empty and dry, the water shut off, the machine unplugged. His shoulders drooped. "I almost *want* to find one," he said.

"No, you don't," Prasad said.

"Just to get it over with."

"The hardest part is they used to be human, like you can still see that in them."

"Still…"

"Believe me, once you've seen one you'll wish you hadn't."

Munroe slammed the dishwasher lid down, the clang reverberating throughout the kitchen. "Nah, I want to find one," he said. "Just to prove they're not as scary as Everett says."

Outside, Xavier marched until he came upon the familiar shed with the massive hole smashed through the rear of it, Evelyn hurrying behind him. He poked his head in, examining the ATV, half a dozen canoe paddles upright in the corner, a pile of broken bows and arrows strewn across the filthy floor.

"Is this where it happened?" she asked.

A shiver ran through him as he tried to keep the horrific thoughts at bay, the beast crashing through, chasing him back to his truck.

"Yeah, this was it," he grumbled.

He stepped out from it then circled the shed. He stopped and peered down at the snow. There was a set of prints, five massive toes with serrated claws above each one.

"Guess we now know these aren't from a wolverine," he muttered.

They moved toward the kettle lake, a line of mouldy and tattered lifejackets hanging off a wire. Evelyn scanned the water and shuddered, a disturbance passing just beneath the surface. She crouched and dragged her finger through the dark current, ripples cascading to the other side before disappearing.

"You think there's any here?" she asked.

"A part of me would like to find a few down here, some stragglers," Xavier said.

"Why?"

"Would be easier to contain them one at a time."

"Makes sense."

"But I don't think we're that lucky."

"What do you mean?"

"They seemed organized, disciplined almost. Like someone was directing their behaviour."

"Did you see anyone else?"

"No."

"So, how's that possible?"

"I don't know. Just have a bad feeling about all this."

"Yeah."

Xavier joined her at the water's edge. "I saw other things in that barn, you know?" he said. "More than I told you."

Evelyn swallowed then stood from her squat. She motioned for him to continue.

"A dead buck, like they had hunted it," Xavier said.

"Okay, but the ones last winter hunted us," Evelyn said.

"Sure, but *a buck*? Hunted it with no weapons? And this thing was mangled, twisted all to hell."

"You said these ones are smarter."

"I guess, but it's like someone's taught them or…" Xavier shuddered, then turned and looked up the escarpment, the grey barn in the distance. "I don't know, Ev. But I think they're up there now, watching us."

"Why?"

"They're just waiting. Waiting for us to make a mistake."

Thirty minutes later, everyone reconvened along the main pathway. Everett and Powell were the last pair to arrive, their flashlights flicked on, the daylight nearly sucked from the sky.

"Alright, circle up everyone," Everett said as he came upon the group. The officers shuffled over. "Find anything?" he asked.

"All clear for Jackson and I," Dunvey said.

"Us too," Singh added.

"We found nothing," Munroe said. He took a final pull off a cigarette then tossed it to the ground, grinding it into the dirt with the toe of his boot. "Just like we said we would."

"So, are we going up to the barn now?" Prasad asked.

"Well…" Everett said, surveying the darkening sky.

"I mean, that's where they all are, aren't they?"

Everett hesitated. "To be honest, I'm at a bit of a loss as to what to do next," he said. "Whether we should search the barn now or wait until there's more light."

"We could head back down to the cars," Dunvey said.

"We'd have to clear all these buildings again tomorrow if we leave the area," Powell said.

"Yes, I suppose that's true," Everett muttered.

"So, we're not going to the barn?" Munroe said. "What was all this for then?"

"I mean, we could hunker down in one of these cabins for the night," Everett said. "Set out for the barn first thing."

"You want to sleep here?" Jackson said. "No thanks. This place gives me the creeps."

"Yeah, let's head back to the cars and make a plan from there," Dunvey offered.

"Well, it's quite a ways back," Everett said. "And with night upon us…"

"We knew it was going to get dark, so how does this change anything?" Munroe said. "Let's just go up to the barn and clear these things out. Let's get this over with!"

Everett removed his hat. He dug the heel of his hand into his forehead then turned to Xavier. "What would you do?"

Xavier glanced around the circle of officers and then at the sky. "There's no good answer here," he said. "It's too dark to travel back to the cars and it's too dangerous to approach the barn. If any were to attack, we wouldn't see them coming."

"Why would they attack? I thought we were here to just gather intel?" Munroe sneered.

"They don't know that."

"Look, we've all got flashlights, and Singh and Jackson

have the Mag's," Munroe said. "We'll be fine."

"Still," Xavier said. "Probably best if we set up here 'til morning and advance on the barn then."

"But what if they come out at night," Munroe said. "Like the boogie man."

"We can rotate watch so others can get some sleep," Xavier said, ignoring the hot-headed officer. He turned to Everett. "Anyway, that's what I would do. But it's your call."

Everett nodded. "Okay, then that's our decision."

"Are you serious?" Munroe said.

"We're here for one night," Everett said sharply. His jaw tightened. "Be prepared to leave at first light."

Munroe huffed then spat in the snow. He hoisted his gear bag and sidled up to Prasad. "Just because the great Xavier Stone says it, the Staff Inspector does it."

"I don't agree with everything either," Prasad whispered. "But he knows what he's talking about. I've seen him in action."

"Overrated if you ask me."

"First time around, he and his brother tracked those things like nobody's business. Could always pick up their trail."

Munroe snorted. "He's just a dude with a gun. No different from you or me."

The officers holstered their weapons and picked up their bags, moving through the campground. They piled into the closest cabin, nibbling on protein bars and beef jerky, preparing their equipment for morning.

Caldwell spread out on a musty mattress, balling up a sweater under her head. Singh climbed the ladder and tried to get comfortable on the top bunk, his feet dangling off the end.

"Whose feet stink?" Caldwell called out.

"We've been hiking for hours. Whose feet *don't* stink?" Singh said.

Jackson climbed the ladder across from Singh, burrowing into the plastic-sheeted foam. "These mattresses are tiny, eh?" he said.

"You're telling me," Singh said.

"The only one who has a lot of room is Dunvey."

"Ah, shut up, will ya?" Dunvey hollered from the lower bunk.

"These must feel king-size to you, huh? Like a gnome in a garden."

"Do you two ever quit?" Dunvey said.

"Like a hobbit in his hole," Singh said then snorted as Dunvey kicked the plywood of the top bunk, shaking Jackson as he smirked down at him.

Powell shuffled to Evelyn's bunk. "Sorry about these idiots," she said. "They'll calm down soon enough."

"It's okay. They're kinda funny," Evelyn said.

"That's being generous. Annoying is more like it."

Evelyn smiled. "I don't mind."

"So, you gonna be okay in here?"

"Yeah, I'll be fine. My brother and I used to camp a lot so, compared to a tent, this is luxury!"

"Damien, was it?"

"Yeah."

"You miss him?"

"Yeah, we'd do everything together. Camping, canoeing. He was kind and always looked out for me—" She stopped suddenly, her jaw quivering. She met Powell's eyes, her face scrunched up in anguish.

Powell placed her hands on the girl's. "I know you probably think it's brave to hold it all in, but you're allowed to cry. You're allowed to let it out."

Evelyn nodded, a shudder running through her.

"Listen, this will all be over soon," Powell said.

"I hope you're right."

"I am. You'll see." Powell smiled and patted Evelyn's shoulder. She shuffled toward her bunk but then turned back. "Oh, and by the way, that's quite the aim you've got," she said. "I mean, back at the house and all."

Evelyn smiled softly.

"Who taught you to throw a knife like that?"

"X."

"He watches out for you, huh?"

Evelyn nodded.

"Yeah, I can see that," Powell said. "Well, he better watch out or you're gonna be better with that knife than he is!"

Evelyn smirked.

"You're a good kid, Evelyn. Brave, with a lot of grit," Powell said. "Make sure you don't lose that through all of this."

Evelyn blushed but said nothing.

"Well, goodnight then," Powell said and lumbered over to her bunk.

"Goodnight," Evelyn said.

She kicked her boots off and laid her rifle beside the bed. She slid her knife from her belt and took the flashlight from her pocket, placing both items beside the gun. She laid down and closed her eyes.

She tried to focus on her missing mother, on the last hours spent with Damien, but she was drained from the day, the constant worry of it all like a pulsing hum, an uneasiness simmering beneath the surface. The tension it carried exhausted her and she soon fell into a deep slumber.

Chapter Ten

November 1995
Day 640 | Night

Evelyn tossed and turned until she began to dream. She dreamt of the summer cabin, her and Damien running off the dock and into the cool June water, their mother smiling as they splashed in the shallows.

"Be careful, Ev," her mother would say. It was a nagging voice, but she meant well.

"I will!" Evelyn shouted before disappearing under the surface.

"Watch out for her, Damien," her mother hollered. "She's not as strong a swimmer as you."

But Damien was already reaching out to her, treading water close by, watching over her from a young age.

She remembered how, later that evening, her father prepared the pit for a fire, positioning the logs in a square border, then crisscrossing several others until they were two or three high. He filled the gap in the middle with dry kindling and bark. He called it a Log Cabin, although she didn't see how it resembled anything beyond just a messy pile of wood.

"That's 'cause he does it wrong," her Uncle Joe would tease, whispering to her and Damien as the sparks struggled to catch.

His slick, jet-black hair was tied back and his thick moustache moved with his smile. The red and black plaid shirt he seemed to always wear was rolled at the sleeves, his jeans dark and filthy.

"You can do better?" Simon said.

"Your father always had his nose stuck in a book," Joe said, ignoring the comment, his laughing brown eyes resting on the children. "Couldn't tell north from south out here. If he got taken in by a family of wolves it'd probably be the best for everybody."

"Don't go on teasing him, Joe," Evelyn's mother said. "Simon's plenty smart and you know it."

"Sure, but he was never good at this stuff—building a shelter, making a fire." He turned to the children. "Hell, he probably hasn't even taken you hunting yet, has he?"

Damien shook his head.

"'*Keep your grip loose and you'll bag a moose.*' That's what our dad taught us," Joe said.

"You always loved his idiotic sayings," Simon huffed.

Joe shook his head. "Kids need to learn this stuff. The important stuff."

"Important stuff, huh?" Simon grumbled, just as the flames took. "Oh, I'm doing important stuff, dear brother, don't you worry about that."

"How's that?"

"The advances I'm making in my research. It's something to behold, truly."

Joe huffed and waved him away. "Don't mind him, kids. He's just distracted with his work and all."

"All of a sudden you have an interest in my work?"

"Oh, I've always been interested in it. Don't agree with it, but still interested in it."

"Don't agree with it? You've got no idea what my research can do!" There was a manic excitement in his words, something unsettling with his mannerisms.

"I know enough," Joe said. "Have a good sense where it all leads."

"And where's that?"

"Revenge always ends up at the same place."

"Oh, that's rich! The carpenter telling the scientist all about it."

Joe's face darkened. He sprung up, fists clenched.

"You gonna hit me now?" Simon said. "Get in line behind every other bully in my life!"

"Oh, I know all about them bullies, don't I?" Joe said. He gazed upon the scar etched into his forearm. "And that night in the bar?"

Simon looked to the ground. "Well, I suppose that's true. Ended up being your problem as much as mine." He dusted the dirt off his jeans. "No matter. What's in the past is in the past."

"Doesn't seem like it's in the past, the way you're going on about all of it."

"Knock it off you two," Evelyn's mother said. "Not in front of the kids."

Joe unfurled his fists then sat down again. He turned to face the children. "Don't mind all that, just some grown-up nonsense." He exhaled and adjusted his cap. "You two wanna learn how to camp? How to hunt?"

Evelyn and Damien nodded and Joe lowered his voice. "Then you stay close to me," he said, his big smile returning. "If he won't teach you, then I will." He winked and Evelyn

and Damien giggled, an innocent secret shared between uncle, niece, and nephew. "We'll go out tomorrow, alright? I'll
teach you all that stuff. All the *important* stuff."

Evelyn's dream shifted and she found herself staring up at
a large century home with a slanted gable roof, the grounds
immaculately manicured, a dusting of snow over the lawn and
hedges. Andrew was there too, slumped beside her, bleeding
from his face with his legs splayed out in front. He looked exhausted and his breathing came in sudden bursts as if his
lungs had forgotten how to inhale.

They sat like that for some time, watching the house, the
night cold and silent.

A woman sped up the driveway in a black Porsche. She
stumbled out of the car muttering under her breath, a briefcase in one hand, something shiny in the other. She scurried
to the side of the house, disappearing behind a line of tall
shrubs.

Evelyn stared up at the second-floor window, the beam of
a flashlight bouncing around the space.

There was a gunshot followed by another and then a long
painful wait. Minutes went by—tick, tick, tick—until Rachel
emerged from the front door, her face hot and flushed, her
eyes red with tears. Xavier staggered close behind, his shoulders shaking, a thin burgundy briefcase in one hand, a small
metal box in the other.

"Where's Damien?" Evelyn had asked. But before the
words left her, she knew the answer. She knew what the gunshots were.

Rachel knelt beside her, whispering in her ear, but she
didn't hear any of it. She had already felt the sting of the
words before they were spoken. The pain and vomit spewed

out onto the white-stone walkway. Xavier dropped the items and hoisted the girl, holding her tight as she wailed.

Evelyn saw Damien then. He was a blurred image edging closer, a transparent likeness, maybe his spirit. He was smiling.

You'll be safe with him, he said. *He'll protect you.*

Evelyn punched and kicked at the air, struggling to get free of Xavier, desperately craving one last touch from her brother.

You'll find your courage, Damien said. *You'll find it and you'll see how brave you really are.*

Damien stepped back, his image evaporating, his silhouette melting into the shadows.

But you need to wake now, Ev, he said, his voice loud as if he stood right beside her. *You need to wake now. And listen.*

Evelyn shot up in the bottom bunk, her shirt damp with sweat. She frantically felt along the floor for her flashlight, eventually locating the cool metal. She flicked it on and there, staring down at her, were two children.

She squealed, dropping the flashlight, and instantly Xavier was out of bed, knife drawn. Everett shook awake as well, shuffling his heavy frame from the mattress and staggering to his feet.

"Wh-what is it?" he stammered, trying to steady himself. He flicked on his flashlight and shone it at Evelyn and the two kids. "Who the hell are they?"

The other officers began to rouse and soon all were awake, a loose circle formed around the small visitors.

"Do we know who they are?" Caldwell said.

"Or how they got in?" Powell said. "I mean, who's on watch?"

"I switched off with Dunvey about an hour ago," Prasad said.

"My word!" Powell said and she left the group and went outside, loudly reprimanding Dunvey from the other side of the cabin door.

Evelyn picked up her flashlight from the floor and shone it up the length of the children. There was one girl and one boy. Their clothing was in shambles and their faces were gaunt and filthy.

The girl's corn-blonde hair was a knotted mess of twigs and dirt, tangled and entwined like a rat's nest. A smudge of dirt was smeared across her cheek.

Several scabs lined the boy's arm and his lips were split and chapped. Dried blood and dirt gathered in the creases of his neck and under his fingernails as if he hadn't bathed in some time. He stood with his eyes down and ankles rolled outwardly, unsure whether to speak or not.

In the beam of the flashlight, they looked ethereal, almost supernatural, an eerie glow about them.

"Are you real?" Evelyn asked.

"Of course we're real," the girl said. "We're kids!" Her voice was squeaky and animated and she seemed oblivious to the anxious circle of police officers surrounding her.

"Right. You're kids, but—"

"You can't see we're kids?"

"Yes, it's just that—"

"We're just surprised that kids are *here*, in this camp, that's all," Everett said, stepping forward.

The girl screwed up her face and stared at him as if he was the dumbest person she'd ever met.

Everett knelt. "How old are you?"

"I'm 10. He's 12."

"How did you get in here?"

The girl pointed to the far wall and as Everett shone his flashlight, he saw a small gap. It was no larger than the length of his boot and about just as wide.

"Through there?" Everett said.

"Yep, we know all the holes," the girl said.

"How did you fit?"

"We watch how the raccoons do it and we just follow them in."

"But where did you come from? I mean, before you got here?"

The boy turned and pointed out the cabin window, signalling up the hill. "The barn," he said.

"And where are your parents?"

The boy made the same movement. "The barn."

A few officers shifted uneasily. Prasad leaned into Everett. "Sir, they could be, you know, contaminated," he whispered. "They might have been exposed."

"Oh, hush, they're just kids," Everett said, waving the suggestion away. "They're just lost or something." He turned back to the children. "Tell me again, where are your parents now?"

"Do you have any food?" the girl said.

Everett rooted through his pocket and pulled out a smushed protein bar. He tore off the wrapper and broke it in half, handing a piece to each child. They shot forward and snatched the food, devouring it in seconds.

"Is that good?" Everett asked.

The girl nodded. "Do you have more?"

"Sure, sure, we'll get you some more," Everett said, motioning for Jackson to grab one of the backpacks. "But first, can you tell me where your parents are?"

"My brother already told ya, they live in the barn," the girl said.

"In the barn?"

"Yeah, a bunch of 'em do. But they got all weird and angry so we just came down here."

"To this cabin?"

"To all the cabins! The whole place is like our fort, our hide-out."

"So, you live in this camp by yourselves?" Evelyn asked.

"Sometimes we go up to the barn to spy, to make sure Mom and Dad are still there. But then we come down here."

"Why do you come back here?" Everett asked.

"They're always fighting up there," the boy said. "And sometimes a man comes down from his cabin to yell at them. So, we always leave when we see him coming."

"Yeah," the girl piped in. "He's a meanie, so we don't want to hear him yelling at 'em."

"We snuck up to his cabin once, but there was a man and a woman screaming inside and the whole place smelled like burnt metal or something," the boy said. "So, whenever we see him, we just run back here."

"How long have you been here?" Evelyn asked.

"It was summer when we got here and now it's cold," the girl said. "So, however long that is."

"Did your parents bring you here?" Everett asked.

"They got sick and then got better and then got sick again, and that's when the man came to get them," the girl said.

"The man who lives in the cabin?"

"Yep."

"He came to your house?"

"Yeah. He said he could make them better," the boy said.

"But they're still not better."

"They're bigger now and their faces changed," the girl added. "We're just waiting 'til they get better so we can all go home."

Powell and Dunvey re-entered the cabin then, Dunvey's face red and embarrassed. Everett stood and turned away from the children, motioning for the others to gather around.

"This is a lot to take in," he said. "I mean, they seem fine. Malnourished, sure; but they don't seem infected in any way."

"You sure?" Jackson said. "'Cause they're creepy as hell."

"I think they're okay. But it sounds like their parents and a bunch more *are* infected up in that barn."

"Just as we feared," Powell said.

"And what about the man she mentioned?" Singh asked. "Should we be concerned about him?"

"I don't know what to make of that," Everett said. "Obviously, proceed with caution when we go up, and we'll just have to assess what we find."

"Probably just some loser hermit," Munroe said. "Nothing we can't handle."

Everett gestured toward the children. "How they've survived this long is beyond me. But I guess they're safe now."

Evelyn turned to face them. "May I ask, what are your names?"

"I'm Alice," the little girl said. "This is Joshua. Sometimes adults call him Josh but that makes him mad 'cause he likes the long way of saying it."

"Well, it's nice to meet you Alice and Joshua. My name's Evelyn."

"How old are you?" Alice asked.

"Thirteen."

"You look older."

"Oh?"

"Yeah, your eyes are older. Older than 13."

Evelyn stood awkwardly, studying the child. She swallowed. "Um, can you tell me how you've survived this whole time?"

"What do you mean?" Alice said.

"What do you eat?"

Joshua turned and pointed to the hole in the wall. "Raccoons," he said.

"You eat raccoons?"

"Yeah! We watch 'em and follow 'em in," Alice added. "My brother kills 'em and then we eat 'em!"

"H-how?"

"We saw how the adults from the barn were doing it—setting traps with wire and stuff," Joshua said. "So, we just copied them."

"Yeah, he's caught lots of 'em!" Alice said.

Xavier raised his eyebrows. "My kind of people," he smirked. "Almost like eating fisher huh, Ev?"

Evelyn made a face, remembering the strange meat sticks Andrew offered her all those months ago in the cellar. "Don't remind me," she said.

She reached into her backpack and pulled out a granola bar. The children snatched it and gobbled it down. She closed the bag and turned to the window. The black night was beginning its transition to a hazy blue-grey. "It's almost dawn," she said.

Everett stepped beside her. "It most certainly is," he said, a sudden sadness in his voice. He sighed then turned to the officers. "Prepare your things. Weapons, camo, everything. We go up in ten."

The officers shuffled and muttered, yawning and stretching the sleep away. Caldwell rummaged through her duffle bag for an extra sweater while Jackson pulled on fresh socks, lacing his boots up tight. Munroe and Prasad wolfed down the last of the beef jerky. Each of them packed extra ammunition, then holstered their revolvers.

"What about the kids?" Evelyn asked.

"They can stay here," Everett said.

"You sure?"

"They've survived this long," he said then ran a knuckle across his chin. "But if what they say is true, we need to go up to that barn." He peered out the window a final time, the sun moments away from cresting. "And we need to go up there very soon."

Chapter Eleven

November 1995
Day 641 | Morning

Rachel sat rigid on the metal chair, her hands flat on the table. Everything was cold to the touch and the air an acrid mix of bleach and body odour. The smells of the prison had always been there, of course, but today they were more pungent, more irritable. She wriggled her nose, attempting to get rid of the stench.

Across the room, a door clanged open, and Angela shuffled through. She wore an orange jumpsuit, her hands cuffed in front. An officer followed close behind.

When they arrived at the table, the guard said something low and Angela nodded. He produced a key and sprung the cuffs from her wrists. She smiled meekly and sat down.

Her eyes were puffy with dark circles under them. Loose skin hung off her arms as if her bones had shrunk. It had only been three days since Rachel's last visit but already Angela seemed more diminutive, as if receding into herself, the usual smugness she carried now gone.

"Are you okay? You don't look well," Rachel asked.

Angela gave a sideways glance and gestured at the bleak surroundings. "As good as I can be in here," she said.

"Looks like you've lost weight. Are you eating?"

Angela shrugged. "I eat enough. Food stinks though. Makes me miss Mom's cooking."

"Yeah, well…"

They shared a long look. Rachel's knee jostled under the table as Angela rubbed her wrists where the cuffs had pinched the skin.

"They've granted me access to scientific journals," Angela said after some time.

"That sounds promising," Rachel said. "Should help you keep up with your research."

"I suppose."

"Any other news?"

"The psychologist has me on stronger meds."

"Oh?"

"Says it's worth trying a few different options. Experiment with it, she says."

"At least she obtained your consent before experimenting," Rachel said, but regretted the dig the moment she said it.

"Let's not get into it today. It always exhausts me. The arguing. The yelling."

Rachel nodded, but something about Angela's words caused her to think back to when she and Xavier were new in their relationship. It was late September and he had come over to find her crying, Rachel muttering through tears about some guy at work. The arguing. The yelling. Those are the words she used to describe the scene in the office lunchroom.

She didn't tell Xavier much more. Just a name: Jayson. It had slipped out while she was rehashing events.

Xavier held her a while longer then got in his truck and left. He was gone most of the night.

The next day, Jayson ran to her with flowers, apologizing

for his behaviour, saying it would never happen again. As he finished grovelling and turned to leave, that's when Rachel caught it. The dried blood at the corner of his mouth, the plum swelling just above his collarbone, the slow exhale and flinching as he grasped at his ribs.

She shouldn't have smiled, but she did. And for the first time she thought maybe this Xavier fellow had deeper feelings for her than he let on.

Sitting across from Angela, she cleared her throat. "So, the psychologist here is nice?"

"She's okay," Angela said. "Young. A recent grad."

"Hm."

"But good at her job, takes it seriously."

"So, I guess the trick with these new meds is you actually need to take them."

"Ha! Wasn't something I was always consistent with, was it?"

"Not by a long-shot."

Angela shrugged and lazily looked around the room. There were three other couples just like her and Rachel huddled together. Heads tilted, hushed whispers.

Half a dozen guards ambled around the space, monitoring the exits, discouraging physical contact between visitor and prisoner. Rachel tuned in to the jingle of keys, the tap of night stick against thigh as the burly officers sauntered between the tables.

Angela drew in an uneasy breath. "Is this really my life now?"

Rachel motioned to respond but realized the question wasn't meant to be answered. It was an admission of regret. Maybe remorse. They sat in silence, neither sure how to navigate this new dynamic.

Eventually, Angela turned to face Rachel. "So, two visits in one week. I feel spoiled. What brings you up this way?"

"I'm picking Andrew up at the airport," Rachel said.

"Now which one is he? I can't keep up with all your new friends."

"He's Xavier's brother. Well, half-brother, if you want to be specific."

"Ah yes, I remember. You see, even in here I try to keep up with the comings and goings of the bustling town of Barn Wood."

"Do you now?"

"You'd be surprised. There's more gossip in here than at work!"

The guard who had uncuffed Angela stepped forward. "Ten minutes, ladies."

Rachel nodded, then turned to Angela. "Anyway, the airport is a little beyond here so I figured I'd stop in on the way."

"Why can't Loverboy pick up his own brother?"

"Xavier? Well, he and Evelyn went up to some campground with a bunch of cops to look around."

"Look around for what?"

"He's convinced there are some leftovers up that way."

"Leftovers?"

Rachel lowered her voice. "You know, infected creatures left over from last winter."

"What are you talking about?"

"People still acting crazy."

Angela scrunched up her face. "People are still sick from the vaccine clinics?"

"The term *sick* doesn't really cover it. These people are running around like possessed lunatics."

Angela shifted in her seat, swiping the bangs off her forehead. "What are you saying? These things are resurfacing?"

"I guess so. The cops figure some are still in hiding, some still missing from the inoculation push last summer."

"Well, my solution was only temporary," Angela said. She leaned forward. "So, I suppose it makes sense some are reverting."

"They're reverting all right."

"But why haven't they developed something permanent? I gave the cops the temporary one along with all my research notes months ago."

Rachel shrugged.

"Surely, they have access to scientists that can create something permanent," Angela added. "They need to develop it soon, otherwise this will just keep happening."

"To be honest, I didn't think you'd be interested in all this anymore," Rachel said.

"The science behind it is fascinating," Angela said. "There were mistakes made for sure, but—"

"*Mistakes made?*"

"Oh, please, don't get all high and mighty on me. Our intentions were to find a cure."

"And to make a shit-tonne of money."

Angela rolled her eyes.

"Regardless," Rachel continued. "Xavier says they're either leftovers or new ones."

"New ones?"

"Says he thinks they're different from the originals as these ones are stronger than anything he fought last winter."

Angela twisted her mouth. "Actually, thinking about it, that doesn't surprise me," she said. "I was beginning to see that in my own research."

"Smarter too."

Angela moved her hand to her chest. "What do you mean, smarter?"

"I don't know, he says these new ones are smarter."

"Smarter how?"

"Okay, ladies, time's up," the guard said, sidling up to the table. He swung the cuffs with his index finger as if spinning a frisbee at the beach.

Angela spread her hands on the table. "Smarter how?"

Rachel glanced at the guard then rose from her chair. "Looks like this will have to wait until next visit, sis."

Angela lunged across the table and grabbed Rachel by her collar. "How are they smarter, Rachel? How do you know that?"

"Hey, no touching!" the guard yelled, forcing Angela's arms behind her. "I already told you this visit is over!"

"Rachel, you need to go to him!" Angela shouted.

"Pipe down!" the guard barked.

Another guard hustled over and tackled Angela. She thrashed wildly, tugging out a hank of his hair. Soon, a third guard was on top of her, his knee on her back, fumbling with a set of handcuffs.

"When I studied it, the virus changed, the subjects got stronger," Angela said, nearly out of breath, the weight of the officer straining her voice. "But never smarter."

The guard clamped the handcuffs on and hoisted Angela up. "I said this visit is over!" he shouted, spit flinging from his mouth. He marched Angela toward the exit, her legs dragging behind.

"If they're getting smarter, then someone's behind it,"

Angela hollered over her shoulder.

Rachel rushed forward. "What do you mean?"

"Someone's altered the drug. Or enhanced the virus somehow."

"What do I do?"

"You have to go to him, to Xavier. He's not safe!" Angela screamed as the guards pushed her through the door.

"He's not safe how?" Rachel said, her voice panicked.

"They've mutated beyond recognition. It's unpredictable now, it can't be controlled!"

The metal door slammed and the room fell silent.

Rachel looked around, the other inmates and visitors staring at her. One of the visitors made eye contact. "What was that lady saying?" the woman asked.

"Oh, uh, nothing," Rachel muttered.

"Was she talking about the virus from last winter?" the visitor asked.

"I-I'm not sure."

"Is it coming back? Is that virus coming back?"

A second visitor rose from her chair. "Who was that woman? Why was she so scared?"

"Sh-she's not well," Rachel stammered, lowering her eyes. "They have her on new medication."

"Hey, I lost someone last winter," the second visitor said. "We damn near all did!"

"I'm-I'm sorry, I—"

"So, if you know something about this virus coming back or those crazy people coming back then you better damn well tell us!"

"I-I don't know," Rachel said. She tried to gather herself, adjusting her blouse and smoothing the front of her jeans.

"You'll have to excuse me. I need to go."

She wobbled toward the exit, motioning to one of the guards to be let out. She followed him through the maze of corridors until she arrived at the front desk.

"Ready to sign out?" the clerk asked.

"Yes," Rachel said. Still shaking, she handed the visitor badge through the narrow slit in the glass. She breathed deeply several times, trying to calm herself.

The clerk moved the mouse then typed out the exit time. But as she did, something on the screen caught Rachel's eye. A name. And the exit time entered beside it was only one minute before her own.

"I don't mean to pry," Rachel said. "But what's the other name listed for Dr. Angela Till?"

"Like I told you last time, that's privileged information," the clerk said.

"Oh, right, of course," Rachel said. "Sorry for being nosy. It's just that—I thought I recognized the name."

The clerk looked around the empty foyer. "You're her sister, right?"

Rachel nodded.

"Normally we ain't supposed to give that information out," the clerk said, her voice lowered. "But given she's your sister…" She scrolled down the screen. "It was a Mr. Pak. Checked in then checked back out a minute later."

"He stayed for only a minute?" Rachel asked.

"Yeah. Got spooked when I told him Dr. Till already had a visitor. Scurried right outta here."

"Thank you," Rachel said then hurried down the hall.

As she pushed through the metal door, her eyes squinted from the sun. She scanned the parking lot until her eyes caught on a slim Korean man hunched outside a jet-white BMW. He was finely dressed, a gold ring on his pinky, his silver hair slicked back. His faint moustache was meticulously clipped and his hand anxiously roamed up and down the length of a cane, a twisted head of a stag at its collar. He stared at the front door, his piercing black eyes digging into Rachel.

A squat man with a black overcoat and driving gloves stepped forward. "Ready to leave, Mr. Pak?"

Pak dropped his eyes from Rachel as he stepped into the vehicle, his driver closing the door behind him. But as the car pulled away, Pak glared at Rachel again. And the hatred in his eyes shook her deeply, troubling her in a way she would not easily forget.

Chapter Twelve

March 1994
Day 45 | Night

In the dank basement, Evelyn sat on the cold metal stool. Her father had his back turned at the bench. A bare light-bulb swung slack from a wire above.

"You ready?" Evelyn asked.

"Almost," Simon said, fidgeting with something. "Just another few seconds."

"Okay, 'cause I've got a bunch of homework."

"Homework in grade six? Seems a little early, doesn't it?"

"Tell that to Mrs. Reynolds."

"Oh?"

"She gives homework every night and twice as much on the weekends! But no one likes her so that's probably why."

"She sounds nasty," Simon chuckled. He spun to face her, holding a needle. "Alright, you know the drill. Roll up your sleeve."

Evelyn begrudgingly slid her sweater up. Simon rubbed the inside of her elbow with an alcohol swab then adjusted the needle between his thumb and finger. Evelyn looked away as the prick of metal pierced the vein under her skin, followed by the warm heat of pain and then the suck of scarlet up the tube.

Simon pressed a cotton swab on the wound followed by a bandage. "Not so bad, huh?"

"But do we have to do this every month, Dad?"

"Until I find what I'm looking for," Simon said.

"But what *are* you looking for?"

"I'm trying to manipulate a drug, to see if there's a way to control it."

"And you need blood for that?"

"Certainly. I test the drug with your blood—see what it can endure and what it can't."

"But aren't you trying to find a cure?"

"Um, I guess so. But also, more than that. It's a bit complicated, I suppose."

"But why don't you take Damien's blood? Why is it always me?"

"I do take his blood. He's just not as…as willing a subject as you are."

"What does that mean?"

"He resists. Puts up a bit of a fight," Simon said. Then he smirked. "Must be because he's a teenager. You know how moody they can get!"

Evelyn giggled. "But what will you do when all your tests are done?"

"Ah, you never mind that. Besides, I think it's time for that homework, don't you think?"

"But I was just wondering what happens after you use the blood—"

"You don't want to anger that mean Mrs. Reynolds now, do you?"

Evelyn grimaced then hopped down from the stool. "I guess not," she said, sliding her sweater over the bandage and back down her arm. "But Dad, I don't understand why you need *my* blood."

"Ah, don't worry about all that. It's a bit…*science-y*…a bit complicated. Time for you to run along now."

Evelyn huffed and moved to the door then paused, her back still turned. "It's just that I overheard Mom say something and I wasn't sure if it was true or not."

"What did she say?" Simon asked, his voice suddenly tense.

"That she didn't know if what you were doing was helping people or…"

"Or what?"

"Or hurting people."

"Who did she say that to?"

"Uncle Joe. I overheard her on the phone. She was whispering, but I could still hear."

"Listen, Evelyn. Your mother knows very little about this stuff."

"Maybe. But she sounded sad. A bit scared."

"I wouldn't listen to her. She doesn't understand any of this."

"She also said—"

"It's time for your homework!" Simon barked.

Evelyn nodded then jittered from the room, closing the door behind her.

Simon exhaled then turned back to the bench. He took the newly filled vial and wrote the letters 'E.S.' upon it in black marker. He dipped the end of a pipette into it and extracted a small amount of blood.

He stepped to the microscope and switched it on, the bright glow of the staging area illuminated from below. He tilted the pipette and a few drops dripped onto the glass slide. He reached across the table and unscrewed a clear glass bottle, the label of a dark, menacing buck affixed to it.

"Good thing you're as stupid as you look, Mr. Mackenzie," he sniggered to himself. "Snatched this right out from under your nose at our first meeting."

With a separate pipette, he added several drops of clear liquid from the glass bottle. He stared down the ocular lens as he mixed the liquids.

After several seconds, the texture changed from an opaque fluid to a dense gel. The substance began to ripple, quivering and clotting upon itself, shaking the slide until it abruptly turned to ash.

He pressed his lips together, his eyes squinting in confusion.

He reached for a second bottle. This one contained a cloudy gas-like vapour, a curl of mist. It was hot to the touch and as he unscrewed it, it released a scent of burning metal. He tilted the bottle over the slide, mixing it with the existing smear. The ash began to reverberate again. It was swirling and swaying as if trying to leap from the slide, something propelling it upwards.

"Interesting…" he mumbled.

He watched, fascinated, as the ash shrouded away, leaving only the blood and clear liquid on the slide once again as if nothing at all had happened.

"In all my years…"

He stepped back from the bench and switched off the microscope, a look of panicked excitement curdling across his face.

"Maybe just a few more tests," he mumbled to himself. "A few more tests and then, well…I just may finally crack this!"

Chapter Thirteen

November 1995
Day 641 | Morning

Everett shivered as he led the others through the desolate campground, up the path, and past the sleeping cabins and run-down storage unit. His boots crunched over the night's dusting of snow as the group crept up the steep incline and through the tall timber toward the barn.

At the top of the escarpment, it came into view—its grim and hulking shadow taking shape in the misty haze of dawn. As they approached, Everett unclipped his holster and gripped his revolver, a tremor troubling his hand.

"Xavier, why don't you come up front," he said. "You, um, you seem to know this place best."

Xavier wormed his way to the front. He sniffed the air then motioned for Evelyn to join him. They both turned, skulking forward, leading the others through the long grass and fescue.

"You remember how they smell?" Xavier whispered.

Evelyn nodded.

"Last time I was here this place reeked," he said.

Evelyn raised her nose to the wind. "I don't smell any-thing."

"That's my point. And last time that barn was full of

them fighting and screaming. Hear any of that now?"

Evelyn shook her head.

"Me neither."

"What's it mean?" she asked, although the quiver in her voice suggested she might already know the answer.

"They know we're here."

Evelyn clenched her rifle. "But wouldn't we be able to smell them?"

"Something's different this time," Xavier said. "Something's not right."

The group continued through the waist-high ryegrass and weeds. Evelyn stopped then turned with a puzzled look. She squinted into the trees on the far side of the barn but the morning fog hadn't lifted and she couldn't see but for a few yards beyond it.

"See something?" Xavier asked.

"No, it's not that," Evelyn said. "I feel like I've been here before."

"How's that?"

"Something familiar about this place. The barn or…I don't know…the trees are familiar, if that makes sense."

"Well, it's unfamiliar to the rest of us so keep your eyes and ears sharp!"

When they reached the barn, Xavier slid the rifle from his back. "Stay tight to me," he whispered to Evelyn.

He stepped to a window and peered in, his eyes darting around the large empty space. There was nothing. No movement, no noise. He turned back to Everett and shook his head.

"There's nothing in there?" Munroe blurted out.

"Shut up!" Caldwell said in a forced whisper. "Keep your voice down!"

"Why? Big man just signalled there's nothing in there."

"We don't know that."

"They've probably cleared out already," Munroe said. "Or were never here in the first place."

Everett faced Xavier. "What do you think?"

Xavier peered in the window again. There were none of the signs he had spotted last time: the blood on the walls and floor, the half-eaten buck, the dusty prints on the floorboards.

He shook his head. "I don't get it," he said. "It's like they've abandoned it. And someone's come and cleaned it all up."

"These creatures got a maid now?" Munroe said.

"I don't know what to tell you," Xavier said. "They were there and now they're not."

Everett stood with his lips pursed, staring at the foreboding structure. A wind picked up from the south and some of the loose boards under the slanted eaves began to rattle.

"Looks like a big haunted house," Jackson whispered.

"Maybe we just head down then?" Dunvey offered.

"Well, we've searched the campground and now the barn…" Everett said.

"So, we just head back to the trucks?" Dunvey said.

"I suppose," Everett said. "Could radio back to headquarters. Update them on the situation, wait to see what they say."

"We should burn it down," Munroe said.

"Burn what down?"

"The whole thing," Munroe said. He rummaged in his pockets, pulling out his lighter. He flicked it twice until the flame caught. "From pillar to post. We take the whole thing down to the ground."

"What are you talking about?" Powell asked.

"Look, if those things are in there, then we burn it down and get rid of 'em."

"And if they're not?"

"Then all we've done is burned down their so-called hideout. It's a win-win."

"We're just here to gather intel," Everett hissed. "We're not burning anything down. We haven't even identified a threat!"

Prasad cleared his throat. "I agree with Munroe. It actually makes sense."

"Have you two lost it?" Powell sneered.

"Look, if they're in there, we get rid of them," Prasad said. "If not, it's just a dilapidated barn nobody uses anyway."

"Get rid of them?" Everett said. "How many times do I have to repeat myself. We're not here to get rid of anything!"

"Besides, you heard the kids," Powell said. "Said their parents were in there."

"We taking tactical advice from a pair of rug rats now?" Munroe huffed.

Powell turned on him. "At least they appreciate what we're up against!"

"Look," Munroe said. "Whether those things are in there or not doesn't really matter if it all goes up in flames."

"You're not making any sense."

"All I'm saying is we were sent to neutralize a threat, right? Well, burning the barn down neutralizes it."

"*Neutralizes it?* Your plan *obliterates* it!"

Munroe clenched his fists and moved toward Powell, but Xavier was already standing between them, his stare burrowing into the rookie officer.

"Easy there, soldier," Prasad said to Munroe. He put an

arm around him, pulling him away. "Let's just take a breather, okay?"

"All these clowns wanna do is tiptoe around the problem," Munroe said.

"I know, I know. Let's take a walk and everyone can have a minute to calm down, okay?" He guided Munroe away from the group, pacing through the long grass and out of sight behind the barn.

Xavier unfurled his fists, a line of sweat carving a path through his dark stubble.

"Sorry for that," Everett said. "He's new. Still wound up, still full of that go-getter energy."

Xavier exhaled. "I think we should go in," he said, motioning toward the barn. "Get a closer look."

"You sure that's a good idea—"

"They were here, Tom. Dozens of 'em. It doesn't make sense they all just up and left."

"I suppose…"

"I'll go in quietly, look for any signs we might be able to pick up on."

Everett chewed the inside of his cheek and squared his hat. "Alright. Take Singh and Caldwell with you."

"What about us?" Jackson said, motioning to himself and Dunvey.

"You two keep watch with me, Sheila, and Evelyn," Everett said.

"Sounds good," Jackson said with a sigh of relief.

"And Xavier," Everett added. "You've got ten minutes. See anything suspicious, you come right out so we can make a plan. Understood?"

Xavier nodded. He moved toward the barn door, Singh

and Caldwell following at a distance. When he was close, he pulled at the door, making a rough, grating sound as it scraped along the wooden floor.

Inside, he inched forward. He paused and listened and then waved for the two officers to join him. They each moved from the entrance and down a short hallway, weapons drawn.

"Are t-they as big as you say?" Singh stuttered, his vinyl coat scratching noisily as he walked.

Xavier faced him. "Little late to be asking, don't you think?"

Xavier turned and continued down the hallway until they reached the main area. He scanned the room for any movement or sound but all was silent.

"Even the rats are gone," he mumbled.

He peered into a darkened corner, his eyes travelling up the wall to the vault of the barn, across the bowed and rotted trestles. He thought he saw something move, something trussed up in the rafters.

"See anything?" Caldwell whispered.

Xavier stared a moment longer than shook his head. "Thought I did…but maybe not."

"That's good, right?" Caldwell said. "Means nothing's here."

"Yeah, that's what I'm worried about."

"What's to worry about? They heard us coming, got scared, and ran off."

"These things don't run. They hunt."

A shrill beep sounded and Singh jumped until he realized the noise was coming from his wrist. He clicked the side of his watch, the noise stopping.

"That's ten minutes," he said.

"You set an alarm?" Xavier said.

"Everett said ten minutes, so I just thought…"

"What's wrong with you?"

"We were told to go back after ten minutes," Singh said. He shuffled down the hallway, but as he did, his revolver dropped to the wooden slats below, the metallic thud reverberating throughout the space. Everyone froze, their panicked eyes shifting around the room and then to each other.

After a strained silence, Xavier exhaled and swung the strap of his rifle across his shoulders. "I think we're okay," he said.

He walked past Singh and down the narrow hallway. "Who sets an alarm?" he huffed, heaving the barn door open, the three of them trudging back outside.

"Anything?" Everett asked.

"Nothing," Xavier said.

"What's it mean?" Evelyn asked.

"I don't get it. They should be there."

"So, it's settled then?" Dunvey said. "We head back to the trucks?"

"I guess so," Everett said. "We'll go down and radio headquarters."

"What are they gonna do?" Dunvey said.

"We'll have to tell them there was a sighting a few days ago, but these things must have cleared out since then."

"Just a minute, Tom," Powell said, something threading her attention back to the barn. She stood on her toes and peered into the window.

"What is it?" Everett asked.

"Thought I saw a light."

"What kind of light?" Caldwell asked.

"I-I'm not sure," Powell said. "Just looked like a light or—"

"Want us to go check it out again?"

"No…it's…it's probably nothing," Powell said.

But as she was about to lower from her tiptoes, there was a flash again. An orange haze, shimmering along the window on the opposite wall, black fingers of smoke curling about the pane and sill. Her eyes followed the flare, rippling along the wooden floor, until she saw something else.

A yellow marble. Perhaps a kid's toy, lodged within the floorboards. It was moist and midnight-black at its centre, salt-white flakes peppered around its edges. She began to turn from it until the marble shifted. Then a second marble appeared, just as yellow and black as the first, until a bloody eyelid blinked over it.

Powell watched as a clawed hand wormed up through a crack in the floor and peeled the floorboard back onto itself, a second set of eyes now shifting into the light. She gasped as a second clawed hand and then a third came up, stripping the thick planks away as easy as wet wallpaper.

"They're beneath the floor," she said, her voice barely above a whisper. "They're hiding beneath the floor."

Her eyes rolled up and her knees wobbled. She lost her footing, her head crashing hard against the side of the barn, her body crumpling into a heap.

"Sheila!" Everett yelled and ran to her side.

He brushed her hair out from the large gash in her forehead then fumbled around her neck, pressing his pudgy fingers along her throat, searching for a pulse. The others ran to her as well and together they yanked the unconscious officer to standing.

"Is she breathing?" Evelyn gasped.

"She's breathing. A weak pulse though," Everett said.

"There's med kits back at the cars," Jackson said.

Everett draped Powell's limp arm over his shoulder. "I'll take her back, but I'll need you to—" But his words were cut short as something caught his attention.

He sniffed at the air. "Smoke?" he said.

He turned back to the barn as wisps of flame clamoured up the cedar shanks. "They're burning it down! Those idiots are burning it down!"

Xavier hoisted Powell's other arm over his shoulder. "We need to take her down. She needs medical attention right away," he said.

"What about the barn?" Everett said.

"I'll come back and deal with the fire after."

Everett nodded. "Yeah, yeah, sounds good."

They hobbled over the snow and through the slick grass, Powell drooping between them, her neck swinging lifelessly as the others followed close behind.

And then everything seemed to stop as a scream pierced the air.

Evelyn stiffened and the colour drained from her face as the force of the noise brought her to her knees. Her shoulders slumped forward and she felt nauseous. Her eyes twitched wildly as a desperate look swirled about them just before the panic set in.

She knelt on the snow, frozen to the spot, unable to will herself forward. How many nights had that sound shocked her and Damien awake? How long would it haunt her still?

At the sound, Everett turned, the barn now fully alight. He went still, his mouth ajar. "Dear, God, what have they done?"

Evelyn looked to Xavier, her face wet with tears, her breaths coming in heaving sobs. She heard the scream again and whipped around to see the creatures surging out from the barn, away from the flames, and across the field toward her.

Get up, Damien said.

And just as abruptly as the tears had started, they stopped. She rose and a different look came over her. Gone was the anguish and fear, replaced now by something close to courage. Or rage.

She reached for her knife and turned to face them just before she heard his voice again.

Run, Ev, Damien said. *You need to run.*

Chapter Fourteen

**November 1995
Day 641 | Afternoon**

Still trembling from the events in the prison, Rachel sped down the highway, following the signs for the airport. Her knuckles were white as she gripped the steering wheel.

She signalled into the arrival's lane and parked the car against the curb. Flipping the visor mirror down, she remedied her eye make-up which had run from tearing up.

After a few minutes, Andrew emerged from the bowels of the airport, backpack over his shoulders. He was holding hands with someone—a red-haired girl—and they shuffled around an elderly couple before arriving at Rachel's sedan.

Rachel stepped forward and hugged Andrew. "Good to see you."

"Good to see you too," Andrew said. "How is he?"

"Left yesterday morning with Everett and seven other cops."

Andrew nodded. "What else do we know?"

"That they want you there straight away, but, um…" Rachel stopped, taking in the girl standing awkwardly to the side. "Who's this?"

"Oh, right, this is Juliana," Andrew said. "We met back in April and she came to visit me a couple days ago. Juliana, this is Rachel. Rachel, meet Juliana."

The women shook hands, but then Rachel pulled Andrew to the rear of the car. "What's she doing here?" she said, her voice low, tense.

"Her ride bailed. I just figured—"

"Then put her in a cab! You can't bring her with us."

"She lives quite far. A cab would cost a fortune."

"Andrew, you know what we're walking into."

Andrew looked to the ground. "Look, Everett wants me there right away, right? So, drop me first and then drive her home after."

Rachel crossed her arms and glared at Andrew.

"She just needs a ride home," he said. "It's been a shitty trip for her. The last thing I want to do is put her in a taxi by herself. She'd never speak to me again."

He reached down to open the trunk, but as he lifted the lid, Rachel slammed her hand against it.

"Whoa," Andrew said.

"I brought your…your *supplies*," Rachel said. "You don't want to be flashing them around an airport."

"Right. Okay, I'll just throw the luggage in the back."

He tossed his backpack to the floor and jostled Juliana's bulky suitcase into the rear seat then slid in beside it. Juliana eased into the passenger seat as Rachel hopped back in the driver's side. She put the car in drive, accelerated off the curb, and sped down the express ramp.

"So, where is he?" Andrew asked.

"I have a vague idea, but he left me this map with coordinates," Rachel said, grabbing the folded papers from the dash and handing them over her shoulder. "Figured you'd be able to locate it. Camp Clearwater or something like that."

"They're at a camp?"

"It's abandoned. He kept talking about a barn up that way as well."

"Okay, let me take a look." He unfolded the map and examined the documents, muttering to himself, double-checking the numbers scrawled in Xavier's chicken scratch. "So, what's in the trunk?" he asked a few minutes later. "Like what *supplies* are we talking about here?"

"Food, water, your boots, camo, rope, your knife," Rachel said, as if reciting a list. "Your rifle, of course. Lots of rounds."

"My word," Juliana said. "Are we walking into a war zone?"

"Just about," Andrew mumbled. "Welcome to my life."

"Is the camp safe?"

"X and I did something similar last winter. If everyone keeps their wits about them, we should be fine."

"Well, that's just it, Andrew," Rachel said. "There's some other things I need to tell you."

"Such as?"

"X says these things are bigger. And faster. Says it's not like last time."

"Yeah. I could hear it in his voice when he called."

"There's more. You see, I visited my sister today."

"Your sister's Angela, right?" Juliana said.

"Mm-hmm."

"Andrew told me some things about her. She's the *doctor-scientist* person?"

"That's right. She got arrested so I visit her in prison every few weeks," Rachel said. "Good Lord—that's a sentence I never thought I'd say."

"So, what'd she say?" Andrew asked.

"I told her about some of the new creatures X found," Rachel explained.

"And?"

"She said something about them getting bigger and stronger was predictable. How her tests were already showing that."

"Okay…"

"All that she was fine with until I told her they're getting smarter. That threw her into a full-fledged panic."

"Why?"

"I didn't hear all of it, the guards dragged her away."

"Did she say anything else?"

"Said if they're getting smarter then someone must be behind it, that this wouldn't happen through natural means."

"These mutations?"

"I guess. She was convinced someone needed to initiate it."

Andrew's brow furrowed. "Maybe it's that Alan Mackenzie guy."

"Why do you say that?"

"His name's all over those reports from your sister's house. Maybe he's still trying to finish the experiments. Juliana actually knows him—used to work with him."

Juliana turned to Rachel. "He was a client of my former firm. A real creep."

"I'd imagine anyone involved in this is a creep," Rachel said. "Real low on the morality scale."

Andrew sighed. "This is a lot to take in twenty minutes after landing."

"Sorry, I know, but there's more," Rachel said.

"Was afraid of that," Andrew mumbled.

"One of the last things she said was the whole thing was now out of control."

"It was out of control a long time ago."

"I know, but she said something like there used to be safeguards, but now…"

Andrew sighed, his mind fishing for answers. The reports from Angela's study, the textbooks about the virus. There had to be something he wasn't seeing. A clue, some sort of hint.

"Seriously though," Juliana said. "Is it safe where we're going?"

"I'm just dropping him and then driving you home," Rachel said.

"You're not staying?"

"They only asked for Andrew. And believe me, I'm totally fine with that."

Juliana drew in a breath. "But is it safe for him?" she asked, lowering her voice so only Rachel could hear. "Because, you know, I wouldn't mind getting him back when all this is done."

"To be honest, I don't know anymore."

"Doesn't exactly ooze confidence."

"Last winter, he and X had this figured out pretty quick. How those things behaved, how to track them."

"And now?"

"This time around feels different, feels like…" Her voice trailed off, something gnawing at her.

They drove in silence for a long time, the afternoon light gradually dissolving from the sky. After a while, Rachel turned to Juliana. "You mentioned a firm? What do you do?"

"I'm a lawyer," Juliana said.

"Wow, that's so cool."

"Well, kind of a lawyer. I used to practice, but now I'm, well…I'm in-between careers, I suppose."

"I always wanted to be a lawyer."

"Oh yeah? Well, you still can, I'm sure."

"It was always just a silly dream, that's all."

"There's loads of studying involved, lots of late nights. But Andrew tells me you're super smart, so maybe you'd be fine."

"Yeah, but a lawyer? I don't know, seems like a fantasy," Rachel said. She went quiet for a minute. "Anyway, what area of law do you practice?"

"The firm I worked for did patent law, copyright law, things like that," Juliana said. "Mostly for pharmaceutical companies."

"Pharmaceutical? Then this whole nightmare is right up your alley?"

Juliana smiled. "I just executed the contracts. I never understood the science behind it. That's more Andrew's thing."

"Still…" Rachel said. She surveyed Andrew in the backseat through the rearview mirror. He was examining the map in his lap, deep in thought. She cleared her throat and lowered her voice. "So, you and Andrew, are you two…?"

"I'm actually not sure what we are," Juliana said.

"I see."

"I mean, I think we're just feeling it out, seeing where it goes."

"Sounds familiar."

"Oh, really? So, you and Xavier?"

"Same answer."

Juliana laughed.

"I mean sometimes he's touchy-feely and sometimes it's like I'm not even there," Rachel said.

"Aren't all men like that?" Juliana said.

"I suppose," Rachel chuckled. "Seems like the Stone brothers have the same approach to dating. They both keep their women guessing."

"Ha! Confirming their relationship status isn't high on their priority list."

"Definitely not after last winter," Rachel said, a sudden soberness to her words. "Staying alive was the only thing on their list. Mine too."

"That's when you met Andrew and Xavier?"

"Yeah, I was with a few others when we came across them, a few weeks after everything hit the fan."

"And it was only going on in your town?"

"As far as we know. There's been rumours," Rachel said. "But from what Everett tells us, his team has only seen this sort of thing in Barn Wood."

Juliana adjusted in her seat. "It must've been so scary."

"The whole thing was a nightmare," Rachel said. "Didn't know who to trust. Didn't even trust Xavier."

"My word."

"And then he saved my life."

"What? How?"

"Shot a creature that was about to attack me. Didn't think about his own safety. Just thought of me. And that right there gave me a pretty clear indication of who these guys really are."

Juliana smiled awkwardly. "That sounds sweet. Horrible, of course. But sweet."

Andrew yawned then folded the map and handed it back

to Rachel. "X and I used to hunt in that area so I kinda know it," he said. "You're on this road for a while, at least another hour."

He turned to stare out the window, the hazy-orange sun continuing its slow descent behind the rolling fields, the yellow stalks pushing up through the snow, clipped short for the winter. He glanced at a passing road sign: *Gas Station—60 Kilometres; Creekside Motel—120 Kilometres.*

The car meandered along the county road, the grey hills and hollers in the distance. Andrew rested his head against the window. The rush of Juliana's visit, the panic of Xavier's phone call, and then the chaotic last-minute flight arrangements had all but exhausted him. He yawned again then closed his eyes and quickly fell asleep, the sway of the car lulling him into a dream.

It was the one dream he always had. He would lumber up the winding driveway toward his family's farmhouse. He would step through the creek, the vicious leeches gnawing at his skin, and then up to the porch.

He would nudge the front door open, shards of glass beneath his feet, then climb the stairs to the bedrooms. First, his brother's on the left. Then, his parents' down the hall.

His best friend, Jeremiah, was in the house too, cursing Andrew's name, threatening his father would avenge him. And then his mother would appear, shrieking to come find her over and over again.

But this time, an icy cold seeped into Andrew, and the vision shifted. He was no longer in his house but now in a forest, a small clearing at its centre. He was young, maybe 9 or 10, and he warily approached his step-father who was kneeling beside a pile of tarps and nylon slips. Xavier was by his side, a hammer in one hand, a fistful of metal pegs in the other.

Joe looked up. "What do you want?"

"C-can I help?" Andrew asked.

"What do you know about putting up a tent?"

Elizabeth was lounging in a chair several yards away. She shot an annoyed look at her husband.

"Alright," Joe said to Andrew. "Grab another hammer and some pegs. Once I get the poles through, you and X can hammer 'em into the ground."

Andrew ran to the toolbox, a smile teasing at his lips.

Joe unrolled the first tarp then overlaid it with a second. He spread the tent on top and carefully fed the poles through the sleeves. After all the poles were through and erect, he nodded at the boys. "Okay, hammer 'er down."

Xavier worked fast, looping the guy-lines through and then swatting each peg half a dozen times until it disappeared into the dirt. Andrew watched and then followed Xavier's lead, holding the hammer in the same manner, allowing his wrist to lever, pounding the peg into the earth.

A few minutes later, Joe ambled over. "Who did these ones?" he asked, pointing at the lopsided stakes.

"I did," Andrew said proudly.

Joe shook his head. "They're all wrong."

Andrew shirked and looked down at his runners.

"Crooked as hell, the loops gonna slip right off 'em," Joe barked.

"I c-could fix them, if you show me how—"

"Just leave 'em for X. He'll do 'em right."

Andrew drew quiet then dropped the hammer near the pile of tools and walked away from the tent. He bit down on his lip, desperately trying to fight the tears welling up.

"X, come dig these out and do 'em right," Joe said.

When Xavier had finished, Joe sidled up to him. He tousled the boy's hair. "Nice work, son," he said. "That so called brother of yours ain't much for the outdoors, huh?"

Andrew heard the comment and turned to his mother, her sorrowful eyes resting on his, until he felt a weight on his shoulder. He swatted it away but it came again, this time firmer.

"Andrew?" his mom said. He looked over to where she sat, but she looked different.

"Andrew!" she said again. However, it wasn't her voice this time but another, panicked and urgent.

"Andrew!" Juliana said.

Andrew shot awake, a spittle of drool gathering along his lip. His eyes fluttered as his mind returned to Rachel's car. Juliana was shifted around in her seat, her arm outstretched, her hand on his shoulder.

"Was it that same dream?" she asked.

"Yeah, same one," Andrew said. He sat up straight and wiped the drool away. He kneaded the heel of his hands against the hollow of his eyes and when he brought them away, they were wet. "Must've dozed off. Did I yell?"

"A little."

"Sorry. I've been getting them more and more and they're just—"

"No need to apologize," Rachel said. "I get them too." She held him with soft eyes in the rearview mirror. "About those *things*, right?"

Andrew nodded. "Them and my mom."

"X and Ev get nightmares too," Rachel said.

"Really?"

"Oh yeah. Most nights the house is full of everyone screaming in their sleep. It's a real treat, believe me."

"They feel so real. And it's just strange how so many townsfolk have been found. But not my parents."

"They're out there," Rachel said. "Somewhere."

"Yeah," he said. "Maybe…" He made a noise in his throat. And then: "How are we for gas?"

"Less than a quarter tank."

"I saw a sign for a gas station a while back. Maybe turn in when you come to it."

Rachel nodded and Andrew swiped the last of his tears with the cuff of his sleeve. He looked like someone grieving at a funeral, his head bowed and shoulders slumped, his brow laden with sweat and worry.

Chapter Fifteen

November 1995
Day 641 | Afternoon

Evelyn turned from the black river of monsters flooding out of the barn and sprinted across the clearing.

When she reached the others, she found Caldwell and Jackson fumbling to load their revolvers, Everett and Dunvey carefully leaning Powell against a tree.

Singh dropped to his knees and stared at the approaching onslaught, mumbling a shaky prayer under his breath. Xavier was already firing, several of the beasts collapsing from the steady stream of bullets.

"Take my ten o'clock," he hollered to Evelyn.

She nodded and slid the rifle from her back, trampling through the frosted high grass, a list in her gait. She clicked the safety and wallowed down in the snow. The fog had lifted so she could see clearly through the scope. She closed her eyes and steadied her breath.

"It's just a tree," she whispered to herself, remembering Xavier's lesson those many months ago. "Just like shooting a tree."

Her eyes shot open and she fired two quick rounds as a beast a foot taller than her fell.

A second one lurched forward and she reloaded and fired

again. The first shot nicked it, but the second shot landed true, the hot lead tunnelling its way into the creature's throat. It buckled, wrapping its massive hands around its neck. Wheezing, it soon went still, its body crashing to the ground, the thirsty snow drinking its black blood.

Another creature tripped as it lunged for Evelyn and she rolled out of the way as it thumped beside her. She took her knife and stabbed it repeatedly, the beast howling before its head dropped and it went silent.

A fourth creature, obese and marred, reached out for her, but she spun and flicked her wrist, the knife curling through the air, plunging into its chest. She marched over and pulled the blade from its clammy skin. It gurgled and spluttered blood over its teeth and tongue before collapsing.

In her periphery, she saw something else coming for her: a gaunt, emaciated figure with grey, soggy skin, one of its eyes hanging loose. The creature stumbled toward her, arms flailing and with a lame gallop—a macabre marionette.

Evelyn moved to reload but fumbled, the cartridge disappearing in the snow. She ducked low as the beast sprang for her, but it snapped back as a bullet went through its forehead. When she turned, the smoke was still wafting from Xavier's barrel.

He trained on it again, a second round scything off pieces of flesh, its blood spraying out behind it. He reloaded and then ran for Evelyn as another beast lurched toward her, digging its gnarled claws into her.

She screamed as Xavier grabbed the monster and heaved it into the air before throwing it to the ground. He wrestled it as it bucked and shrieked. He held it down with his weight, pinning the creature, punching it over and over again like a furious carpenter hammering a nail.

Another beast howled and charged at the girl, but Xavier was already poised to strike, a possessed rage about him. He drew out his knife and split the beast's throat. The creature dropped where it stood.

He raised his knife and swung it down, cleaving the creature's skull in two. He stood over it while it died, wiping the blade on his inseam, black blood leaking out from the blunt hole.

He looked to Evelyn. "You okay?"

She trembled and stepped back as she took him in: his feral eyes, his fevered breathing, blood streaming off his fingers. There seemed to be something dark in him, something she hadn't seen before, something that frightened her.

"Ev, you okay?"

"I'm-I'm okay," she said. She located the cartridge in the snow and reloaded her weapon, never dropping her gaze from him.

A shot rang out and she spun to find Caldwell and Jackson shooting at creatures still streaming out of the barn. Dunvey and Singh hurried to join them, yelling instructions, advancing toward the burning building until Caldwell screamed.

"I'm out of ammo," the officer shrieked, patting her vest pockets.

Singh ran to her with extra cartridges but the pack of monsters was faster. They ran Caldwell down, slashing her chest. She wailed as they trampled her into the earth.

"Fiona!" Singh shouted.

He quickened his pace just as a creature grabbed Caldwell by the leg and tossed her violently against the barn. The flames curled around the wood siding, licking at her uniform.

"Fiona!" Singh yelled again, his voice strained.

The beast cocked its head and looked down at the unconscious officer as if unsure what to do with her. An unusual look came over it. It wasn't anger or hate. Empathy, perhaps. Or longing.

"Get away from her, you bastard!" Singh shouted, staggering across the clearing.

The creature glanced up and gave a curious look. It turned to stare upon the small cabin in the distance and suddenly, a darkness fell over it. It shook and growled and thrust its claws into Caldwell's chest. It bent awkwardly toward her face and when it raised its head, half her jaw had been torn away, her eyes staring out, black and lifeless.

Evelyn's face crumpled as she watched the dark herd lumber toward them like oil seeping across snow. She glanced at Powell, lifeless against the tree, and a nauseous feeling flooded her.

"We've got to move her," she said.

Xavier nodded then whipped around to Everett. "Tom, you need to get Powell to those med-kits!"

Everett stood still, his mouth opening and closing but not making a sound. He looked like a suffocating fish.

"Tom! You hear me?" Xavier said.

Everett shook as if coming out of a trance. "Let me just call for back-up."

With shaking hands, he fiddled with the radio strapped to his uniform. He pressed the call button but there was no tone, no static. "Dammit," he said. "No signal up here!"

"We'll figure it out later," Xavier said. "Just get her down to the cruisers!"

Everett bent and hoisted Powell's limp body from the ground.

"Take Ev with you," Xavier said. "The rest of us will hold them as long as we can!"

Everett nodded then turned to Evelyn. "Bring her stuff and the briefcase," he said, then stumbled into the trees and down the escarpment, Powell's arm loose across his shoulders. Evelyn grabbed Powell's bags and followed close behind.

Singh screamed as he emptied his revolver into a wall of creatures. Jackson followed, labouring across the field, but before he reached him, a beast came up from behind and slashed him down the back. He howled, recoiling in pain, his uniform split open, the white moist flesh along his spine exposed.

The beast grabbed hold of his leg and ambled toward the barn, Jackson thrashing wildly. When it was close to the barn it raised the officer high into the air, bringing him down upon its knee, the crack echoing across the field.

Jackson stared out, his eyes terrified and bloodied, until the creature heaved him into the barn. The officer tried to stand but his mind wouldn't allow it. He wailed as the flames overtook him, his head clunking to the wooden floor seconds later.

"Take me too," Singh cried out. "Take me too, you cowards!"

He tossed his empty revolver to the ground and opened his arms to the advancing beasts just as Prasad and Munroe rushed out from behind the barn.

Several of the creatures turned and charged, but Munroe fired at them, a bullet travelling through the chest of one, the forehead of another.

A third one stormed up the bank and swung at him, but Munroe ducked and fired two rounds into its back, blood fanning out upon the snow. He kicked the beast into the barn, the flames devouring it.

Xavier moved across the field to join them.

"I knew you were lying," Munroe crowed when he spotted Xavier. "These things aren't that bad!"

He steadied his weapon and fired, a bullet entering a creature just below its collarbone. "Woohee! Finally, some action!"

"These ain't nothing like last time," Prasad yelled, putting a bullet through the back of one's head.

"Doesn't matter. These things ain't gettin' away."

"I think we got most of 'em now," Prasad called out.

"Not sure what all the fuss was about," Munroe grinned. "These things die just like everything else—"

But his words were cut short as a creature sprang up from the long grass and drove its claws into him. It was incredibly tall and blinding white, its skin that of an albino. It dug into Munroe's side, its nails like scalpels, fishing along his ribs and up into his lungs.

Munroe dropped his gun and gasped, his breathing rattled, as the monster yelped excitedly. He drew back with all his strength and elbowed the creature in the side of the head, but it shook off the attack, a maniacal look coming over it.

Munroe tried the movement again but he was losing blood and his swings weakened. He reached along his belt for his hunting knife but found nothing, the blade left back at the station.

He twisted around to face the creature. "You ain't that scary," he said, his words slurred and raspy. He spat blood on the ground. "You just got lucky."

The beast twisted its hand inside Munroe. The officer's eyes bulged out and his head drooped forward as blood rippled out from his mouth and down his neck. The beast brayed then hoisted Munroe high above its head, as if displaying a grotesque trophy.

"Steve! No!" Prasad shouted.

Xavier turned at the noise and his breath caught. It was the same monster that chased him days earlier. He hesitated as if an unfamiliar fear came over him.

"Let him go!" Prasad yelled.

Xavier unsheathed his knife, flinging it at the beast, the blade cutting through the air and thumping into the centre of its spine. It shook and dropped Munroe to the ground, falling on top of the officer.

"That thing just killed him!" Prasad screamed, tears welling up.

"I know, I know," Xavier said.

"Like he was nothing!"

"I know. But we've got to focus."

"I hate every last goddamn one of these things!"

"You've got to listen to me," Xavier said, vying for Prasad's attention. "How much ammo you got?"

Prasad breathed in ragged breaths and glanced down at his revolver. "Six, maybe seven rounds."

"I'm nearly out too."

"Wait, where's Everett?" Prasad said, scanning the field. "And Powell?"

"She's unconscious. Everett and Ev took her down to the cruisers."

Prasad nodded then looked at Munroe's body contorted awkwardly in the snow. He turned away, trembling. "What do we do now?"

"Get the others. We need to make a run for it."

"You sure?"

"Hopefully we lose them in the forest."

Prasad hollered and Singh and Dunvey hurried over.

"They killed Fiona!" Singh said. "I watched her die right in front of me."

"They got Jackson too," Dunvey said, his voice breaking.

"Steve's gone as well," Prasad said.

"There's too many of them. We can't hold them off any longer," Dunvey said.

"We're gonna have to make a run for it," Xavier said, sliding his rifle across his shoulders.

"Look," Prasad said. "There's more coming!"

"Listen, if we stick together, we'll be okay," Xavier said.

"But there's just too many," Dunvey said.

"They don't see that well in the forest," Xavier said. "The trees confuse them."

"How do you know?"

"I've had my fill of these things, learned some things the hard way."

Dunvey swallowed then turned to the other officers. "What do you think?"

"I'm nearly out of bullets," Prasad said.

"I'm completely out. Don't think we have much choice," Singh added.

Dunvey turned to Xavier. "Okay, what do we do?"

"Just head for the trees and run like hell," Xavier said.

The officers nodded, turned, and staggered down the escarpment. They trampled over the snow and grass, stumbling through a thick stand of birch, back toward the abandoned campground.

Xavier turned back just once to see the barn engulfed in flames and a horde of rabid creatures in his wake.

Chapter Sixteen

November 1995
Day 641 | Afternoon

Alan Mackenzie's head slumped between his shoulders, his wrists still tied overhead in the cramped closet. His arms were no longer in pain, his shoulder joints numbing long ago, all blood nearly drained from his hands and forearms.

Occasionally, a spasm would jolt through his outstretched legs, causing them to kick and flutter. But for the most part, he remained still.

His voice was raw from screaming for Simon the first few days. With little water, his throat was now hoarse, more of a blunt gravelly groan.

He had been in the closet for five days, although it felt much longer. And it had been nearly just as long since he had heard the voice from the other side of the wall. A man's voice —someone saying 'no' or 'not no'—over and over again.

As the days turned over, he racked his brain around who the person might be and what they were saying. He began to question if the man was really saying 'no'. Maybe he was saying something else. A plea? A clue? Or a name?

And what was it that Simon said? Something about the man's wife? So, there were definitely two more being held hostage. With he and his driver, Milton, that made four. At least.

Frustrated, he would jostle his hands every few hours, trying to get free of the rope. But each time the knot remained true, not budging at all.

Until it did.

He didn't notice it at first. It was a simple reprieve against his bare skin, a slack in the rope. The tension wasn't as sharp, the wire not digging in quite as deep. And then his eyes lit up as he became aware of the subtle sag in the cord.

He began adjusting the lines which curled into the thick bowline. He realized if he shifted his wrists in the exact same motion over and over again, a slight gap would form between the overlapping threads. He continued this movement, gradually loosening the nip of the knot, until he heard the door fling open and heavy footsteps bounding toward him.

The light was blinding when the closet door swung open. He attempted to cover his eyes with the crook of his elbow, but the fluorescent beams shone through nonetheless, his eyes squinting with tears.

When he was able to focus, he saw a massive creature breathing down on him, heavy and drooling. It looked similar to the one he had seen in the glass dome before he was tied and bound in the closet.

"Okay, step aside," a voice from behind the creature said. "He's not going anywhere, all strung up like that."

The creature grunted and took a step back as Simon moved out from the beast's shadow. He was lean and rangy and had a manic look about him, his eyes narrowing to a squint behind his glasses. A metallic-blue briefcase dangled from his hand.

"Still with us, Mr. Mackenzie?" he said, a slight disappointment in his voice. "I would have thought you'd given up by now."

Alan adjusted himself, moving his knees toward his chest. He opened his mouth to speak but only a strained wheeze came out.

"Something to say?" Simon mocked. He pushed his greasy hair back and Alan noticed a patch of burnt skin, long scarred over, along the man's forehead. "You're usually such a talkative fella, always selling people on your lies."

He unscrewed the lid of a plastic water bottle, took a swig then turned to Alan, feigning surprise. "Oh, I'm sorry, did you want some? I suppose it's been a while, hasn't it?"

He stepped into the closet and tilted the bottle. Alan craned his neck as the cold water splashed upon his forehead, most of it dripping into his matted hair and patchy grey beard, some gathering along his chapped lips. He swallowed then stared at Simon.

"What are you looking at?" Simon barked.

Alan let out a stuttered exhale. "What's the point of this?" he said, his voice like sandpaper across knotted wood.

"The point of what?"

"Why keep me here?"

"Oh, you haven't figured it out yet? Well, let's get your neanderthal brain caught up."

He placed the briefcase down and began circling the room—his head held high, hands clasped behind his back—as if about to deliver a lecture. A bare lightbulb hung loosely from a wire, providing a spotlight.

"You remember how it all started, of course. You approached me to develop a cure for the Eastern Equine Encephalitis Virus. A silly request, mind you, as not many people contract the illness," Simon said with a rueful grin.

"We had reason to believe—"

"Yes, yes, I've heard your marketing pitch," Simon interrupted. "You had reason to believe there would be a resurgence so wanted to get a cure to market before anyone else."

Alan nodded.

"But before you came to me, I'm assuming you went to others with the same idea, yes?"

Alan looked away.

"And they all said no, because, like me, they knew it was a waste of time. Am I correct?"

Alan pressed his lips together but said nothing.

"But the difference between them and I is I saw an opportunity."

"To poison a whole town?" Alan said. "Real ethical."

Simon's cheeks reddened and his breathing became laboured. "You dare speak about ethics? It was BioHealth Pharmaceuticals that ruined me! A smear campaign designed to discredit my research!"

"I wasn't even with the company back then."

"You are now!"

Alan dropped his gaze.

"After they spewed their lies, there were so many cruel things said about me," Simon said. "I became a pariah, a laughing stock amongst colleagues, a punchline to their jokes!" Simon glanced at the briefcase. "But then, as fate would have it, you approached me years later with an offer."

"I didn't know your history with the company," Alan said, nearly out of breath. "I was just the broker, the link to investors."

"What you did or didn't know is irrelevant! Financial resources presented themselves. So, under the guise of creating a cure, I used your money to further my research, contort your drug into something wonderful. All while tarnishing the reputation of BioHealth."

"That was your plan?"

Simon pushed his glasses up the bridge of his nose. "Most of it. Until I realized I couldn't get close to the company men as some might remember me."

Alan's brow narrowed in confusion.

"So, I planted the idea of engaging a second scientist. Someone to be the face of it. An attractive distraction."

"Angela," Alan said.

"You've always had a propensity for approaching the—how do I put this?—those on the fringes. Those of us society has not been kind to."

"She was the medical officer of health for Christ's sake."

"She was stewing in so much loss and pain and pent-up rage. Loses daddy to cancer and then mommy dies from the same virus you ask her to cure."

"We didn't know that until later."

"Oh, please. You were looking for someone a little off, someone with lapses in their meds."

Alan closed his eyes for a long time then opened them again, his energy waning. "She tested your formulas," he said finally. "We were confident in her."

"That's what you get when you hire a sub-standard scientist to review the work of an exceptional one."

Alan shook his head.

"Remember, Alan, I've studied this virus a long time. I know how to hide flaws within a drug supposedly designed to cure it, how to ensure *impurities* go unnoticed."

"But she gave us reports each month. Everything looked clean."

"Well, here's another thought for your boorish brain to wrap around. Maybe deep down she wanted this too."

"Why?"

"Perhaps she had grown tired of no one listening to her. Perhaps a bit of justice for her late mother."

Alan bit his lip then ran his tongue over it. "So, what happens now?"

"It's still a work in progress," Simon said. "I'm researching how to cure the things, sure. But also altering the drug to advance the illness."

"You're making them sick on purpose?"

Simon pursed his lips. "I'm amplifying the effects of the virus, learning how to control it," he said. He hooked a thumb toward the beast. "That's why these ones are bigger than the first time around, growing smarter each day. I mean, soon they might even hold down a conversation, Alan! Can you imagine?"

"What are you doing to the man next door?"

Simon whipped around. "What do you know about him? How could you…?" He stopped and walked into the closet. He put his ear to the wall. He knocked, the sound echoing within the neighbouring room. "You've been communicating, haven't you?" He knocked again then shrugged. "Well, no harm done. He's not there anymore anyways."

"Why are you hurting him?" Alan said.

"I'm not hurting him. I'm-I'm helping him."

"The screaming suggests otherwise."

"Just part of the process. You accept some bad with the good."

"It sounds all bad."

"Not at all. He's family…I mean, he's like family to me."

"And the others? What will you do with them?"

"Well, for starters, no one's laughed at me since I've had them around."

Something shook and beeped from within the metallic-blue briefcase. Simon bent and unlocked it. He extracted a metal object the size and shape of a bowling pin, cradling it as if it were a newborn. He pressed a button on the side of it and a small number three glowed as the device began beeping louder, the tip glowing red.

He grinned. "Looks like Hiltsville's nearly ready."

"What's that?" Alan asked.

Simon lovingly gazed upon the device. "This is the next phase, Alan," Simon said. "This is when things get exciting."

Alan shook his head. "And to think, we trusted you to find a cure."

"That's true. But when the altered drug began to show promise, showed what it could really do—"

"You're sick, Simon. You need help."

Simon's head shot up. His cheeks burned red and his eyes teemed with hatred. "I am not to blame!" he thundered, spit flinging from his mouth. He glared at Alan as he struggled to breathe. "They terrorized me, tormented me…they, they… you can only poke someone so long before you get what's coming!"

"Simon, this isn't the way."

"Interrupt me again and you'll be sorry about what happens next!"

Alan drew back. He swallowed, staring at the mad man in front of him.

"Besides, what I've done is nothing compared to what your boss is up to," Simon said.

"Mr. Pak?"

"Yes. Mr. Pak and his grand plans. It's Mr. Pak that has—"

A clawed hand grabbed Simon's shoulder and he spun to see the beast standing behind him. The creature pointed to the tiny window across the room.

Simon shuffled over, his eyes narrowing as he approached the glass. "What is that?" he said. "Is that…is that smoke?"

He turned back to the creature, but it just stood there, staring straight ahead. Simon turned back to the window and squinted. "It *is* smoke. But that's in the same direction as the—" He gasped. "The barn! It's coming from the barn!"

He jolted around. "The others are in danger! We need to go!"

The creature growled and bounded out of the room, plodding down the hallway. Simon knelt and grabbed the briefcase, nudging the bowling-pin-shaped device into the padded tray. He clicked it shut.

"Sorry to end our chat early, Alan, but something's come up," he said. "I'd like to say we'll pick this up where we left off, but by the looks of you, you'll be dead by morning. So, I'm afraid this is goodbye."

He stood and rushed out of the room, yelling orders. He followed the roars and howls down the narrow hallway, up the stairs, and out of the cabin, hurrying toward the dark columns of smoke.

Chapter Seventeen

November 1995
Day 641 | Late Afternoon

"Just a little bit further," Everett said. Powell's limp arm was draped across his shoulder as he guided her down the steep hill leading into the valley. "You're doing great. You're doing fine."

"She's unconscious," Evelyn said, trying to keep pace. "Probably can't hear you."

"Who says I was talking to her? I need all the positive self-talk I can get right now," he said, his breathing laboured, the soft flesh under his chin wobbling.

He grabbed Powell's uniform just above her belt in an attempt to keep her upright. He leaned into her for stability and continued the slow trek to the cruisers.

Fleeing the barn, Everett and Evelyn had navigated the slope and spurted into the brush quick enough that none of the creatures seemed to notice. They traversed over snow-covered ferns and slick rocks until they disappeared under tree cover.

They had rushed through the abandoned campground, shuffling along the dirt path, passing the kettle lake, the maintenance shed, the sleeping cabins, and mess hall. The second pitch was trickier, the route riddled with ruts and roots, the uneven ground treacherous.

Over time, the police cruisers came into view, and the sound of the gunshots and howling grew faint, now just an eerie thrum in the distance.

"Let's stop a minute," Everett wheezed.

He lowered Powell to the ground and guided her head onto a pile of leaves. He bent at the waist, breathing deeply, then stood, wincing as he rubbed the back of his hand across the small of his back.

"My body ain't what it used to be," he said. "Nor my lungs."

Evelyn placed the stainless-steel briefcase on the ground then swung Powell's bag off her shoulder. As if seeing the bag for the first time, Everett's eyes lit up.

"Hey, there might be something useful in there," he said. "Unzip it, let's take a look."

"Like what?" Evelyn asked.

"I dunno. An ice pack or smelling salts or something. Who knows what she keeps in there."

"Shouldn't we keep heading down to the cars?"

"Yes, yes, but at the pace I'm going, the cruisers are still half an hour away. Open it up and see what we got."

A howl rang out and Evelyn whipped around. The barn was out of sight but she knew what was still up there. And maybe, it was making its way down here.

"How close do you think that was?" she asked.

"Sounded far away," Everett said. But something in his inflection was off, as if he didn't believe his own words. He stared beyond the crest of the hill. The wind picked up and he angled his hat low.

"Do you think the others are okay?" Evelyn said.

"We can't worry about that now," Everett said. "We can

only worry about ourselves. And getting Sheila down."

He snapped his fingers over Powell's shuttered eyes and pinched her cheeks and chin. "She's still out cold," he mumbled. He turned to Evelyn. "What's in that bag?"

Evelyn undid the zipper. She reached in and pulled out wool socks, a compass, extra rounds of ammunition, a spoon. She rummaged through the bag until her hand grazed a small picture frame. She brought it out and turned it over. Two young kids stared out from the photo, smiling at the camera; all buckteeth and tight curls.

"Powell has kids?" she asked.

"Yes, I've met them a few times," Everett said.

"She's married?"

"Her husband left her a few years back. Anyway, she's got some real cute kids—"

"The kids!" Evelyn yelped, remembering the pensive boy and his firecracker sister from the cabin.

Everett stood and nervously patted down his pockets as if he had misplaced something. "I-I had forgotten about them," he stammered. "With everything up at the barn and then with Sheila I forgot they were up there."

"We have to go back!"

"I-I'm afraid I wouldn't be able to make it up that hill again. Not with my knees…or my back."

"We have to go!"

"We can't just leave Sheila. She's defenceless out here in the open."

"But we promised those kids."

"I know we promised them, but…" Everett paused. "Look, if I could, I would go back up for them, but I just won't make it."

"We need to go."

"Those kids have survived this long on their own. I'm sure they'll be fine——"

"I'm going."

"Now listen, when the others return, I'll send one back up to sort it out."

Evelyn zipped up Powell's bag. She shoved it into a nook at the base of an alder, then placed the briefcase on top. She adjusted her knife along her belt, Damien's rifle taut against her. "I'm going up."

"You need to stay here," Everett said. "With us. With Sheila and I."

"I'm getting those kids."

"But you're a child yourself!"

Evelyn turned and glared at him. Her breath was hot as it funnelled from her nose. She stood erect, her shoulders back and proud. A strange chill moved through her. "I'm going up."

"Now listen here, I'm in charge. You stay right here and that's an order!" Everett shouted, but she was already climbing, her powerful legs propelling her up the steep bank.

A distant shrill echoed again through the trees. Evelyn hesitated but then was running again, careening over rocks, swatting branches from her path.

When she reached the campground, she passed under the faded camp sign.

"Alice?" she called out, her voice nearly lost to the wind. "Joshua?"

She hustled to the cabin where the children last were and peered through the window. The room was empty. She stepped away, frantically scanning between the trees. "Alice?"

She jogged toward a second cabin when a noise caused her to stop. It was a gurgling sound, like someone choking on water. The noise was close. Then closer still. She crouched amongst the high grass and after a few moments, sprang up to move again.

Get down! Damien cried out.

She dropped, her silhouette barely sheltered by a sparse stand of saplings. She burrowed down at their trunks as a shadow passed over her, the creature close, sniffing at the air.

Its head was shaved raw and blotches of blood and pus rutted its skull. Its thick red tongue moved across its lip, a stench of decaying flesh dripping off it. Three of its fingers were chewed away.

Evelyn stifled a scream as her hand fretted for her knife. The creature stepped away and she watched as it pushed in on the boards of the cabin, trying to gain entry. It moved around the wooden structure, out of sight, and Evelyn shot to her feet.

Not yet, Damien said.

She dove to the ground again just as a second creature emerged from hiding. It looked into the trees where Evelyn lay, snuffling and snorting, until a noise pulled its attention elsewhere. It grunted and the other creature joined it, both trudging down the icy path away from the cabin.

Go! Damien yelled.

Evelyn pushed herself from the ground and sprinted in the opposite direction. She was less than a dozen yards from the third cabin when a flicker of light caught her eye.

She crept beneath the window and raised her head to the glass. Alice's dirt-stained face stared back at her, smiling.

"We saw them coming so snuck in through one of the holes," Alice exclaimed.

Evelyn waved both her and Joshua out of the cabin then raised a finger to her lips. "We've got to stay quiet."

Alice grabbed her, hugging her tight. "You came back!"

"We've been waiting since summer," Joshua said. "No one's ever come back."

"You're gonna be okay," Evelyn said. "I'm gonna get you down where it's safe."

"Are there more of those things?" Alice asked.

"There might be. Will you be able to run if we have to?"

Both children nodded.

"Okay, then stay right by my side, as quiet as you can."

The three of them crept through the grass and snow, away from the cabins, treading down the path. They snuck past the mess hall and maintenance shed until a sound caused Evelyn to turn.

It started quiet and far in the distance—a crunch of snow, a hum of voices—but the noise quickly grew. She could soon make out Xavier's hoarse shouts and then an officer screaming.

And then the howling came; such evil sounds upon the air.

Run, Damien said.

"Run!" Evelyn said.

She and the children sprinted down the path until Alice stopped. "I have to go back!"

"For what?" Evelyn hollered.

"My friends!"

"What friends?" She twisted around but the small girl was already scampering up the hill toward a thick stand of trees.

"Wait!" Evelyn shouted. "Those things are coming!"

But the child ignored her, swatting the low branches from her path until she came to the base of a wide trunk. She looked up to the trees: six yellow and pale blue shapes swaying in the wind.

By the time Evelyn and Joshua caught up, Alice was already halfway up the tree, scurrying up the trunk and springing through the canopy like a squirrel. She untied the reef knot from one of the branches and a small figure fell, its blue dress fluttering until it thumped to the ground.

"Dolls?" Evelyn shouted up at her. "You came back for dolls?"

"They're my friends," Alice shouted back, hopping to a second branch, working quickly as she loosened the knot. "And can you catch the next ones please? I don't want them to get hurt."

A second doll careened down, followed by a third. Evelyn reached out, fumbled with them, before securing both in her arms.

"What's she doing?" she asked, turning to Joshua.

"They're her friends," the boy said. "Never goes anywhere without 'em."

"But why are they in the trees?"

"She thought they were safer way up there, like those weirdos couldn't get them."

"But we don't have time for this!"

He shrugged and then lunged for a fourth doll whistling down through the branches.

Evelyn looked skyward. "Alice, we don't have time for this!" she hollered as a fifth and sixth doll found Joshua's outstretched arms.

"That's all of 'em," Alice said, leaping from the tree. She grabbed the dolls tight in her arms and began rushing down the hill. "We can go now," she called back, her little legs propelling her down the slope.

Joshua took off after her with Evelyn close behind. When they arrived where she had stopped with Everett and Powell, she bent at the trunk where she had hidden the duffel bag and briefcase.

"What's in that case?" Joshua asked.

"Our way out of this nightmare," Evelyn said.

They continued toward the cars until a howl cut through the trees. The sound clawed its way deep into Evelyn so that when she twisted to face the children, all colour had drained from her face.

And then, as if all the noise of the forest concentrated into one tiny area, Xavier and the officers crashed through the trees, a dozen beasts close behind them.

Xavier absorbed the steep incline, his knees jittering, yelling instructions as the group traversed the rutted terrain. He caught sight of Evelyn and the kids.

"We gotta go," he yelled. "As fast as you can, run as fast as you can!"

They all turned and sprinted, Xavier's rifle slapping off his sweaty back as he coughed out ragged breaths. Dunvey was close behind and as he leapt off the crest, he misjudged the distance and fell awkwardly on his ankle, yelping out in pain.

Singh hustled over to him. "Get up!" he shouted, hoisting the chubby officer to his feet. Dunvey stepped forward and grimaced as his weak ankle rolled over.

"Can you run on it?" Singh asked.

"I-I'm not sure," Dunvey said, gingerly taking another step. "I don't think so."

"You better decide quick! Those things are right behind us!"

Dunvey nodded and followed Singh down the hill, flinching with each step.

Prasad ran past them and caught up to Xavier. "How much further?"

"Maybe two hundred metres," Xavier said.

"Dunvey's hurt. Twisted his ankle. He's moving slow."

"Tell him to suck it up. We'll deal with it when we get out of here."

"No, like he's real slow," Prasad said. "Like, *'he'll put us all in danger'* slow."

Xavier peered up the hill. Although he could no longer see the beasts, he could hear their grunts and growls as they stumbled their way through the trees.

"There another way down?" Prasad asked.

"This is it," Xavier said. "Run or get eaten…" But his voice trailed off, his mind returning to something. "The ATV!"

"The what?"

"It had a key in it, I'm sure of it."

"What are you talking about?"

"Just get Ev and the kids to the cruisers. I'll find another way outta here."

Prasad nodded. He shuffled Evelyn and the children forward while Xavier sprinted back up the hill. When he reached Dunvey, he slid his shoulder underneath the officer's armpit, steadying him against his body.

"How you doing?" he asked.

"Been better," Dunvey said.

"Grab his other arm, we'll support him between us," Xavier said to Singh. "We gotta go up."

"Up?" Singh asked. "But those things are up!"

"With his ankle…we need a different way outta here."

"What way is that?" Dunvey asked.

"You won't like it much, but believe me, the alternative is worse."

Xavier grabbed Dunvey's shirt along his waist as he and Singh yanked the officer up the hill, under the camp sign and past the mess hall, until they reached the maintenance shed.

Singh peered in as panic washed over him. "Nothing in here will work!" he said. "It's all junk!"

"Hold him up," Xavier said, leaning Dunvey into Singh. He stepped into the darkened room. "There was an ATV in here. Just need to move some things to get at it."

Singh's head shot up at a snap of branches. "Whatever you're doing, hurry it up!"

"Found it. It's right at the back." Xavier mounted the vinyl seat. It was covered in cobwebs and the tires were nearly flat. The key stood upright in the ignition, but when he turned it nothing happened. He tried a second time, but again, nothing.

"This was your big plan?" Singh shouted. "A broken-down ATV?"

"I just thought…"

"You dragged us even closer to those things and now we have no way down!"

Xavier noticed a ring of orange about the ignition. "It's rusted out," he said.

He slammed his hand on the handlebar and swung his leg off the seat. But as he headed to the door, something caught his attention: a jug of CLR. He unscrewed the cap and dumped the liquid onto the key hole, wiping away the rust, lubricating the metal. He turned the key. On the third try, it sputtered alive.

He smirked at Singh. "Okay, get him on the back."

Singh hoisted Dunvey onto the seat as a howl rang out.

Xavier revved the engine and shot out from the shed. Singh jumped on the back as a roaring crash came through the trees, a beast galloping toward them. He pulled out his revolver but it only clicked, the chamber empty.

"Take mine!" Dunvey said.

Singh unlatched Dunvey's holster and jerked the revolver out. He aimed it at the beast and shot it in the chest just as it leapt for the ATV. "Let's get outta here!" Singh hollered.

Xavier jerked the handle bars as he navigated a sharp turn. He gunned the engine and the ATV careened down a steep hill, a thunderous sound of branches breaking and the engine whining as he maneuvered the bulky machine toward the road.

A second beast came out from the brush, swiping at Xavier, its claws slashing through his thick jacket. Dunvey screamed as Singh aimed and unloaded, the bullet channelling into the creature's jaw. It roiled and dropped to the ground.

"Jesus, that was close," Dunvey gasped.

Xavier steered the ATV around gnarled roots and loose shale until he saw the police vehicles, Evelyn frantically waving her arms at him. He yanked the handle bars and gunned the throttle, the tires spewing up snow and mulch as the ATV charged down the last pitch of the hill.

It bottomed out just as they crashed into the ditch, the engine sputtering, the stench of motor oil blooming out.

"We're running from here," Xavier said, swinging his leg off the seat. He ducked under Dunvey's arm, hoisting him from the ATV, and pulled him toward the squad cars.

Singh slid off the back, firing the last of the bullets into the trees. "I'm out, I'm out!"

Prasad rushed over and began firing as Everett hustled over to Dunvey. "Where are the others?" he shouted.

Dunvey stared at him blankly.

"Did any of 'em make it?" Everett said.

"They're still up there, sir," Dunvey said. "They didn't… they're still up there."

Everett hoisted Dunvey into the SUV as the officer cradled his injured ankle. Everett slammed the door, then turned to the others.

"Time to go!" he hollered.

Singh sprinted to the lead car to find Powell's body spread across the backseat. He held the back of his hand to her mouth, checking for breathing. "She gonna be okay?"

"Not if we stick around here," Everett said. "We gotta move out."

He guided Alice and Joshua into the second SUV, then spun when he heard a crunch, a clutch of creatures creeping out from the woods. He slammed the door and tossed the keys to Prasad. "Get them kids the hell out of here!"

Prasad jumped in the driver's seat and turned the ignition over. He hammered the gas pedal, the tires spinning, eventually gaining purchase.

Everett turned to Singh who was climbing into the driver's seat of the other SUV. "Go! Go!" he yelled. "Get out of here!"

Singh reefed the key forward then peeled away.

"C'mon, we'll take one of the cruisers," Everett shouted, throwing the keys to Xavier.

"What about the other one?" Xavier said.

"Leave it. We've got no one left to drive it."

With Evelyn in tow, they climbed into the cruiser and took

off. Several beasts sprinted through the ditch and down the road after them. They howled as Xavier pinned the gas and the vehicle sped away. Xavier glanced in the rearview mirror to see the monsters hunched over on the road.

His eyes caught on one in particular. It was lean, unnaturally tall, and bleached white. And as the creature turned, he recognized the hilt of his own knife, the blade still lodged deep within the beast's spine.

Chapter Eighteen

November 1995
Day 641 | Evening

Rachel signalled and pulled into the gas station, edging the car beside the nearest pump. She slid out and unfastened the gas cap, shoving the nozzle in then squeezing the lever.

The sun had nearly set, the sky a dark-grey threat, as she scanned the area. There was an overturned garbage can with flyers and candy wrappers littered on the ground, sand and ice-salt lining the curb. The sign overhead was filthy and smudged, its writing illegible.

Juliana and Andrew stepped from the car. Andrew reached for the squeegee but it was ripped and tattered, the water bucket bone-dry. He noticed two cars parked beside the cashier booth: a maroon late-model station wagon and a compact peacock-blue sedan.

He marched over to the newspaper stand and unfolded a copy of *The Chronicle*. "Been gone for three months," he said. "Let's see what I missed."

Flipping through the first few pages, he paused then read aloud: "*Chief Medical Officer mum over criminal charges.*"

"Do I really want to hear this?" Rachel said.

Andrew cleared his throat and continued reading. "*Nine*

months after disaster struck Barn Wood, Medical Officer of Health, Dr. Angela Till, has still not spoken publicly nor apologized for the shocking experiments she was involved in, reports columnist Brad Moseby."

"Moseby? That guy went to see my sister," Rachel said.

"Really?" Juliana said.

"Yeah. But she said she didn't tell him anything."

"I'm getting to that part," Andrew said. "*Upon entry to Brayfield Penitentiary, our columnist was granted access to Dr. Till for an exclusive interview. Unfortunately, the disgraced former health officer declined to comment on her sinister plot to poison the residents of Barn Wood with a tainted drug, even refusing to provide information about a pending cure. This act of cowardice shown by a once prominent community figure continues to keep readers in the dark and delay finding answers to this horrific mystery."*

"That's enough," Rachel said, yanking the nozzle from the tank and slamming it back in its cradle.

Andrew folded the paper and tucked it under his arm.

"It's true, all of it," Rachel said. "I just don't need to keep hearing about it."

"Yeah, sorry…" Andrew said.

Rachel reached for her wallet. "I'll settle up for the gas," she said, walking toward the booth.

"I'll come with you, I want to get something to drink," Julianna said. "Let me just grab my money." She ducked her head into the car, rummaging through her purse.

Rachel stepped into the booth and froze. She whipped around to face Andrew, her eyes panicked. Andrew knew the look well. He had seen it many times in the woods last winter. Her eyes would grow wide and she would become rattled. Nothing that came after ended well.

"Get back in the car, Juliana," Andrew said.

"But I'm gonna get something to drink. You want any-thing?"

"Get in the car," he said. He slid to the trunk, opened it, and pulled out his rifle, never dropping his eyes from Rachel.

"Why do I need to—" Juliana said, but then stopped. She looked at Andrew and something about his expression made her slide back into the car and close the door. She pressed down on the lock.

Although the booth was only a dozen yards away, it felt like forever for Andrew to close the gap. His boots rolled over the packed snow and gravel and he leaned his shoulder into the door. The wind chime clanged as he stepped through.

A whiff of aluminum fouled the air. He looked to Rachel and then at the cashier.

The girl was maybe 20, sunken and emaciated, and she sat slumped on the stool behind the counter. Her eyes were open wide, red and swollen, not blinking. Her straw-blonde hair was unevenly cut as if she had barbered it herself: one side long, the other hacked close to the skin. Her arms dan-gled by her side, one longer than the other; a lopsided puppet.

Several knife wounds gutted her chest, black blood stain-ing the front of her shirt and dribbling onto her white tennis shoes.

"Jesus," Andrew said.

Rachel stared at her, taking the girl in. Her gaze drifted and she squinted into the corner.

"What do you think happened?" Andrew said, his eyes trained on the girl. "Who do you think did this?"

"Andrew…" Rachel whispered.

Andrew turned to face her. She motioned toward the cor-ner and as his eyes adjusted, he could see the shape conjure out from the dark. He gasped and swung his rifle toward it until a shout caused him to stop.

"Wait!" the shape shouted. It was a woman's voice. "Don't shoot!"

She remained crouched, her dark skin smudged with dirt. She was short and round with a wild mane of brown and grey. Her jeans were ripped and her faded plaid jacket was frayed at the cuffs.

She stood and held out her hands as if to signal she had no weapon. Andrew paused on the yellow and red string along her wrist.

"Who are you?" he said, his rifle levelled.

"I'm not one of them."

"Did you do that?" Rachel asked, pointing to the cashier.

"Yes," the woman said coldly. "She had turned. Or almost."

"Did she attack you?" Andrew asked.

"I didn't let her. Was quicker than she was."

"She had the virus?"

"Look, I know how this stuff ends."

"You stabbed her!" Rachel said.

"Most of time it's either me or them. That's just how it is these days."

"How long have you been here?"

"Look, can cowboy here just lower the gun? It's difficult being interrogated with that thing pointed at me."

Andrew reluctantly lowered the barrel to the floor. "Anyone else here with you?"

"Just me," the woman said, a sharpness to her words.

"We just walked into a murder scene so you're gonna have to give us more than that."

The woman glared at him, sizing him up. Andrew sensed something dark in her, could almost taste it, a metallic tension swirling around his mouth.

"Something's wrong with my car," she said finally. "The blue one out there. Been stalling every few hours."

"Okay. And?"

"So, I pulled in here to see if they sold parts. And that's when I ran into blondie here."

She wrung her hands, a smear of red across her palms.

"I asked her a few questions and could see she wasn't totally with it," the woman continued. "It was like she didn't even notice me. And then she snarled."

"Snarled?" Rachel said.

"That's when I…well, that's when that happened."

"Where were you coming from?"

"Just outside Barn Wood. We, uh…I live on the outskirts."

"Where were you headed?"

"Nowhere, really. Just running."

"Running from what?" Andrew asked.

The woman sighed as she glanced around the booth and then back at Andrew. She looked haggard, like someone exhausted and worn down. She took a deep breath and hesitated, as if about to divulge a dark secret. "They're turning back," she said.

"What?"

"The antidote isn't holding. You can see it."

Rachel took a step back. "How do you know about that?"

"It was fine for a few months, things back to normal. But it's beginning again."

"What-what do you know about that?"

"All along I said it wasn't over. He's going to make us relive it all over again."

"Who?"

Andrew tugged at Rachel's sleeve. "We're leaving," he said. He pulled her toward him and they both stumbled through the door and bounded across the parking lot. "Start the car," he said.

Rachel fumbled for her keys as the wind chime above the door rang out. Andrew moved for the safety on his rifle until the woman's voice caused him to stop. He spun around, her hard eyes holding his.

"I need to go with you," she called out.

"I don't think so," Andrew said.

Juliana rolled down her window. "Who's that?" she asked as Andrew marched toward the car.

"Long story."

"Please," the woman said, this time softer.

"Not a good idea," Andrew said, swinging the back door open.

"You don't understand. I need to go with you."

"You go your way and we'll go ours."

"Please!" the woman said and the inflection in her voice caused Andrew to halt. She took a few steps toward the car, her arms raised as if surrendering. "I'm looking for my children," she added.

"We're looking for people too," Andrew said.

"I need to find them."

"Listen lady, after what we just saw in there—"

"I'm not a murderer."

"And yet you just murdered someone."

"She murdered someone?" Juliana said. "Oh God, I shouldn't be here, I can't be here."

"She was already turning," the woman said. "If not for me, the virus would have taken her anyways."

"You don't know that," Rachel said.

"She was a goner. Had a few hours at most."

"But you don't know that…"

"I'm sure of it," the woman said. There was a sudden sadness to her words. "I've seen my share of these things."

"Andrew, what is she talking about?" Juliana said, panicked.

Rachel turned back to the woman. "Maybe we could have helped her. Gotten her the antidote."

"And how's that working for you?" the woman said. "You got any on you? We got it coming out of the vending machines now?"

A strained silence hung between them. Eventually, Andrew spoke. "You have kids?"

"Two. A son and a daughter," the woman said.

"How long have they been missing?"

"Too long." The woman sniffed, a break in her voice. "I've been out looking, but…I just need to find them."

Andrew looked to the sky. Eventually he turned to the others. "What do you think?" he said.

"It's your call," Rachel said.

"I just want to go home!" Juliana said.

"I'm afraid we're beyond that now," Andrew said. He sighed and pondered things over. He turned back to the woman. "Okay, you can come with us," he said.

"Thank you," the woman said. She approached the car, her arms still raised.

"Got a gun on you?"

The woman shook her head.

"Sit in the back with me," Andrew said. "Any funny stuff —anything at all—and we drop you at the side of the road. Understood?"

The woman nodded.

Andrew put Juliana's luggage and his backpack in the trunk then sat in the car, his rifle resting along his thighs. The woman turned to sit, and as she did, her shirt slid up so that Andrew saw a glint of light, a slender shape of steel—something shiny tucked beneath her belt.

Chapter Nineteen

November 1995
Day 641 | Evening

Xavier breathed heavily as he gripped the steering wheel of the cruiser, his knuckles white, his palms slippery with sweat. "Son-of-a-bitch, that was close," he huffed.

"You're telling me," Everett said, his breathing laboured as well. His eyes caught on Evelyn in the backseat and then out the rear window.

"Any following us?" Xavier asked.

"Hard to see, it's nearly pitch black," Everett said. "And looks like a storm's rollin' in."

"Do you see *anything*?"

"I think we're good, but my word, we almost didn't make it out."

"Believe us now?" Evelyn said.

"Oh yeah! No doubts now."

"X told you they were different."

"That's for sure," He dug into his pocket and pulled out a used napkin to dab his forehead. "Scary how vicious they are."

Xavier skidded off the county road and onto a main thoroughfare, closely following the black SUVs. "How many you think were in that barn?" he asked.

"Nearly fifty, I'd say," Everett said.

"Yeah, that's what I thought."

"But why hide beneath the floor?"

"To draw us in, maybe? Create an element of surprise?"

Everett rubbed the scruff along his cheek. "You were right, these aren't like the others. They're clever. Like they're trained."

"They seem to vary. Some are smart, some not yet," Xavier said.

"I never would have believed how big they were until I saw them myself."

"We peeled out of there pretty quick and still they were right on us."

Everett exhaled. "The others? They, uh…they didn't make it down?"

Xavier bit his lip and shook his head.

"Definitely could have used your brother back there," Everett said. "Might've…it might've made a difference."

"He was flying in today," Evelyn said. "Rachel was going to get him."

"Should have landed by now," Xavier added. "Might be on his way."

"Should've waited for him," Everett mumbled. He shook his head then turned and stared out the window, the ryegrass and rotted wheat whipping past in the glow of the headlights. "Where we headed?"

"On our way in, I saw a motel about forty klicks from here." Xavier said. "Maybe we pull in, make a plan from there."

Everett nodded and gripped the police radio in his meaty palm. He pressed down on the call button. A burst of feed-back crackled through the radio until he started talking.

"Singh, everyone in your car alright?"

There was a pause followed by a shock of static. "Sheila's still out," Singh said. "Dunvey's okay. Ankle swollen as hell, but says he'll pull through."

"How 'bout you, Prasad? Everyone in your car okay?"

"We're alright," Prasad radioed back. "Kids ate my whole bag of food. They're dozing in and out now."

"Okay, listen," Everett said. "Xavier says he saw a motel about forty kilometres from here. Watch for it and we'll pull in there to regroup."

"Copy," Prasad said.

"Should be there in less than an hour," Everett added.

"Copy," Singh said and the line went quiet.

"Now that we got a signal, you gonna radio this in?" Xavier asked.

"Would they send anyone anyways?" Everett huffed. He chucked the radio to the floor. "Goddamn useless headquarters," he muttered. He turned to the window, his brow knitted as if deep in thought.

The cruiser sped on, past paddocks and pastures, fields bordered by splintered posts and rusted wire. Some properties had animals on them: calves huddled against heifers, a foal galloping within its pen. Others were crowded with crops, unharvested stalks shoulder-high, burnt and hardened and frosted with snow.

Xavier motored on, past Earl's Bait and Tackle, past Henry's Burgers and Shakes. Both were empty, the lights turned off, the windows and doors boarded up.

He glanced in the rearview to see Evelyn's head bobbing against the window, her eyes struggling to stay open, fatigue forcing them shut. Watching her, a rush of exhaustion swept over him, the adrenaline from the day finally leaking out of him, leaving a depleted shell of tired bones and sore muscles.

He yawned and pressed the heel of his hand above his eye. He blinked, struggling to focus beyond the headlight beam, when something darted in front of the car. He swerved but still the thud came, the animal ricocheting off the undercarriage, fur and limbs rolling into the ditch.

"Dammit!" he shouted.

"What was that!" Evelyn yelped, now fully awake.

"I got a raccoon," Xavier said, righting the car.

"Was there anything else?"

"No."

"You sure?"

"Just a raccoon, Ev. Nothing else."

She exhaled. "Good."

"Try to go back to sleep. We're still a ways away."

She yawned, burrowed her shoulders into the vinyl seat, and was soon asleep once again.

After a while, Everett cleared his throat. "Ever heard a rabbit scream?"

Xavier made a face. "Come again?"

"A rabbit. You ever heard one of 'em scream?"

"I didn't know they made any noise at all."

"I was driving my wife's sedan," Everett started. "Well, ex-wife. Anyway, truck was in the shop so I took hers to run a few errands."

"Okay."

"It was dark as stink. Driving past some high school when the first rabbit darted out. Ran right through my headlights like a shot." He slapped his hands together for effect.

"Anyway, that first one was fine. Made it across the road, its bushy tail bouncing and whatever. But the second one..."

He swallowed. "My wife's sedan was lower than the truck, you see. My truck would have cleared it, but the sedan... Anyway, I see this little guy go under the car and then hear this horrible crunch. I slam on the brakes and a second later I see it out the rearview. At first, I thought it was rolling across the road, like it'd been flung. But that wasn't it."

He took his hat off and wiped his forehead then returned it low on his brow and turned to face the window.

"I stopped the car and that's when I heard it, this high-pitched wail. It was terrifying. Full of fear and pain. It was so strange that I thought it was a child at first, like a kid had seen what had happened."

"Hm."

"It took me a second to realize it was the rabbit. I mean, you picture them as these quiet little things. Just sniffing around, stealing a bit of lettuce and whatnot, but otherwise harmless. Just innocent things."

Xavier moved to speak but said nothing, waiting for Everett to gather himself.

"So, there's this rabbit, screaming all hell. I jump outta the car and that's when I saw what it was. It hadn't rolled across the road. It had *dragged* itself."

"How so?"

"The crash had paralyzed its back legs. This guy was pulling himself with only his two front ones. Right up over the curb and under a rosebush."

"Jesus."

"As I got closer, it noticed me and stopped screaming, pulled itself deeper into the bush. It was shaking. And its eyes —oh, if you could've seen its eyes. Not dull and stupid like in all the hunting books. They were brown and alive and full of fear. I stood over it a while, considered standing on its throat, you know, to put it out of its misery. But I couldn't quite reach it, and even if I had, I'm not sure I'd be able to."

He took a deep breath, steadying himself. He cupped one hand in the other as if to present an offering.

"And then something inside me just broke. Seeing how much pain this guy was in, an innocent thing like that, everything just… I tell you, I sobbed the whole way home. Couldn't hold it together."

He pressed his lips together and went silent. His shoulders curled in as his breathing swelled then settled. He fidgeted with his watch then ran the back of his hand across his moist eyes.

"Stupid, eh?" he sniffed. "I mean, it's just a rabbit. There're tonnes of 'em. A few are gonna get smucked and that's just how it is. I mean, I used to hunt the little buggers. But that one? I never got over that one."

"Hm."

"And the noise it made? Fiona made that same noise up at the barn. When that monster dug its claws into her, bent down and gnawed at her face like it was a goddamn sandwich." He struggled with a button on his uniform, his hands trembling. "The sound of that rabbit haunts me to this day," he said. "And now, she will too."

He drew quiet, just the hum of tires and the faint whine of the engine filling the silence until he spoke again. "She didn't sign up for this. None of 'em did."

Xavier exhaled. "For what it's worth, they died with honour."

"How's that?"

"They died protecting each other. Did what they were trained to do."

"That supposed to make me feel better?"

"Not sure how you're supposed to feel."

"You saying I should be proud of them or somethin'?"

"Just know they died fighting for each other. They died with purpose."

Everett scoffed. "And still, this isn't a priority for my supervisor."

"Like you said, he's looking into rumours from other towns. Maybe there's something to that."

"Or maybe my whole unit needs to die before he takes notice." Everett shook his head. "You lost a few too, huh? The first time around?"

Xavier nodded. "Ev's brother, Damien. And a nurse named Maddy."

"How'd you get over it?"

"You don't."

"Ever?"

"The pain's always there. It's that simple and it's that hard."

Everett gestured at Evelyn asleep in the backseat. "How's she dealing with all of it?"

"She's coming through."

"Hm."

"Some days better than others."

"Her brother's gone and her mother's missing. She's been through so much."

"She's stronger than you think."

"We're all stronger than we think until you hit a rabbit with your car. Then you sob like a child all the way home and learn just how fragile you are."

Xavier swallowed.

"We're pursuing Ev's father," Everett said after a while. "Your uncle—this Simon fella."

"Any leads?"

"Just dead-ends so far."

"Hm."

"We interviewed some ex-colleagues of his. Said he's become a real nut job over the years, a bit of a recluse."

"But nothing to go on?"

Everett shook his head. "Something will come up. Just a matter of time."

"And the others? I know Angela's in prison, but it wasn't just her and Simon behind it all."

"The documents from Angela's study name several people. A Mr. Pak, a Mr. Mackenzie, a shitload of investors. We're looking into all of them."

They drove a while longer until Xavier nodded at a roadside sign: *Creekside Motel, 5 Kilometres.* "That's us," he said.

Everett picked up the radio. "Okay fellas, motel is just up ahead. I want everyone to park around back so we don't draw attention from anyone passing by. We'll assess from there, go in through the back if we need to."

Both Singh and Prasad acknowledged the message and when they came to it, the three vehicles pulled in, parking side by side in the back lot. They cut the engines and killed the headlights, the vehicles dark and silent.

And so too were the occupants. Each person quiet and still, no one saying a word, staring ahead at the run-down motel. Their eyes darted from window to window, squinting through the sheer curtains, trying to see what might be lurking in the darkened rooms.

Chapter Twenty

November 1995
Day 641 | Night

Rachel navigated the sedan along the winding county road. Slender trees clambered out from the snow-crusted soil along both shoulders, bent and hunched over, as if to hem the small car in.

There were no streetlights. Just the faint beam from the headlights guiding the group to the campground.

In the passenger seat, Juliana dozed in and out of sleep, the fatigue of frequent flights and the emotional rush of the past three days catching up with her.

In the backseat, the woman they had picked up had dozed off as well. She leaned her head against the window, her eyes pulsing beneath her eyelids.

Andrew sat to her left, rifle across his lap. He hadn't taken his eyes off her since they had left the gas station. He surveyed her overcoat which was stained and dirty, her brittle hair like a frenzied rat's nest. There was dried blood along her thumb and forefinger. She smelled like fish.

She was short, maybe an inch or two above five feet, but even beneath her coat, Andrew could see she had a powerful build. As he stared upon her, a pang of familiarity surged through him although he didn't quite understand why.

The woman called out in her sleep and then twitched awake. A blush darkened her cheeks as she noticed Andrew eyeing her.

"Sorry about that," she said. "I get these nightmares, can't seem to shake 'em."

"I get them too," Andrew said.

"Of those things?"

Andrew nodded.

"Of what, exactly?" she asked.

"Mostly their screams, the hate in their eyes."

"You've seen them up close?"

"Plenty. They hunted us back in March. When all this began."

"Has it only been since March? My God, it feels a lot longer."

"The nightmares came soon after that."

"But you came out alright? Lived to tell the tale, as they say?"

"Not all of us." He rubbed the stock of his rifle and remembered the feistiness of Maddy, the friendship of Jeremiah, the sacrifice of Damien.

The woman cleared her throat. "You don't need your gun out like that."

"Why's that?"

"Well, for starters, you're about a foot taller than me, and by the looks of it, a shit-tonne stronger."

Andrew smirked but said nothing.

"I ain't gonna try anything," the woman said. "You were kind enough to bring me with you, so…"

Andrew studied her and then lifted the rifle from his lap, balancing it upright between his leg and the car door.

"What's your name?" she asked.

He drew in a breath. "Andrew."

The woman's brow furrowed and she turned to face him, her eyes moving about him as if searching for something. He turned away and pointed at Rachel. "This is Rachel. She's a good friend who's also dating my brother."

The woman nodded.

"And this is Juliana. Her and I are, well, we're—"

"We're dating!" Juliana chimed in, now awake. She twisted in her seat to face the woman. "I just spent five hundred bucks on airfare to go see this guy so we better be dating!"

"Nice to meet you both," the woman said.

"Nice to meet you too," Juliana said. "Even though the circumstances are right screwy!"

"They've been screwy for so long now it almost feels normal."

"What's your name?"

"I'm Wanda," the woman said, her tone creeping towards a threat. She shifted in her seat. "Sorry, I just realized I haven't said my name in nearly eight months." She brought a hand to her mouth. "No one's bothered to ask."

"Yeah," Andrew said. "It was touch and go there for a while."

"It got somewhat back to normal by the fall," Rachel offered. "Schools opened up, some of the shops. Not firing on all cylinders yet, but things slowly ramping up."

"I wouldn't know," Wanda said. "Been in hiding. Haven't really come out since rumours of the first cases."

"I wouldn't know either," Juliana quipped. "All this madness seemed to have only happened here."

"Really?"

"Sure! I was just living a normal life in a normal town when this guy calls me out of the blue last summer, tells me all this stuff about viruses and mad scientists and folks turning into nut jobs. I didn't believe him of course—thought he'd gone insane!"

"Yeah, I could see how that might sound."

"Right? It was so outlandish!"

"Those early days were a nightmare, that's for sure."

"Where were you when it first started?" Andrew asked.

"At home," Wanda said. "Early on there were rumblings, rumours."

"Did you run or…"

"My husband and I left our house to find out what the hell was going on. But even then, you could see it happening."

"See what happening?" Juliana asked.

"That some of those folks just weren't…right."

"Those first few weeks are seared into my mind," Rachel said.

"My husband got our kids to a neighbour's house, thought it'd be safer while we investigated what was going on," Wanda continued. "But when I went back, my kids weren't there."

"Where were they?" Juliana asked.

"She told me they hadn't been dropped off. Had no idea what I was talking about."

"Your husband never dropped them?"

"I don't know. She just kept saying she hadn't seen them. And then my husband disappeared."

"My word."

"So, I readied myself to go find them. But that's when the first attack happened."

Andrew cocked his eyebrow. "You were attacked?"

"I was caught off guard. The guy was acting weird and then turned violent." Wanda snapped her fingers. "Just like that."

"Did he hurt you?" Juliana asked.

"I was able to get away but the whole thing spooked me."

"What'd you do?"

"More of those things kept coming around my house. I finally left and holed up in my neighbour's house."

"Those same neighbours?"

"Yeah, but by then they had already fled. The house was empty, so I stayed."

"How long were you there for?" Andrew asked.

"Months."

"You survived for months there?"

"They had plenty of food, a full freezer," Wanda said. "Taps worked fine."

"You never left?"

"I was just so scared. I wanted to go out but…well, that first attack frightened me to the core. Just couldn't build up enough courage to leave."

"Did you at least go back to your own house?"

"Didn't really need to. Besides, I could see my house from the neighbour's so I would watch."

"Anything happen?"

"First those things were there, and then a few weeks later, the cops."

"Cops?"

"They taped it all off, started carting boxes away."

"Like a crime scene?" Juliana asked.

"I guess so," Wanda said. "But I don't really know."

"Did your husband come back?"

"No."

"Never?"

"Never. I phoned my brother to see if he knew anything. Lives a few towns over. But even he didn't know what I was talking about. And soon after, the phones cut out."

"And your kids? They never came back?"

Wanda turned to the window, a sudden sadness washing over her. "Those first few months I was worried sick about them," she said. "I was so tired. So alone." She bit her lip, a mist forming across her eyes. "Anyway, it was thoughts of them that brought me out. I finally found the courage to go search for them. And I've been on the road ever since."

"No luck yet?"

"Been driving everywhere, spending nights in abandoned homes, sometimes in the woods. Then the car started acting up."

"That's when you pulled into the gas station?" Andrew asked.

"More or less." She grew quiet and then turned to Andrew. "What about you? Who are you looking for?"

"My mom and step-father," Andrew said. "Been missing since March."

"Any sign of 'em?"

"No."

"Sorry to hear."

"I was at school overseas when it all happened. My brother told me they got real strange for a while and then disappeared."

"Is he missing too?"

"No, he's good. He's helping the cops with some surveillance stuff."

"Really?"

"He and I kinda got roped into it last summer, helping them track those things and all."

Wanda nodded. "I bet you miss them. Your folks, I mean."

"Yeah, my mom especially," Andrew said. "My step-dad…well, that relationship's a bit more complicated."

"Usually is. Blended families can be hard to navigate, depending on how they all shake out."

"He's a good man and all. We just don't see eye-to-eye. Or he doesn't want to."

"My brother, Dennis—he's separated now, been through the wringer," Wanda said. "But he says when life gets hard you just gotta remember the good stuff and throw away the rest."

Andrew nodded, then turned to the window, light rain pinging the glass. "It's getting late," he announced.

"What do you suggest?" Rachel asked.

"I saw a sign for a motel a while back. Maybe pull in there."

"You sure?"

"I don't want to pull into some abandoned camp in the pitch black," Andrew said. "Besides, I'm sure we could all use a few winks before starting out again in the morning."

"All of us are staying?" Rachel said. "I thought this was a drop-you-off-and-turn-right-back-around type of scenario."

"Plans changed. After seeing that gas station cashier, best if we stick together."

"Think we'll be able to sleep with all this going on?"

"We'll sleep in shifts."

Rachel nodded and continued down the dark stretch of road. Thirty minutes later, the sign came into view: *Creekside*

Motel—1 Kilometre.

"That it?" she asked.

"Yeah, that'll do," Andrew said.

Rachel signalled and turned into the empty parking lot, the front sign flickering. She killed the engine. "So, what's the plan?"

"How many guns did you pack?" Andrew asked.

"Just your rifle."

He scrunched up his face. "Then I'll lead and you three follow."

"How do we know it's safe?"

"We'll go in through the front. If no one's there, we'll take it room by room."

"Search the whole place?"

"We'll have to. Once cleared, we can hunker down 'til morning."

Juliana swallowed. "I'll stay in the car, at least until you guys check it out."

"Best if we stick together."

"No, no, I'm not meant for this."

"No one's meant for this," Wanda said.

The four doors swung open. Andrew stepped out then moved in front, his rifle levelled, the others scanning the parking lot. When they reached the front door, Andrew propped the door open and they all stepped in, the linoleum squeaking beneath their wet boots.

Brochures and pamphlets were strewn across the floor, a thick layer of dust and spiderwebs coating the panes and sills. Crusty coffee stains were ingrained on the check-in counter. There was a lumpy red liquid in a glass, curdled into something rank.

A display of local maps, keychains, and kitschy tourist items took up space on a side wall; a painting of a menacing stag hung on the other.

The place was deserted and quiet until Andrew tuned into a faint sound: the scuffling of socked feet. He motioned for the others to stay as he stepped toward the front desk. As he inched closer, the noise grew, and he stretched himself over the counter to see behind it.

At first, he couldn't make out what it was. There were limbs and bright colours all moving in a flurry, like people wrestling on the floor. He cocked his head and made a noise in his throat, and then a young man jumped up, his neon orange vest shining bright under the fluorescent lights.

"Ah, ah, ah," the man stuttered. He became frazzled as he took in the four new faces. "I, uh…I, uh, well, look at that, look at that. Yes, ah yes, welcome to the Creekside Motel!"

Under the vest, he wore a flannel shirt several sizes too small, the cuffs torn and tattered. He was tall and weedy and his bulging spine twisted jaggedly down his back, causing his shoulders to hunch forward. There was a sour smell about him, like spoiled milk, and his hair was matted and full of lice.

"May I-may I check you in?" he asked. He fidgeted along the counter, knocking over a pile of papers, a clatter of pens. He reached for a pencil and gripped it upside down.

Andrew stepped back, his thumb rubbing along the rifle's stock.

"Um, well, um, well, let's see now, what comes next?" the man nattered, chuckling to himself. "Ah yes, we have lovely rooms, the loveliest of rooms."

When he spoke, Andrew noticed most of his teeth were black and rotted, his gums raw and swollen, and the stench of burning metal overtook the small foyer.

"Andrew?" Juliana asked nervously, her eyes glued to the strange man. "What's wrong with him?"

Andrew swallowed and raised his rifle. The motel clerk began to tremble.

"Now, now, there's no need for that," the young man cackled, his wily eyes narrowing at the sight of the gun. "I have lots of rooms. I can check you in right away." He rummaged through the papers, his head swinging side-to-side. "Oh, right! Let me just check with my manager!" he bellowed. He picked up the phone and yelled into the receiver. "More rooms, fine sir! We need more rooms!"

He slammed the receiver down as his breathing quickened, like a bull preparing to charge. He ripped the phone from the desk and hurled it down the hall. "We have lovely rooms, the loveliest of rooms, you'll see," he said. "I can check you in now, yes, my manager said it's fine to check you in."

Andrew clicked the safety, his pulse thrumming in his ears, unable to break from the young man's gaze. The clerk began to shake violently and when he spoke again, it was in a different voice altogether.

"We can check you in right away," he shrieked. "Will you be staying for one night or two, one night or two?"

His arms were outstretched, bracing himself. And then he reared forward and smashed his head on the counter, over and over again. A deep gash split his forehead as blood dribbled onto the desk. He looked up, out of breath, and snarled at Andrew.

"Put down the gun or you don't get a room!" he screeched, a most devilish sound.

He sprung onto the counter and lunged at Andrew, but

Wanda was already between them and she dug her knife into the man's throat.

The clerk dropped to the floor, wringing his hands around his neck, gasping for air. Juliana shrieked as the man bled onto the tiles, then stopped shaking, an eerie stillness seeping into his eyes.

Wanda wiped the blade on her pants then tucked it behind her back under her belt. "That one far enough along for ya?" she said, eyeing Rachel. "Or you think we should have waited for the antidote to arrive?"

Andrew shuddered. He clicked the safety then turned to Wanda. "Thank you. I, uh, I froze. Must have clammed up."

"Don't worry about it. None of us saw that coming."

"I just-I've just never heard one speak so much."

"He was a talkative one, that's for sure."

"They usually just grunt so the whole thing threw me off."

Wanda stared down at the clerk. "Must be a leftover from the original outbreak. Not like this new breed we've got now."

"Wait, what do you mean *this new breed?*"

"I, uh…well, it's-it's pretty obvious," she stammered.

"I thought only the cops and my brother knew about the new ones," Andrew said. "How could you possibly know?"

"What I mean is, I mean, just look at him. You can see it, he's just like—"

A loud clang came from the other end of the hallway.

Andrew swung his rifle, pointing it into the darkness. He and Wanda exchanged a glance. "We're not alone," he whispered.

"No, no, no, we're not doing this!" Juliana squealed. "Let's get the hell out of here!"

Andrew stood still, squinting down the hall, the sound of

his heart like thunder in his ears. "We can't," he said.

"Why not?"

"They already know we're here."

"But if we make a run for the car—"

"They're likely watching the car. Running for it would make us easy targets."

"I don't want to go down there! I want to go home," Juliana said, her voice weak and panicked.

"I know you're scared. And this isn't what I wanted—"

"Please, Andrew, let's just go. Please drive me home!"

"I wish, but right now, you're safer with me."

Juliana dropped to her knees, frantically murmuring under her breath. "Let's just go, let's just go, let's just go."

Andrew reached down to hold her hand and then turned to Rachel.

"What do we do?" Rachel asked, a familiar fear creeping into her voice.

Andrew released Juliana's hand and stared into the dark. He gripped his rifle and flicked the safety off as Wanda pulled her knife from her belt again. He stepped from the foyer into the darkened hallway, his boots rolling from the linoleum to the threadbare carpet, the others following close behind.

Chapter Twenty-One

**November 1995
Day 641 | Night**

Xavier chopped his hand through the air, signalling to the officers to move forward. Everett, Singh, and Prasad shuffled passed him.

He held up a hand to Evelyn. "Wait," he mouthed.

He pushed up to join the others and surveyed the motel hallway. He ran his tongue along his teeth, sucking at the air. Squinting into the dark, he remained motionless, his wrist cocked over the trigger guard of his rifle.

He swung his arm and Evelyn was beside him in seconds.

Everett reached for a doorknob—*Room 103* stencilled into the flimsy door. His other hand held his revolver and as he inhaled, he shoved his shoulder against the door, swinging it open.

Prasad and Singh sprang into the room, guns drawn, one going left, the other right. Everett and Xavier followed, providing cover until both the bedroom and bathroom were cleared.

Evelyn remained in the hall, rifle pointed down the corridor. "We good?" she asked as Xavier exited the room.

"Yeah, it's clear," he said.

"We have to do this to every room?"

"You wanna sleep tonight?"

The group advanced to the next door and took their positions. Everett gripped the doorknob and angled his shoulder. He was just about to heave against the door when Xavier pulled him back.

"Wait," he said.

Xavier pointed to the ground where a sliver of light escaped between the door and carpet. A shadow passed through it from the other side of the door.

"What is it?" Everett whispered.

"Dunno."

"Do we need to go in?"

"If it's one of those things, then we aren't safe here."

Everett nodded and approached the door a second time. He looked back at his officers and breathed through his teeth as Singh and Prasad gripped their weapons close to their bodies.

"Stay right on me," he said. "If anything's in there, I want you to shoot first and think second. Understood?"

He hammered his shoulder into the door and stuttered into the room, Singh and Prasad a step behind.

They inspected the main area as Xavier pushed through the bathroom door. A slow drip from the showerhead caused him to pause and he ripped the shower curtain down, but the tub was empty.

"We're clear in here," he hollered.

"Good in here as well," Singh said from the main room.

"Did you check the closet?"

"Yep. Everything clear."

"Then what was that shadow?"

"Maybe it came from outside, like headlights from a

passing car or something," Prasad said. He marched to the window and drew the curtain to one side. "Hey, was there a car out front when we pulled in?"

"I, uh, I can't recall," Everett said.

"Well, if there wasn't one before, there's one there now."

"Doesn't change our approach," Xavier said. "We still need to clear all the rooms."

Everett nodded and the group exited, continuing in the same zig-zag pattern down the hall. They moved efficiently, room by room, until most of the floor was cleared.

"One final hall of rooms," Xavier said. "After that, we should be safe to hunker down and—" He stopped abruptly, tuning into a noise.

Everett swallowed. "Sounds like voices."

Xavier brought a finger to his lips. "Let's get closer," he whispered.

The group inched forward until they came to a bend in the hallway. Xavier crouched in front. An illuminated 'Ice Machine' sign flickered above a large metal appliance beside him.

"Hear anything?" Everett asked.

"People are talking," Xavier said. "Or arguing."

"Let me see if I can get closer," Singh said. But as he shifted, the handle of his revolver banged into the ice machine, a loud clang echoing down the hall.

The voices at the other end stopped and Singh's eyes grew wide with terror.

Thirty seconds earlier, at the other end of the hall, Andrew looked up from the clerk and stared at Wanda. "I thought only the cops and my brother knew about the new ones," he said. "How could you possibly know?"

"What I mean is, I mean, just look at him," Wanda said. "You can see it, he's just like—"

There was a clang and Andrew swung his rifle up, pointing it into the darkness. He stepped from the linoleum to the carpet, passing several guest rooms, the four of them slinking down the hallway.

"They're just up ahead," he whispered.

Wanda edged beside him, clenching her knife. He looked to her. "We end this threat here, okay?" he said. She nodded.

"I'll shoot down as many as I can," he continued, "but you may need to—"

A sudden movement caught his eye. He stopped and squinted, and just like in the forest last winter, his senses heightened and he could begin to see shapes within the dark.

There were five of them, most of normal height, except for the one in front. That one was crouched on one knee, but Andrew could still see the size of it—wide and muscled like a bear.

So, these are the new ones, he thought, a tremor coursing through him. *The new breed.*

He sniffed at the air for the familiar stench of burning metal. Instead, he smelled the tart sting of sweat and body odour, the grime of dirt and muck. But there was something else. Something from his past, something familiar. It smelled of forest oils and woodsmoke and a sudden panic rushed through him.

"X?" he said. His voice was quiet, unsure. But as he breathed in the smell once more, he spoke again, louder. "X?"

A strained hush hung in the air until the sound of

Xavier's deep growl broke through. "Andrew?"

The massive shape stood and plodded forward. When he was within a dozen yards, Andrew could see Xavier's wide grin. He lunged for Andrew and wrapped his arms around him, a hearty laugh liberated from his barrel chest.

"Jesus Christ!" he exclaimed, releasing Andrew. "What in the world are you doing here?"

"I was going to ask you the same thing!" Andrew said.

"We thought you were something else."

"Us too! You scared the shit out of us! After that psycho at the front desk, we didn't know what was down here."

"There's one at the front desk?" he said, but an excited shriek caused him to turn.

"Xavier?" Rachel yelled.

"Rachel?" he said, pushing past Andrew and rushing toward the voice. The couple embraced, Rachel holding his face in her hands before kissing him.

"I don't understand," he said.

"I'm just so happy to see you, that you're safe," she said.

"What are you all doing here?"

"My sister said you were in danger and well, I'm just so happy you're okay!" She placed her hand at the base of his neck, fingering the fine hairs along his nape. "It's so good to see you," she said, then rose on her toes and kissed him again.

Everett marched toward Andrew and shook his hand. "Good to see you again, Andrew," he said, the words excitedly spilling out of him. "You remember Constable Prasad from the summer? And this is Constable Singh."

Andrew shook hands with each of them as the others around him hugged and slapped shoulders. Juliana brayed with laughter at the sheer coincidence of it all. Even Wanda, a coiled ball of tension, relaxed and introduced herself to the officers.

Andrew stepped away and pulled Xavier close. "It's good to see you, brother."

"Good to see you too," Xavier said. "Thanks for flying back."

"Of course. Crazy meeting here though, isn't it?"

"Not much around here. You probably saw a safe haven for the night, just like we did."

Andrew nodded. "How's Ev?"

"She's good."

"Still makin' you a better man and all that?"

"Ah, come on now. You make me sound like I was awful before her."

Andrew chuckled. "She stay back at the house?"

"Not quite." Xavier swung his arm and the fifth figure at the end of the hall rose and scurried forward. "Here she comes now."

But as the girl came close, Andrew noticed a concerned look upon her, one of puzzlement and panic. Her breathing was laboured and her cheeks were wet with tears. She stepped out from the shadows, quivering, staring at Wanda.

"Mom?"

Chapter Twenty-Two

November 1995
Day 641 | Night

Evelyn silently studied Wanda.

She smiled then scowled, a whirlpool of emotions cascading through her until Wanda reached out and wrapped her arms around the girl. She held her close as Evelyn shook with sobs.

"Oh, thank God, thank God, I found you," Wanda said through stuttered breaths. "I've been praying to find you, providing offerings." She wept as she held her, a visceral release from months of separation.

She stepped back and held Evelyn's face. She ran her hands through the girl's black greasy hair. "You look so different," she said, smiling. "So strong, so big now."

Evelyn dug her head into Wanda's chest and continued to sob, a river of grief bubbling forth. She breathed in her mother's familiar scent: the musk of her sweater, the oily sweat of her skin. She looked into her mother's eyes and the words tore out from her. "It's been nine months! Where have you been?"

"I tried to find you, but—"

"Why didn't you come for me?"

"I was so scared," Wanda said. "I couldn't leave the house."

"Not even for me?"

"I wanted to, I did, but I didn't know what was out there. The horrible things that happened to me, that were happening all around—"

"But it's been so long!"

"I know, I know, but you know what? I'm not scared anymore."

Evelyn bit her lip, shook her head.

"No, it's true," Wanda said. "I became brave. Like you."

"Like me?"

"Yes! Look at you. Travelling with these guys, a knife and a gun. I mean—"

"But how did you find me?"

"I looked everywhere, drove everywhere looking for you and your brother."

But at the mention of him, Evelyn went limp. She pulled away, her eyes red and swollen. She moved to speak but her voice snagged, such was the pain in her chest, and a deep sorrow welled up within her.

"What is it?" Wanda urged. She squeezed her hand. "Where's Damien?"

Xavier cleared his throat and motioned to the others. "Let's give them some space, huh?" he said and the group turned and trundled into the nearest guest room.

Alone in the hallway, Evelyn told her mother everything.

She explained how she and Damien never went to the neighbour's house that first morning. How they instead fled to the forest and were attacked, and how they found refuge with Andrew and Xavier and Rachel and Maddy.

She described how they tracked Angela and how Damien sacrificed himself to save Xavier. She told her how Dad was somehow involved, his name all over some confidential documents, and that the cops were looking for him.

She revealed that her, Andrew, and Xavier were cousins, and that she lived with Xavier at his family's farmhouse. She told her how Xavier came across the mutated beasts, about going up to the barn, and then fleeing the abandoned campground.

When she finished, she exhaled, as if relinquishing the last of an evil spirit.

"And where is he now?" Wanda asked.

"Who?"

"My son."

Evelyn swallowed. "He's buried at Xavier's. At the foot of an oak."

Wanda trembled, her eyes red and glassy.

"Mom, I didn't know what to do, it was all happening so fast! And you and Dad weren't there. I figured putting him there might be the best thing. I couldn't remember all the traditions and I thought—"

"Did you bury him with anything?" Wanda asked.

Evelyn nodded. "His knife. And a medicine bundle."

Wanda stood stoic, a distant look upon her. "He always liked oaks," she said after a while. "When he was a boy, he'd gather up the acorns that fell from them and throw 'em up to the squirrels. Put 'em in his pocket and toss 'em up as if the squirrels were gonna catch them. Throwing all these acorns up as if the buggers couldn't figure it out on their own—" But she choked up then, her stubborn tongue shoving the remaining words back down her throat.

Eventually, she motioned to the guest room. "So, that big one? He's been taking care of you?"

"Yeah, that's Xavier."

"And you live at his house?"

"Yeah, and his girlfriend, Rachel, kind of lives there too. But I guess you already met her."

Wanda smiled weakly. "Whirlwind of a day, huh?"

Evelyn nodded then wiped the tears from her cheeks with the cuff of her jacket.

"Suppose we should gather up with the others," Wanda said. "Apparently, I have two nephews to meet. Or meet again."

"You've met them before?"

"Sure. Although the younger one was just a little squirt back then so likely wouldn't remember me."

"I didn't know that!"

"Your father and I would occasionally visit, go out to see Joe and Liz every few months."

"What are you talking about?"

"It was a long time ago."

"How come I never knew about it?"

"Well, it got confusing after that."

"But why did Damien and I never meet them?"

Wanda looked to the floor. "Listen, how about we join those cousins of yours. Sounds like we all have some catching up to do."

She wrapped her arm around Evelyn's shoulder and they followed the loud chatter to one of the guest rooms. When they entered, the room was buzzing, as if they had walked into a surprise party. Everyone was yakking and laughing, rehashing the events of the past few days.

Officers Dunvey and Powell had already been assisted in from the SUVs along with the two children. Dunvey was still favouring his injured leg as he hobbled toward one of the twin beds. Powell was now conscious, propped upright on a chair in the corner, her eyes like tired slits. She was nodding at Everett as he knelt beside her, animated as he spoke, holding her hand in his. She looked up and spotted Evelyn with Wanda. She smiled and waved them over.

"Who do we have here?" she said.

"Ms. Powell—this is my mom!" Evelyn said.

The officer nodded then weakly extended an arm. "Name's Sheila," she said, shaking Wanda's hand.

"Pleasure. I'm Wanda."

"You've raised a wonderful child, Mrs. Stone," Powell said. "Kind and brave. And skilled with that knife too," she added with a sly smile.

She leaned close to Evelyn. "There's a couple other ones waiting for you." She motioned to the drapes puddled at one side of the window and that's when Evelyn noticed the children. "That little one was talkative as hell at the campground, but she's gone quiet since," Powell said. "Said she's waitin' on you. Seems to have taken a liking to you."

Evelyn approached the kids, her mother in tow. "Mom, this is Alice and this is Joshua," she said, pointing and smiling at each child. "Guys—this is my mom!"

"Hi!" Alice said while Joshua bit his lip and nodded.

"Nice to meet you," Wanda said. "And how do you two fit into all of this?"

"We live in the cabins," Alice offered.

"Cabins?"

"Yeah, and we were watching these guys, spying on them. And then we woke them up!"

Wanda gave a puzzled look.

"They were at the campground we were scouting," Evelyn

clarified. "They were abandoned there so we brought them with us."

"You were alone?" Wanda asked.

"No, our parents are in the barn," Alice said.

"Oh?"

"But they were acting like weirdos, so we just left them there until they turn normal again."

"Oh…I see," Wanda said. She turned to Evelyn. "What campground was this?"

"Camp Clearwater, I think, something like that."

A flash of recognition rippled across Wanda's face. But the look faded as someone behind her cleared their throat. She turned to find a brute of a man towering over her.

"You must be Xavier," she said, extending her hand.

"Yes, ma'am."

"My, you've grown."

"Sorry? We've met before?" he asked, just as Andrew sidled up next to him.

"Oh, yes. And your brother too." She turned to Andrew. "Although you had just turned 5 the last time I saw you so I don't expect you to remember."

"But you remember me?" Andrew asked.

"I had an inkling in the car. Joe would show us pictures of you boys when he'd visit. But it's been more than fifteen years since I've seen you in the flesh so it was hard to know for sure."

"Your bracelet," Andrew said, pointing to the bright yellow and red strand wound tight to Wanda's wrist. "I noticed it at the gas station. Our mother wears the same one around her ankle."

Wanda fingered the thread, adjusting it between the two

nubs of bone on her wrist. "Evelyn made these each time Joe came to visit," she said. She looked up with a sad smile. "I suppose Liz took a liking to them. Wore them to remember us, perhaps."

"Evelyn's told us our father would come see you each summer," Xavier said. "But I didn't fully believe it until now."

"You didn't believe me?" Evelyn said.

"It just…it just didn't make sense. Still doesn't, really."

"What we can't figure out is why keep it all hidden?" Andrew added. "Like, why has it been so long since you've seen us?"

"We better grab a seat," Wanda said, gesturing to a cluster of chairs by the window. "This may take a while."

Away from the others, the four of them sat. Wanda nervously picked at a metal bar in the track of the window, jammed in to keep the rickety pane in place. She exhaled, peered hard at the brothers, and began to tell her story.

"My husband, Simon, he was a good man, you see. When we got married, he was finishing his doctorate in chemistry and he had this intense interest in immunology. Very smart, very ambitious. Didn't have a lot of friends, but he kept busy with his studies so that never seemed to bother him."

"And Ev?" Xavier asked.

"We didn't have kids yet. But we had a dog, a cozy house, a small cabin we spent summers at. We were happy. For a while anyway."

"What happened?" Andrew asked.

"One night, he came home furious. He had been at a research conference. He didn't say much, but I got the sense his colleagues didn't agree with his research methods. Sounded like he wanted to test his ideas on people, but such a thing wasn't allowed."

Andrew gave Xavier a look.

"Anyway, whatever happened at that conference stayed with him," Wanda continued. "Lingered. Gnawed at him until he became obsessed with it. He couldn't shake it. He would turn violent, trashing the house, cursing all to hell, saying things like 'they don't respect me' or 'they don't understand me.'"

"Why?" Andrew asked.

"He was trying to do something he shouldn't, and he didn't like his colleagues standing in the way. And so that anger fuelled him, made him bent on some twisted idea of revenge."

Wanda dragged her tongue across her lips, her gaze cast down at the stained carpet.

"Something happened to him during those next few years," she continued. "Something dark came over him, something rotting inside. He changed, felt like he didn't belong."

"He told you that?" Evelyn asked.

Wanda nodded. "Look, it doesn't excuse what he's done, but he was bullied as a child, you see. Simon was awkward, didn't know how to fit in. At school, he ate lunch alone in the bathroom, got picked on. He had very few friends, no one talked to him really."

"That's awful."

"I mean, the stories he told. One kid in science class—Rusty Roeden—set fire to his hair! Can you believe that? Set fire to his goddamn hair!"

"Jesus," Andrew said.

"And in high school, at some river beside the school, a group of 'em held him under water until he went limp. One of the teachers ran over to revive him but if she hadn't… And home wasn't much better. His father was rough with him, you see. I mean, he just had a slew of these God-awful stories. And he carried them with him, wore them like a burden wherever he went."

"I never knew any of that," Evelyn said.

"Anyway, this work conference seemed to put him over the edge," Wanda said. "Dug a wound in him that wouldn't heal." She raised her eyes to Andrew and Xavier. "And I guess that brings us to you two."

"How so?" Xavier asked.

"Joe and Liz noticed a change in Simon as well. We were close back then, visiting each other several times a year. But as Simon became angrier, he pulled back. Retreated into himself, like a recluse. And the visits dried up."

"Meaning what?"

"Eventually, it was just your dad who would come over once a year—sort of an annual rekindling. He'd take the kids camping, out to the woods, that sort of thing."

"Why wouldn't he bring us?" Andrew asked.

"He shared with me that it was best to keep you two away, given the…the unpredictability of Simon."

"Unpredictability?"

"Yes, but it was more than that. Simon was becoming immoral. Doing things he shouldn't. And your father saw all of it."

"Did he do anything about it?"

"In his own way, I suppose. But mostly he just watched until he no longer trusted Simon. Your father saw where it was headed."

"And where was that?" Xavier said.

"It pains me to say but…he's gradually turned from the man I married into…" She trailed off, a tremor moving through her. "Now, there's this darkness in him, this anger, simmering just beneath the surface."

"But he loved Damien and I, I know he did," Evelyn said.

"Oh yes, he loved you both very much. He would always make up silly rhymes to make you laugh. *'It's freezing as a deezing, it's windy as a bindy,'* he would say. Or *'keep your grip loose and you'll bag a moose.'* None of it made any sense, really."

"Joe would say the same things to us," Andrew said.

"Now you know where he got it from! Those two had a quirky way about them. Maybe that's just something brothers share—no one understands them except the other. They were thick as thieves, those two. And Joe was always protecting Simon, wouldn't let anyone get away with hurting him.

"Simon was a good father though. But over time, he became distant, the kids less and less a priority, and then…" Her gaze dropped to her lap. "He began testing on them."

"Testing? Like experiments?" Xavier said, a tension in his voice.

"No, no, not like that. He would just extract blood. Although I think…sometimes…he would add something, to see the effects."

"To his own kids?"

"I didn't know much about it," Wanda said, her voice rising in defence. "He kept it all secret, all hush hush."

"How long did he do that?" Andrew asked.

"Just a few times, I think."

"Does it have anything to do with all this?" Andrew said, gesturing out the window. "This virus? These lunatics?"

"I–I'm not sure."

"You seem to know a fair bit about it," Andrew challenged. "You spoke about it just after you knifed the desk clerk."

Evelyn gasped. "Mom, you killed someone?"

Wanda looked away. "What I know is Simon was working to cure a virus known as EEEV."

"Yeah, we know that already," Andrew said.

"He was obsessed with it, hellbent on curing it."

"Curing it or making it worse?"

"How should I know? I'm not a scientist!"

"I think you know more than you're telling us."

Wanda's breathing intensified, her eyes flicking between the brothers. They eventually settled on Andrew. "Before he disappeared, he spoke about developing a drug," she said. "He was excited about what he was seeing in his experiments, how it produced a heightened response. He referred to it once as 'a new breed.' At the time, I didn't know what he meant, but now…"

"What else do you know?"

"Nothing, I swear."

Someone touched Wanda on the shoulder and she spun around.

"Sorry to interrupt," Everett said. "I'd like to do a final sweep of the remaining rooms before we hunker down for the night, so I'm gonna need these two for a little while."

"These *three*," Evelyn said. "I'm coming too."

Everett rolled his eyes. "Sure, come along," he conceded. "I'm done trying to reason with you lot."

Andrew and Xavier stood and joined several officers in the hallway, Evelyn following behind.

"We have enough to split into two groups," Everett instructed. "Xavier, you take Andrew and Evelyn, clear out the south wings. Prasad, Singh, and I will head the other way to clear the north side."

"Gotcha," Xavier said.

"While you're at it, look for food, supplies, that sort of thing."

"I'll come too," Dunvey said, hobbling from the bed.

"You sure? You're still banged up pretty good," Everett said.

"Wasn't much help at that campground. Feel I need to redeem myself."

"Only if you're up for it. We could use the help though."

Everett poked his head into the room. "Sheila, you okay holding it down here while we're gone? Should be quick and then—"

"We'll be fine," Wanda interrupted.

Everett peered at the blade extending from the woman's belt. He nodded then disappeared down the hall, barking instructions as he went, the officers swinging their revolvers nervously around each corner.

Down the south corridor, all was quiet. Andrew, Xavier, and Evelyn moved silently and efficiently through each room. Andrew would lead, followed closely by Xavier. Evelyn would hold firm in the hall, watching for any movement creeping up from behind.

"Feels like the first time around, huh?" Andrew whispered.

"Don't remind me," Xavier grumbled.

"Back to survival mode."

"At least here there are beds. I spent two weeks sleeping on a milk crate in that damn cellar!"

As they came to the final room, Xavier grabbed the doorknob. He swung it open and Andrew was already halfway across the room, rifle levelled, prodding behind the window curtains then peering under the bed.

Xavier pushed open the closet door, then shuffled into the bathroom, his rifle stretched out in front. He nodded and both returned to the hallway.

"Good?" Evelyn asked.

"We're clear," Andrew said.

"Should we head back?"

"Yeah, let's meet up with the others. Might be able to actually get some sleep."

He plodded down the hall but Evelyn remained where she stood and she pulled Xavier to her.

"I um, I wanted to talk to you about something," she said.

"What's that?" he asked.

"Just, um, just at the barn...I, um, I..."

"Ev, what is it?"

"At the barn, something came over you."

"What do you mean?"

"Like you changed, somehow."

"How so?"

"When those creatures charged at me, it was like you became possessed, just full of this rage."

Xavier exhaled, squeezing his eyes shut. "I just saw them coming for you and I-I..."

"It's okay, X."

"When I saw them attack you, something...something just broke."

"That anger though, I've never seen it. It was like you couldn't control yourself."

"But I need to protect you."

"I know you feel that way, but—"

"I owe him that much."

"I know, but listen…you need to control it, okay?"

"Hm."

"I'm serious. That anger—it could get you hurt. Or worse."

Xavier pursed his lips and stared at his boots.

"And I need you, X," Evelyn said. "I need you around. Okay?"

He looked at Evelyn and smiled. "Don't worry about it. I ain't going nowhere."

He tousled her hair then trounced down the hall. But as he made his way toward the others, he became distracted, as if something in Evelyn's account caused him pause. Her words seemed to unsettle him, something haunting about them, like a warning.

Chapter Twenty-Three

November 1995
Day 641 | Night

In the closet, all was silent.

Earlier, Simon had seen something at the window, hollered orders, and stormed out of the room. Alan Mackenzie had remained still until everything had quieted around him.

He stared out from the closet into the room. The doors which had secured him for the past six days were now open and unlocked, Simon failing to secure them in his panicked exit.

Alan glanced at the knot above his head binding his wrists —the same knot he had loosened moments before Simon had barged in. There was still a sag in the cord and wire—too discreet for Simon to have noticed, but there all the same.

Alan turned one of his wrists into the knot. The rope became tighter, but the wire wrapped around it sprung loose. He then turned his wrist in the opposite direction, the knot growing slack as the rope feeding into it began to sag. No longer worried about the wire digging into his skin, he repeated the movement, over and over again, until the rope loosened from his wrists. Excited, he worked quicker, but froze when a bang rang out from the adjoining room.

"Hello?" Alan said. "Is that you? Are you back?"

There was a gargling sound followed by a whimper.

"Are you tied up as well?" Alan asked.

"Yes," someone said. But it was a different voice from the previous day, a woman's voice.

"Are you okay?" Alan said.

"They took him," the voice said although the sound was slurred and muffled, like someone speaking underwater.

"What's that?" Alan said. He pressed his ear against the wall.

"They took him," the woman said again. "Simon and those things took him."

Alan glanced at the knot again. "Listen, I'm working on getting out of here. Give me a few minutes and I'll try to get you out as well."

He kneaded the knot several more times, rotating his wrist until it came free. He shook the cord off as if it was a poisonous snake and then pried his fingers into the second knot until it too came loose.

He braced against the floor and pushed himself to his knees. He tried to stand but his legs were wobbly, and they crumpled so that he fell back to the ground. He paused to catch his breath and then tried once again, clambering his way up the wall.

Once the blood returned to his limbs, he hobbled across the room and out the door then stood outside the room with the woman in it. He turned the knob but it was locked. He shook it harder, leaning his shoulder into the door, but it didn't budge.

"I'm sorry, I can't get in," he said through the door. "But I'm gonna go look for a key. Just hold tight, I'll be back soon."

He braced himself against the narrow walls and scuffled down the darkened hallway. He soon came to a second door. He turned the knob and to his surprise, this door was unlocked. It creaked open, and when he flicked on the light, he recognized it to be Simon's lab.

The ceilings were unusually high—well over twelve feet—and a large oval dome with thick glass panels stood in the centre. There were empty test tubes scattered along the bench, calculations scribbled on a whiteboard fashioned above reams of paper. A cluttered desk sat in the corner, bowed bookcases along the wall, a centrifuge with several murky vials. Simon's black overcoat and Tilley hat were tossed over the back of a chair.

A second coat laid over it, dark grey and with a tailored cut, made for someone much taller. Black driving gloves rested upon the coat and beside it was a folded pair of trousers, a suit jacket, and a wrinkled pinstripe shirt.

Alan hustled over and picked up the shirt, turning it over, a stain of blood along the collar. He held it to his nose and breathed in the familiar cologne.

"Milton," he shuddered.

Reaching for the overcoat, he rummaged through the pockets and fished out a ring of keys, a Mercedes symbol imprinted on one of them. He reached deeper into the pocket, stumbling upon a fold of leather. He yanked it out—a bulging wallet—and flipped it open. Milton stared out from a faded driver's licence.

"What has he done with you?" Alan mumbled.

He squinted into the glass dome and the answer was before him. Shadowed in the far corner was Milton. He was laid out on the metal floor, naked with legs splayed, as if on display.

Alan's hand shot to his mouth as he drew back in horror. He examined his driver's burned face, his jugular ripped open. It was clear one of Simon's beasts had killed Milton at the throat, its hungry jaws tearing through the sternum to arrive at the warm organs beneath. Both of Milton's feet were missing, his long legs severed at the ends, the white and red flesh curling upon itself. His eyes were open and lifeless and Alan began to well up as he stared down at him.

"I'm sorry," he whispered. "You didn't deserve this."

He wiped a hand across his eyes and turned away, hustling from the room. He continued down the hall toward a faint light, but when he was halfway there, a massive shadow passed through it. As the silhouette turned the corner, Alan leaned tight against the wall, trying to melt into it, but it was too late. The creature had seen him and it squealed as it lunged toward him.

Alan shrieked and darted the opposite way, his legs still clumsy and wooden. He wobbled forward, a terrified hare navigating a macabre warren. He came to a set of stairs and awkwardly climbed them, pushing through a door and down a second hallway, the heavy breathing of the beast not far behind.

Alan went through another door and entered a room drenched in fluorescent light. He drew back and covered his eyes, the intensity of the light pounding his head, still acclimated to the dark of the closet.

He spun around and found himself in what appeared to be a living room. It was quaint and tidy and elegantly decorated. A polished cast-iron fireplace sat idle in the centre, a bucket of kindling and newspaper beside it. Lakefront paintings hung prominently on the walls, a calming adage to cottage country.

He heard the grunts of the beast as it ascended the stairs and Alan ran to the front door, heaving it open. He caught sight of the Mercedes parked in the driveway and stumbled toward it. He unlocked it and fell clumsily into the driver's seat, forcing the ignition to start.

The engine came to life and he threw the shifter in reverse just as the creature burst through the front door and lurched across the porch. It ran for the car, slashing its claws at the tires, but yelped in pain when the wheel seized its hand, wrenching it from its body.

Alan threw the car in drive and hammered the gas, swerving along the snow-slick county road and then onto the main thoroughfare.

Weak and exhausted, he drove for nearly thirty minutes, frantically glancing out the rearview mirror. He swiped at his sweaty, dishevelled hair and constantly rubbed his knuckles across his patchy grey beard. He scrunched his face each time he caught a whiff of his own stench.

As he drove, he saw the dimmed lights of a gas station up ahead. He pulled in. He wobbled from the car and through the door of the small kiosk.

"Water!" he shouted at the clerk, his voice hoarse and raw. "I need water!"

The clerk stepped back, alarmed. "There's a tap out back, sir," he uttered.

Alan went to the rear of the shop and put his lips to the faucet. He gulped the water down, but then bent over and heaved, the liquid coming up as fast as it had gone down.

He wiped the vomit from his lips and tried to drink again, but his stomach rejected it once more.

He went back inside and stumbled along the aisles,

snatching a bag of beef jerky, ripping the package open. He shoved the meat into his mouth and chewed violently, but again his body rejected it and he gagged and vomited on the floor, a mushy pile of brown slop splashing onto his pants and loafers.

He looked up to see the clerk staring at him with troubled eyes. "Sir?"

"Police station," Alan said, his breath uneven. "Where's the police station?"

"'Bout fifteen kilometres north, down this same road," the clerk said, pointing. "But sir, you need to pay for that. You can't just eat it and—"

Alan raised his eyes to the clerk and the anger circling within them caused the young man to draw back. Alan threw the door open and staggered to the car, starting the engine once again and driving north.

He was faint when he arrived at the station. He teetered from the car and pushed through the glass doors, nearly collapsing onto the front counter.

"Who's up in Barn Wood?" he said.

The startled officer behind the desk jumped from her chair. "Say again, sir," she squeaked.

"Who's dealing with the maniacs up in Barn Wood," Alan said, nearly out of breath. "Who's in charge up there?"

"Sir, you're…you're injured," the officer said, her eyes examining the raw skin around his wrists. She motioned toward a second officer. "Riley, call for an ambulance."

The fatigue flooded him then and Alan dropped to his knees. He looked up, exasperated, white spittle foaming around his lips and nostrils. "Who's in charge of the Barn Wood case?" he shouted.

The officer flipped through a pile of papers on the desk. "That um, that would be Staff Inspector Tom Everett," she said. "He's been leading the…the *situation* up that way since March."

"I need to speak with him."

"He's not here. Went up to some campground. Rumours of activity up that way."

"I need to speak with him," Alan pleaded just before his eyes rolled back and he fell unconscious, his head bouncing off the stippled tiles.

Chapter Twenty-Four

November 1995
Day 641 | Night

Juliana paced in front of the door, wringing her hands. She bit her nails, glancing out the peephole every few seconds.

"It's been less than twenty minutes," Wanda said. "Just calm down. They'll be back soon."

"She's right, I've seen them boys in action," Powell said. She was seated by the window, Alice and Joshua at her side. "Believe me, they can handle themselves."

"I know, it's just that Andrew and I…" Juliana started. "Well, we don't know each other that well and I just thought…"

"Wait, you guys just met?" Powell asked.

"No, we've been on a few dates. But our most recent one was cut short."

"She flew over to see him, but they had to fly right back because of all this," Rachel explained.

"And he brought you here?" Powell asked. "Geez, what a romantic."

"I don't think either of us expected this," Juliana said. "Not quite what I imagined as our first night in a motel."

"He'll be back soon, all of them will," Rachel said. "Then we'll laugh about the whole thing."

There was a loud scratch down the door—long nails grating across the flimsy particle board—followed by a strained gurgling sound.

Juliana scurried behind the bed as the room fell silent. Wanda crept forward. Rising on her tiptoes, she peered out the peephole.

"I don't see anything," she whispered. "Nothing's there."

"Then what was that sound?" Rachel said.

Wanda cocked her head as the sound came again: a raspy inhale as if someone was short of breath, and then a faint burbling, like water sloshing about a toilet bowl. She gripped the doorknob.

"What are you doing?" Juliana said.

"There's nothing there," Wanda said.

"If there's nothing there then why open the door?"

"I'm gonna take a look, just to be sure."

She unlocked the deadbolt and turned the knob.

"No!" Juliana squealed. "Let's wait for the others."

"You mean wait for the men?" Wanda scoffed. "Not really my style."

She tilted the door and it swung open with such force that she flung backward, slamming against the floor. Juliana screamed as the creature tore into the room, a flurry of limbs and claws and beady eyes, like a possum defending its den. It lunged for Wanda, black blood dripping from the knife wound sliced down its throat.

"It's the clerk!" Juliana shouted.

It raised a knotted hand and brought it down on Wanda. With eyes yellow and manic, it repeated the motion, punching and scratching the stout woman with each swing. Wanda kicked at it and reached for her knife, but the creature pinned her.

It seemed to smile, its nails moving over the woman's ribs and abdomen, as if debating the best place to carve out a hole. It drove its claws into her and Wanda wailed in pain, the creature huffing and snorting, mucous and snot spraying down on her. It angled one of its claws against Wanda's throat. It brought its arm back, but Rachel sprinted forward and kicked it in its chest. It spiralled off and thumped against the wall, but then stood and snapped its teeth. Rachel stumbled backward as it pounced, thundering its fists upon her.

She wailed and looked to Wanda who lay limp beside her. She scanned the room and found Powell and Joshua at the back, but couldn't spot Alice. As the clerk continued to hit her, Rachel swivelled and finally saw the girl.

She stood behind the creature, holding the lead bar from the window track above her head. Her stare was stern and fierce and she brought the bar down, splitting the clerk's skull.

It shrieked in pain, huffing at the child, as if confused that such pain could come from something so small. It listed toward her, but Alice swung again, smashing the bar along its jaw, blood spurting out from its mouth.

It collapsed to the carpet. It pushed up from the ground, trying to steady itself, but Alice stepped toward it. She screamed and drove the bar into the clerk with such fury, it did not move again.

Juliana and Joshua hurried over to attend to Wanda and Rachel, Powell barking instructions from her chair.

Andrew rushed into the room. "I heard screaming!"

"It was one of those things!" Juliana shrieked.

"Everyone okay?"

She nodded just as Xavier hustled through the door. "What the hell happened?" he shouted. Seeing Rachel, he charged over and knelt beside her. "Jesus, look at you—are you hurt?"

Rachel nodded then grimaced, her gums bloodied. She winced as Xavier helped her stand. Wanda came to and he turned and pulled her up from the ground as well then sat both women on the edge of the bed.

"Was it just the one?" he asked.

"Yeah," Rachel said.

"Where'd it come from?"

"It was the clerk from the front desk," Wanda said. "We thought it was dead but…well, it is now."

"Who put it down?"

"That one did," Powell said, pointing at Alice. The officer rose from her chair and staggered to the girl. "You got a lot of spunk, kid," she said. "As brave as they come, this one."

Alice smiled and leaned into the officer, shaken and tired now that the adrenaline had left her.

Everett and the others came through the door and Juliana jumped up to retell the events, the officers hanging on every word spilling out of the fiery redhead.

When she had finished, a few of them went out to the vehicles to snatch the med-kits and then tended to Wanda and Rachel, stopping the bleeding, wrapping gauze and bandages along their sides and chest.

"Get the antidote," Everett hollered, pointing at the stainless-steel briefcase. "We best give a shot to everyone who came in contact with that thing."

Powell opened the case. She unwrapped a needle, filling it with the liquid from one of the vials. She injected Wanda, then repeated the process for Rachel.

Xavier stepped forward and rolled up his sleeve. "Best to

do me as well," he said. "Was attacked a few days ago."

"Jesus," Everett said. "We gonna run dry of this stuff if ya'll keep getting attacked."

Powell unwrapped another needle and filled it, piercing Xavier's shoulder. She pushed the plunger down then yanked it out. Xavier rolled his shirt down then grabbed the clerk by its collar, dragging it from the room and out behind the building, a moist smear of black blood streaking the carpet.

"Will there be any more of them?" Alice asked, turning to Everett.

"Don't you worry about that," Everett said. "We cleared the whole place. And we'll keep a few on watch, just in case." He turned to Prasad and Singh. "Bring some more mattresses in, will ya? We'll hunker down here together, just to be safe."

The officers dragged several mattresses in from the adjoining room, angling them into the corners. They left again, returning with blankets and pillows.

When Xavier returned from outside, Andrew pulled him aside. "Quite the scare, huh?"

"Yeah, just glad everyone's okay," Xavier said. "Quick thinking by that little one."

"Remind you of anyone?"

Xavier looked to Evelyn. He smiled. "Yeah, a little bit," he said. "Same kinda fire in her."

Andrew nodded. "Hey listen, have there been any updates on Mom and Joe?"

Xavier shook his head. "Ev and I have been looking, but so far there's nothing."

"How about the cops? They found anything?"

"Everett says he'll let me know as soon as something comes in."

"Rachel told me most folks in town have been inoculated?"

"Yeah, things slowly getting back to where they were. Though they're signs the initial inoculation isn't holding."

Andrew glanced at the bloodied carpet where the clerk was dragged. "That much is obvious."

"Suppose so."

Andrew hung his head, a few moments ticking by. "I have nightmares of them, you know? Mom and Joe."

"Rachel says visions can be good. Says it means the people in them are still alive."

"Nothing good about these visions, brother," Andrew said. "Nothing good at all."

Xavier gripped Andrew's shoulder. "We'll find them, okay? We'll find them."

Andrew wiped a finger under his nose then fidgeted with the buttons of his jacket. "I shouldn't have gone back to school," he said. "It was selfish, never felt right."

"What are you talking about?" Xavier said. "I told you to go."

"Still."

"Why'd you come back then?"

"Because you asked."

"You leave your studies and fly six hours just 'cause I asked?"

"Yeah. I mean, you're my brother. All you need to do is ask and I'll be there."

Xavier regarded Andrew. "Well, let's try to get some sleep, huh?" he said. "Been a hell of a day."

"Mm-hmm."

"And don't worry. This will all look different in the

morning."

Andrew glanced once again at the blood-stained carpet. "Not all of it," he said.

Xavier stepped away as Andrew turned to the window. There was a peal of thunder, water sheeting the glass. His thoughts drifted and he was 16 years old again, he and Xavier wet from the rain, trekking through the trees at night. They had learned of the missing boy from their mother, whispering into the receiver, trying to calm the frantic mother on the other end.

"Even if the cops come, they won't go out 'til daybreak," Andrew said. He was sitting at the kitchen table with Xavier and Jeremiah, bits of phone conversation drifting in from the other room.

"Mm-hmm," Xavier said.

Andrew shifted uneasily. "The boy won't survive the night."

"What are you suggesting?" Jeremiah said.

"You already know what I'm suggesting."

"That's what I was afraid of."

The boys shrugged into their raincoats and tied up their boots, checking their rifles for ammunition and the strength of beam from their flashlights.

"Jer, why don't you hang back in case the cops show," Andrew said. "You could lead them out to us."

Jeremiah nodded. "Where you gonna look first?"

"Mouth of the river, where we dip in for the rapids. Kid might've followed the sound of water."

"Alright."

Andrew turned and took off like a shot, Xavier close behind, the screen door slapping shut as Jeremiah stared after them.

They returned within the hour, the boy in tow. He was no more than 10, shivering and afraid, and Elizabeth wrapped him in a wool blanket then phoned his mother. Fifteen minutes later, the headlights of her pickup came bouncing up the driveway.

"Oh, my baby boy," she gasped, rushing into the foyer to hold her son. "Are you okay? Are you hurt?"

After she checked the boy over and kissed his forehead, she turned to the brothers. "I sure am grateful to you both."

"Not a problem, ma'am," Xavier said, his gaze bent to the floor.

"How did you find him?" the woman asked.

"Just followed his signs."

"What signs?"

"Prints in the dirt and snow, broken branches along a path, that sort of thing."

"You can find someone like that?"

"Sure. You could tell where he rested as well. Found a bit of garbage. Must've dropped from his pocket."

"But it's pitch black and pouring rain! How could you possibly—"

"Tracking's not difficult for us, ma'am," Andrew offered. He took off his hat, held it in front by the brim. "Just always been good at it, I suppose."

When the woman and child left, Xavier patted Andrew's shoulder. He nodded but said nothing and Andrew nodded back. It had been a while since they had done something together without arguing. In time, the fights would continue—intense and hurtful, prying them apart—but for now, Andrew just smiled at his brother as he hung up his raincoat, drops of water dripping onto the mudroom tiles.

In the motel, the memory faded. Andrew dug into his backpack for a change of clothes and something warm to sleep on. He leaned his rifle against the wall and curled into a corner amongst a nest of pillows and heavy duvets.

Soon, along with the others, he fell into a deep sleep, the first few hours of rest granted in some time.

Chapter Twenty-Five

**June 1994
Day 118 | Night**

In the dimness of the basement, Evelyn sat once again upon the cold metal stool with her sleeve rolled up. "Dad, how many times do we need to do this?"

Simon was turned away, mumbling to himself.

"Dad?"

He shook his head. "What?"

"Geez, you never listen to me," Evelyn said. "I said how many times do you need to do this?"

"Well, I don't know just yet. Until I have it right."

"Have what right?"

"A…a new formula."

"A new formula for what?"

"It's, ah…to enhance certain qualities of a unique virus."

"What virus?"

"Doesn't matter," Simon said. "What's important is there are some investors interested in my research. Well, the parts I'm telling them about anyways."

Evelyn gave a quizzical look. "What does that mean?"

Simon rubbed the inside of her elbow with an alcohol swab then grabbed a needle from the bench. "Never mind, you don't need all the details," he said. "Just turn away. This will all be over soon."

Evelyn felt the sting as the needle pierced through the skin. She felt the suck of fluid and then Simon applying pressure with a cotton swab. "Just hold that there," he said.

Evelyn reached across her body and pressed down with two fingers. Simon removed the vial from the needle. He scrawled 'E.S.' on the side of it before snugging it into a protective foam beside another, the second vial marked 'D.S.'

Evelyn hopped down from the stool and scanned the mess of papers piled on her father's bench. Most of them were academic articles and lengthy calculations she had little interest in. But there were a few newspaper articles with her father's face in them, looking directly at the camera. The headline above the photo read: *Dr. Simon Stone—genius researcher or pathetic hack?*

"Dad, what's a hack?"

Simon turned from the vials and scowled at the news clippings. "It means people are ignorant."

"Huh?"

"It means even your so-called friends grow jealous and make up stories about you, try to defame your character."

"That's what it means?"

"Ignorance is the enemy of progress, Ev. Remember that."

Evelyn shrugged and reached for her sweater. "Can I go now?"

"Not yet. I have one more needle to, um, I mean, one more procedure to perform."

Evelyn bit her lip. "But you always just take blood. One vial a month, like always."

"Yes, yes, that's true," Simon said. "But today I need to

try something new, see if something works the way it's supposed to."

"What's that mean?"

"I think I might have made a leap forward in creating something special."

Evelyn swallowed. "Mom said to just take blood. Nothing else."

Simon turned on her. "You want to help people, right?"

Evelyn shrugged.

"This may help people, if it works," Simon said. "That's a good thing, right?"

Evelyn remained rooted to the floor. She glanced toward the door, but as she did, Simon slid over, standing between her and the exit.

"That's a good thing, right?" Simon said. "Right, Ev?"

A smear of sweat gathered on her upper lip. She looked at him and nodded.

Simon clapped. "Ah, terrific. So, I just need you to lie face down."

She lay on the table. Simon turned away and fiddled with something—a slurping noise, a tick of metal—then spun to face her again. He rolled her shirt up and rubbed an alcohol swab along her spine. He pressed the plunger of the needle, a squirt of liquid spurting out.

"What's that smell?" Evelyn said.

"What smell?"

"Stinks like burning foil or something, like when mom burns something in the oven."

"Nothing to be concerned with," Simon said. "Now just take a deep breath and—"

Evelyn screamed as the needle plunged into her spine.

Simon thrust the plunger down until it emptied then jerked it out, a stream of yellow and milky-white fluid trailing the needle.

Evelyn writhed, a nauseous feeling coming over her. Her eyelids drooped, a sudden wooziness pressing in on her tired brain. Lightheaded, she pushed up, trying to turn over, but her arms failed and she collapsed, her head thumping off the table.

An hour later she came to. Her shirt was still rolled up, her back exposed. An intense heat emanated from her spine and she reached back to feel it, her fingernails tripping over a pinprick scab.

Her father was sitting on a stool beside her, scribbling notes. She blinked and his pencil stopped. She looked at him, terrified, as if he had taken much more from her than just blood.

"What did you do to me?" she asked.

"Do to you? I did nothing to you," Simon said.

"What was in that needle?"

"We're helping people, remember, Ev?"

"But I blacked out."

"Oh, I don't think that's true. You dozed off peacefully."

"It hurt so much though. What was in it?"

"Now, now, Ev, you're fine. I think you just had a nightmare."

Evelyn pushed herself to a seated position and rolled her shirt down. "Did it work?" she asked. "Whatever you were trying to do?"

"Unfortunately, no, something was off," Simon said. "I'll have to adjust some things and try again next month."

"I have to do this again?"

"Don't worry about it for now. Why don't you go upstairs and rest a little?"

Evelyn eased off the table. She moved toward the basement door, a list in her step. "Why does my leg hurt?"

"How do you mean?" Simon asked.

"It feels like this one is shorter than this one."

Simon's brow furrowed as he watched Evelyn hobble across the basement. He studied his notes, running a hand across his stubbled chin. He scratched out a formula and replaced it with a large question mark. He stared at the pages a moment longer before turning to her. "I'm sure it's nothing," he said. "Probably just need to sleep it off."

Evelyn nodded and opened the door. She began climbing the stairs when Simon called out to her. "Oh, and Ev? Let's just keep this between you and I. No need to worry your mother about this."

"But I-I think I should tell her about my leg."

"No!"

"But it hurts so much."

"It will…it will be fine."

"Yeah, but—"

"Remember, we're helping people," Simon said. "People in need. Now, how many people can say that, huh?"

Evelyn sighed and nodded absently. She turned and trudged up the stairs, dragging her limp leg behind her.

Chapter Twenty-Six

November 1995
Day 642 | Before Dawn

In the cramped motel room, the group slept through the night, several of the officers snoring restlessly on the floor. Wanda sat by the window, adjusting every few minutes to relieve the pain in her side. Evelyn was curled in her lap.

"You're getting too big for this," Wanda said.

"I know," Evelyn said. "It's just been so long since I've seen you. But I can move if you want me to."

"No, no, I was just pointing out how much you've grown. But I never said I wanted you to leave."

Evelyn smiled and curled back into her mother, dozing in and out of sleep as the minutes ticked by. The wind had picked up and the rain had turned to snow, thick flakes covering the parking lot. Wanda peered out the frosted window, the nights now cold enough to greedily clutch the snow until the sun stole it away at dawn. She caressed Evelyn's spine then stopped. "Wait," she said.

She lifted Evelyn's shirt. She picked at the scabs along the girls back until they sloughed off. She rubbed her knuckles across the crusted skin as if searching for something underneath. The skin shed until red pinpricks were revealed, the wounds leaking watery pink blood.

Evelyn awoke with a start. "What are you doing?"

"Wait, wait, wait," Wanda said.

"Mom, you're hurting me."

Both Andrew and Xavier shook awake. "What's going on?" Andrew asked.

"It's in her," Wanda said.

"What's in her?"

"The virus," Wanda said. "It's in her."

"She told us all this," Andrew said. "Her and Damien were attacked in the woods last winter. She got infected by them."

"Yeah, she walked with a limp, so we figured she had been exposed," Xavier said with a yawn. "Although, she's starting to limp again so I don't know what that's about."

"That may be," Wanda said. "But she was also exposed by *him*."

"Who?" Andrew said.

"Simon."

"You told us he just took blood."

"He, uh, he may have done more than that once or twice," Wanda said. "He just got so angry when I confronted him about it, you see. But I started to suspect more."

"Meaning what?"

"I noticed these pinpricks. Along her spine."

"That's what those are?" Xavier said. "From a needle?"

"Damien had them too," Evelyn said meekly. She reached into her bag and brought out the photo of her and Damien jumping off the dock. She handed it to Andrew. "I thought they were freckles. But they must be marks where the needle went in."

Andrew studied the photo as a memory pecked at him: Damien's bare back as they lay atop the crest of a hill one afternoon last March. His shirt had bunched up and Andrew had surveyed the scabs down the boy's spine.

"I ignored them, convinced myself the markings were nothing," Wanda said. "But deep down I had my suspicions."

"What did you suspect?" Andrew asked.

"That it must be where he injected them with the virus."

Evelyn ran a hand along her back as if the sting of the needle was fresh again.

Listening, Everett slid from the bed and joined the others. "Hold on," he said. "Simon was purposefully infecting her? Why?"

"I don't know," Wanda said.

"Kinda explains why she didn't fully turn after she was attacked," Andrew said. "If the virus was already in her, her immunity would have been built up."

"And living on the outskirts, she wouldn't have been exposed to the drug in the town's water," Xavier added.

"What was he trying to find though?" Everett asked.

"I don't know, but he said something about manipulating a drug," Wanda said. "To see if he could...I don't know... control a virus with it."

"Control it? How?"

"I don't know. He rarely talked about it."

"I thought he was trying to cure it?" Everett said.

"Yes, but...I don't know the ins and outs of it, just that he slipped once and said something about controlling a mutation or something."

"And you think that has something to do with what he injected Evelyn with?"

"I told you, I don't know!" Wanda said. "I'm not the scientist, he is."

"Hold on," Andrew said, turning to Evelyn. "You've started limping again?"

Evelyn shrugged. "Hadn't noticed."

"She has," Xavier confirmed. "It's becoming worse."

"So, she wasn't limping after we gave her the antidote last summer. But she's starting to show again?" Andrew asked.

"What are you driving at?" Everett said.

"It may mean the virus has reactivated in her."

"How?"

"The antidote is wearing off. Just like everyone else."

"Okay, and…?"

"Well, it's interesting she still hasn't turned, don't you think?"

"I'm not following."

"Well, I don't know for sure," Andrew said. "But with the mix of the antidote and the virus and who knows what else he put in her, Evelyn's blood is different from ours. Maybe even immune. It may contain—"

Everett's radio cackled, startling the group. He reached for the speaker clipped to his shirt pocket. "Everett here, go ahead."

A woman's nasally voice chirped through the static. "Staff Inspector? It's the Clearwater branch."

"Go ahead."

"Well, you see, I have some news about the Barn Wood case."

"Alright."

"A gentleman came into the station. Said his name was Alan Mackenzie."

"Mackenzie?"

"Yeah. We cross-referenced the name with your case file

and it's the same name which is listed as Lead of Operations on those documents you seized from, ah, what's the name? Oh, here it is, a Dr. Angela Till's house."

"You're telling me Mackenzie's at your station?" Everett said. "We've been trying to locate him for months!"

"Said he had some urgent information he wanted to get to you."

"What is it?"

"Well, he hit his head on the floor so everything he was saying didn't make a lot of sense, but when he came to, he told us he had been held hostage for nearly a week by some guy named…hold on, I wrote it down here somewhere. Riley, pass me that notepad there, will ya? Ah yes, here we go, a Dr. Simon Stone."

"We're looking for him too! What else did Mackenzie say?"

"Well, sir, this is where it gets strange. He said the guy conducts experiments on people inside a huge underground laboratory."

Everett looked around at the others, confused.

"Sir, are you still there?" the woman said.

"Yeah, I'm still here," Everett answered. "Please, go on."

"Well, he said this Stone fella was testing different versions of a drug. Said this new drug made folks really tall and strong, something like this."

"These new ones are being manufactured?"

"Said there were others being held hostage too. A man and a woman, along with his driver. Oh, wait, the driver's dead. Sorry, I jotted that part down later."

"What on earth does he need hostages for?"

"I'm not sure, sir. Again, this Mackenzie guy was rambling on, not making much sense. But he did say two things that sent shivers down my spine."

"What was that?"

"Said this Simon fella has created a small army of these things. Says a few of 'em were acting like bodyguards."

"My word. And the second thing?"

"The second thing is even more far flung. Said this same fella has created a cure but that he's not gonna use it. Says something like people are gonna get what's coming to 'em."

"He must've figured out a permanent cure," Andrew said. "Angela's was temporary. Maybe he's concocted a true one."

"Sounds like he's not interested in sharing it though," Xavier added. "Probably using it as some sort of ransom."

Several of the officers were now awake, sluggishly getting into their uniforms, eavesdropping onto the transmission. Everett spoke into the radio again. "Did Mackenzie say if the cure is permanent?"

"No sir, he didn't say," the woman said.

"Well, go ask him."

"Well, the thing is, sir…"

"Yes? What is it?"

"Mackenzie is dead, sir."

"What?"

"The paramedics came and tried to revive him. He hit his head pretty hard. He came to and told us all the stuff I just told you, but then he collapsed again."

"Dead?"

"Yes, sir. They think it was a combination of head trauma and already being in a weakened state. Whatever this Simon fella did to him…well, he wasn't good coming in."

Everett shook his head. "Okay, thanks for calling this in."

He released the call button. He shoved his hands in his pockets and walked to the window, peering out into the dawn. "Just so I got this all straight," he started, "the antidote is losing its hold and folks are turning nuts again. At the same time, this Simon chump is messing about with the virus, making a bunch of 'em bigger and stronger and more violent." He turned to Andrew. "I get all that right?"

Andrew nodded.

Everett sighed and turned back to the window. "Simon's out there, close to the Clearwater branch I'd imagine, if that's where Mackenzie stopped," he said. "Any ideas where to start looking for him?"

"Well, we know where he hides his henchmen," Xavier grumbled.

"Right. I suppose we can start back at the barn then," Everett said. "What's the name of that abandoned camp we passed through?"

"Camp Clearwater."

"Right. Maybe we go back, see what we can find?"

"You want to go back?" Prasad said. "We barely survived the first time!"

"We have Andrew now," Everett said. "And they'll be a lot less of those things since we took most of them out."

"And what if others show up?" Prasad said. "Last time they were hiding in the floor! Who knows where they could be hiding now!"

"Wait," Wanda said. "What did you say the name of that camp was?"

"Clearwater," Xavier said.

"We used to drive right past that place to get to our cabin."

"I knew that place was familiar!" Evelyn blurted out. "I just couldn't figure out how I knew it. But now I remember."

"Actually, I remember seeing a cabin the first time I was up there," Xavier said.

"You did?"

"Way in the distance, but it was there. Too foggy when we were there yesterday—couldn't see anything."

Evelyn snatched the photo of her and Damien jumping off the dock. She turned to Wanda. "It's this one, isn't it? This is the cabin."

Wanda looked away. "Does anyone have a map of that area?" she asked.

"There were some in the lobby," Andrew said. "I'll go grab one."

When he returned, he unfolded the map on the bed as the others gathered around.

"So, where's this camp?" Wanda asked.

Xavier surveyed the map then pressed down in the corner. "It's here," he said. "On this kettle lake."

A flood of memories seemed to wash over her as she trembled, her cheeks going flush. She nodded absently as if working out a problem in her mind. "He's there," she said. "We haven't been up that way in years, but he's there. Has to be."

"How do you know?" Andrew asked.

"Don't you see, it all makes sense," she said. "Why he's been acting strange for so long. The testing on the kids, the secret formulas, why he's been missing for nine goddamn months!"

"But how can you be sure that's where he is?"

Wanda turned to Xavier. "That barn you described? The

one beyond the camp? You can see that same barn from our cabin."

"Really?" Xavier said.

"Yes. And if you say those monsters were in that barn then that's where Simon is."

"But Wanda," Everett said. "I've lost so many already. Before I send any more officers, we have to be sure that's where he is."

"He's there," Wanda said. "I know he is. I know it in my bones."

Chapter Twenty-Seven

November 1995
Day 642 | Morning

Rachel's sedan followed the black SUVs and police cruiser as they peeled down the county roads. Andrew was consulting the map in the backseat. Evelyn was beside him and Wanda beside her.

"Are we going the right way?" Juliana asked from the passenger seat.

"Give me a minute," Andrew mumbled, "I'm trying to pinpoint our exact—"

"This is the way," Wanda said.

"You sure?"

"This is the way," she said again. Her eyelids shadowed her sad eyes like a blind pulled over a window.

"Mom, are you okay?" Evelyn asked.

"I always knew it. Always had a sense he was…this way. It's just hard when you finally have to admit it."

She swallowed and then turned to the window, staring at the snow-covered branches whipping by. After some time, the SUVs signalled and turned and came to a stop at the base of an incline.

"They're stopping," Rachel said, pulling the sedan onto the shoulder.

"Really?" Andrew said, returning to the map. "But I don't think this is it."

"This is it. It's just over this hill," Wanda said. She opened the door and stepped out.

"Well, I guess this is it," Andrew huffed, crumpling the map. He swung the door open and shuffled out. He grabbed his rifle from the trunk and clipped his knife onto his belt. He followed Wanda and Evelyn to the lead SUV, Rachel and Juliana behind him, hustling to keep up.

Xavier and the officers were gathered around the hood, rubbing their hands together for warmth.

"We in the right spot?" Everett asked, turning to Wanda.

She spun around, taking in the swath of trees, the cattails lining the ditch. She closed her eyes, the crisp morning air blowing her black hair across her dark skin. She inhaled. "This is the place."

"You sure? 'Cause these county roads all look the same to me."

"We don't visit in the winter, but this is the place. I can smell it, sense it."

"Okay, so where's this cabin?"

Wanda walked into the middle of the road, the hard-packed snow crunching under her boots. She pointed up the hill. "About a hundred metres this way. Just beyond that crest."

Everett nodded. "Okay, suit up everyone and check your ammo," he instructed. "We approach in ten."

The trunk sprang open and Powell handed each officer a bullet-proof vest.

"These things armed now?" Prasad said.

"No, but this Simon creep might be," Powell said.

Dunvey clicked open a long metal box, the container overflowing with silver cartridges. "Take more than you need," he said. "Y'all remember what happened up at that barn."

The officers shoved extra rounds into their vests and pockets. Singh and Powell flicked on a pair of flashlights, checking the batteries, before shoving each into a side pocket.

Andrew looked up to see Evelyn and Wanda preparing their weapons. "Hey, listen, maybe you two should sit this one out," he said. "We don't know what to expect, and considering—"

"Don't even start with me," Wanda said. "We're coming. This is my husband. He's my responsibility."

"I just mean, given he may be up there, and your relationship—"

"If he's there, he needs to see me," Wanda said. "He needs to see Ev. And he needs to know what happened to Damien. He needs to see what he's done to this family."

Andrew turned to Rachel. "Will you at least stay back? Just until we've cleared it?"

Rachel nodded. "I'll stay with the kids."

"Me too!" Juliana blurted out. "No way in hell I'm going up there!"

"We'll come back and get you when it's clear," Andrew said. He turned to Alice and Joshua. "Rachel and Juliana are gonna stay back with you guys, just until we make sure everything's safe."

"This is where all the smells and noises come from," Alice said, her voice panicked.

"You know this place?"

Joshua appeared restless. He seemed to give the question

some thought. "There's a camp near here," he said finally. "Where we sleep and hunt raccoons."

"Yeah, and a barn full of weirdos," Alice added.

"Oh?" Andrew said.

"Sometimes those weirdos go from the barn to the house," Alice said. "Well, not a real house. It's made of logs and is tiny but, well, I guess it's like a house."

"And sometimes a man comes out and goes to the barn and yells at them and they follow him back," Joshua said.

"How do you know all this?" Andrew asked.

"We followed them once," Alice said.

"What did you see?"

"Just what she said," Joshua said. "It stinks and there's always yelling and screaming."

"Yeah, like torture," Alice whispered.

"How far is the barn from the cabin, er, the house?" Andrew asked.

"Pretty far. You could probably see it, but it's still far," Joshua said.

"It's more than two thousand steps!" Alice added. "I counted one time but then got bored so stopped counting and we still weren't at the house, so the barn is way more than two thousand steps."

"I see," Andrew said.

Alice reached for her brother's hand and they marched back to the SUV, sliding into the back. Joshua pushed the lock down as Alice burrowed into the seat and surrounded herself with her dolls, hugging one after the other, then holding them tight to her chest.

Andrew joined the others. He shuddered, the squeaky voice of Alice still in his head.

Like torture.

"If he's there, he doesn't know we're coming, so we have the element of surprise on our side," Everett said, gathering everyone around him.

"And if he does?" Prasad asked.

"Well, I don't know how that's possible. But if he does, then we improvise."

"Roger."

"Singh, Prasad, Dunvey—you come with me to the right," Everett said. "Powell, how are you feeling? You okay with us?"

"Good to go," she said.

"Then you come with us up the right side. Xavier, Andrew, Wanda, Ev…" he paused, taking in the second group. "Basically, if your last name is Stone, then you flank left."

Xavier smirked. "Got it."

"If we clear the outside with no incident then we should all end up behind the cabin," Everett said. "We'll enter through the rear, taking it room by room, just like the motel. Any questions?"

"If he's there, he won't be alone," Wanda said.

"Okay, well, if any of those things are there, you take them out, no hesitation," Everett said, making eye contact with each officer. "We ain't foolin' around with any antidote this time," he added. He turned away from the group. "I've lost enough to these psychos already," he muttered.

The group trudged up the hill, passing over a large storm culvert running beneath the road.

Wanda stopped and sniffed the air. "You smell that?"

"Smell what?" Everett asked.

"Burning metal."

Everett wriggled his nose then shook his head. "Nah, I don't smell nothin'." He checked his revolver a final time. "Let's keep moving. We're almost there."

They continued up the road. And there, just over the crest, stood the cabin.

Everett motioned to the officers and, one by one, they moved into a spread formation and disappeared amongst the wide oaks and tall evergreens. He swivelled to face the other group and chopped his hand through the air.

At the signal, Xavier turned and darted through the wiry brush toward the left side of the cabin, Evelyn and Wanda following close behind, Andrew taking up the rear.

They moved through the trees, over snow-covered ferns and grasses, Wanda feeling for the hilt of her knife every few strides. Shielded by a line of aspens, Andrew spun at the sound of branches breaking, but when he turned, nothing was there.

They reached a knoll and the front porch of the cabin came into view. Andrew sidled up to Xavier and knelt, the cold seeping up his legs. "How do you want to play this?"

"As quietly as we can," Xavier said. "And if it all goes to hell, we go in guns blazing."

"Feels like we've been here before, huh?"

"Hunting nut jobs in a forest? Yeah, we've definitely been here before."

"Except this time, we don't have Damien," Andrew added.

Xavier flinched, as if the name struck a painful chord.

A snap of branches rang out again, somewhere off to the right.

"Jesus, those cops are clumsy," Andrew said. He turned to

Wanda. "Anything you can tell us about the cabin?"

"What you see is what you get," she said. "Like Everett said, it's smart to creep around back."

"Look there," Xavier said, pointing toward the driveway.

"What you got?" Andrew asked.

"Could be tracks."

"Let's get closer."

They jogged to the edge of the driveway. Xavier bent low. "Boot prints," he confirmed. "But there's…" His brow knitted as he scanned the area. "There's three separate sets."

"You sure?" Wanda asked.

"Look here," Xavier said as Wanda crouched by his side. "These two are about the same size, but from a different boot."

"But who else would be up here with him?"

Xavier rose from his squat and marched a few yards up the driveway. "And these ones," he said, pointing to a different set. "These ones are much smaller, narrower."

"A woman?" Wanda asked.

"Maybe," Xavier said.

"Truck tires run right through them. And pretty recent, by the looks of it," Andrew said.

"You can see those same prints coming off the front porch," Xavier said, taking another step forward. "They lead from the front door to here—right where the truck was."

"And another set of tracks over that way," Andrew added, pointing across the driveway. "Not as heavy as a truck. A sedan, maybe."

He walked over to the tire tracks, splotches of blood in the snow. Prints of massive bare feet could be seen heading into the woods. He sucked at the air then looked at the others.

"We should go," Wanda said. "Everett wants us in the back as soon as we've cleared our side."

"Right. We good to move?" Andrew asked.

Xavier and Wanda nodded.

Andrew turned to Evelyn. "Ready?"

"Yeah," she said. "Let's just get this over with and—"

Behind you, Ev, Damien said. *They're behind you.*

Evelyn spun. Trembling, she traversed back down the path. And as she squinted through the thick trunks and bare boughs, she saw them. Monstrous shapes, growling and grunting, gushing out from the storm culvert.

They're coming, Damien said.

Evelyn turned to the others, her eyes flooded with fear. "They're coming! Damien says they're coming!"

Chapter Twenty-Eight

November 1995
Day 642 | Morning

Andrew ran to Evelyn. He grabbed her hand and yanked her around a bend just as the forest exploded with a deafening shriek. Xavier swivelled at the noise and stared down the scope of his rifle, beading down on a beast surging toward him. He shot it cleanly, but still it rushed forward. He fired twice more, flesh peeling off the beast's chin and chest. It staggered for a moment then continued its charge.

"A little help!" he shouted, as Andrew and Evelyn bounded over a log to reach him and Wanda.

Andrew brought his rifle up, aimed, and shot the creature twice more. It fell to the ground, the snow around it red and wet. "You weren't kidding," he huffed. "These ones *are* different."

"I've never seen anything like it," Wanda said.

A second beast careened through the trees, its glare like hellfire. Xavier shot it twice in the neck. Evelyn raised her rifle and fired, a bullet ripping through its cheek. The beast howled and collapsed, an exposed tree root impaling it through the eye.

A third one emerged and Andrew fired four straight shots into it. It dropped to its knees, wheezing, its breaths bursting out in small white clouds. It stared up at him with a look of yearning, as if pleading for the life leaking out of it. It was then Andrew realized just how different these new ones were. Their bodies were deformed but their minds had been sharpened, well-beyond the dull intelligence of the creatures last winter. These ones seemed to feel more. Were more human, perhaps.

A sudden crash caused him to spin as another beast bore down on him. He raised his rifle. "Sorry, bud, it's either you or me," he said, centring the creature in his scope. He fired several times, the creature keeling over into the snow and weeds. "And today, it's not me."

He stumbled backward as a ghastly creature came into view. It was incredibly tall, its limbs long and bony, its skin bleached white. It cast a needle-like shadow as it unhinged from the trees.

It had a repugnant confidence about it and it frightened Andrew to the core. It turned and Andrew saw a bowie knife extending from it, one which was familiar. He raised his rifle, but then Xavier was suddenly beside him and he reached out to push down the barrel.

"I've seen this one before," Xavier said. "It's not like the others."

"How's that?"

"Smarter than the rest. Thinks a few steps ahead. Cunning, almost."

Andrew raised his rifle again and peered at the creature through his scope. "X, is that your knife?"

"Mm-hmm."

"What's it doing in that thing's back?"

"I got lucky at the barn. Let's just say that thing can keep it."

The ground shook and Xavier spun to see a dozen more beasts closing in. "There's more coming," he said. "Let's get behind the cabin, wait for the others."

Andrew lowered his rifle. "Okay. You lead; we'll follow."

Xavier sprinted, Andrew, Wanda, and Evelyn following close behind. When they reached the backdoor, Everett and the other officers were already there.

"What took you so long?" Everett asked.

"You'll see in about ten seconds," Xavier shouted, running past them to an old tin shed.

Everett squinted through the trees before drawing his revolver. "Incoming! Take cover!" he hollered as the officers turned and sprinted for the shed. Everett was the last to round it and he leaned up against the wall, sweat pouring down the front of him. "They'll be in the open soon," he huffed. "That's when we give 'em hell!"

"Sir, where's Dunvey?" Singh said.

Everett's face dropped. He peered around the shed to find Dunvey on the ground, holding his injured leg.

"Carl!" he shouted. "Get up, get up!"

Dunvey pushed himself to standing. He tried to run but wobbled, tweaking his ankle once again. He staggered and fell, grabbing at his boot, grimacing in pain. He rolled onto his side, his mouth slack, lame and wheezing, like a sick animal.

"I'm coming!" Everett shouted.

He lurched forward as a pack of beasts came charging out from the bush. He raised his revolver and fired. "Go to hell, all of you!" he screamed.

He hit one in the knee and another in the stomach, but most of his shots missed wildly as he jittered over the uneven ground. "Start shooting, Carl!" he yelled.

Dunvey teetered as he pushed himself up. He slipped his gun from his holster and raised it, but they were already on him like a swarm of wasps. He wailed as they crushed him into the ground, tearing at his flesh, biting through bone.

"No!" Everett yelled, emptying his clip.

Dunvey's pleading eyes bore into Everett. But they soon turned lifeless as Everett watched one of the beasts slice a claw across Dunvey's throat, emptying the officer of blood.

Everett cried out and dropped to his knees, but then a hand was on him and he looked up to find Andrew. Tear-streaked, Everett returned with him behind the shed as Xavier provided cover fire.

"You okay?" Andrew shouted at Everett.

Powell hustled over and put her hands on Everett's face, drawing him close. "Tom, are you okay? Are you hurt?"

"He didn't get one shot off," Everett said, his voice breaking. His legs gave out and he sat on the snow, bringing his knees to his chest. "Not one shot. He never stood a chance."

"I gotta help the others," Andrew said. He turned to Powell. "Stay with him. He's going into shock."

Andrew peeked around the shed. He saw Xavier shooting down several of the beasts. Andrew spun and once again, he spotted the albino. It had a smug look about it, and the way it moved caused him to shiver. The other creatures around it kept their heads low as if in reverence.

It ambled across to Dunvey and stood over him. It hauled Dunvey's body from the ground and held it high as if offering a sacrifice. Or a warning.

It threw the body at the shed, Dunvey's corpse banging off the metal and into a pile of bloodied limbs. The creature howled with excitement and glared at Andrew before drawing back into the shadows, skulking like a spider. The other beasts followed, dissolving into the trees.

Xavier lowered his rifle and Andrew turned on him. "Why didn't you shoot it?"

"I-I couldn't," Xavier said. "I froze…I just …"

"It was right there, you had a clean shot! You saw what it did to Dunvey!"

"There's something…something about that one…"

"Why'd they run?" Evelyn asked, running up to her cousins.

"I don't know," Andrew said. "Something spooked them, I guess." He clicked the safety on his rifle then ran to the rear of the cabin. "Someone get Everett," he hollered. "We need to go through this cabin."

Powell and Singh helped Everett up, the portly officer huffing as he regained his balance. "Are they gone?" he asked, shaking. He struggled to holster his revolver. "Are there any more of 'em?"

"They're gone," Powell said. She wrapped her arm around him as he steadied his weight against her. She held him close and they made their way to the cabin.

"You did good, Tom," she whispered. "The best you could."

He nodded and looked to her with sad eyes. But as they made their way across the yard, he looked back at the crumpled body of Dunvey—all hacked and chewed up—and his look changed. His eyes now held a different emotion within them, something close to rage. And as he stared upon the fallen officer it was as if something dark seeped into him, something terrible taking root.

Outside the cabin, Andrew turned to Wanda. "You know

this place so it's best if you go in first," he said. "We'll be tight on you."

Wanda stepped forward and turned the doorknob. The sun was high and bright so that as the door creaked open, a flash of light cascaded off the cabin floor, causing her to jump back.

"Mom, what is it?" Evelyn asked.

"I-I don't know," Wanda said.

"Did you see anything?"

"I-I don't think so. It was just, uh, just a feeling."

"A feeling?"

"A memory of sorts."

Andrew's eyes held hers. "Something you're not telling us?"

"No, no, nothing."

"Then what did you just see in there?"

"Nothing. Probably just a trick of the light," she said, but still she brought out her knife. She pushed through the door, the others close behind.

The group moved from room to room, rooting through closets and upending mattresses. They rummaged through drawers, kicked at boxes, looking for anything out of the ordinary.

In the kitchen, Xavier studied a water-testing certificate hung on the fridge, Angela's signature prominently strewn across the bottom.

"Ev, check this out," he said. "It's like the one we came across last winter, remember?"

"Yeah, and it had a picture of that hockey player you like," Evelyn said.

"Tony *the Tank* MacAvoy," Xavier said.

"Really?" Andrew said.

"Yeah, we figured the photo was taken at one of the flu clinics the virus was administered at."

Andrew eyed the document. "The certificate's signed by Angela?"

"Who else would sign it?"

Andrew pressed his lips together and pondered the document.

"Why, what are you thinking?" Xavier asked.

"The documents the cops seized said the study site was confined to Barn Wood. But we're far from Barn Wood, way out here."

"Meaning what?"

"Why test the water this far out?"

Xavier shrugged. "Dunno."

Andrew stared at the paper, chewing the inside of his cheek.

In the main room, Prasad approached Everett. "Sir, the place is cleared."

Everett didn't move. He remained at the window, staring at the backyard shed, Dunvey's body beside it. He eventually nodded and turned to the group. He looked haggard.

"Sheila, do you mind getting the others?" he said. "It's safe for them now."

"Sure," Powell said.

As she walked by, she gently rubbed Everett's arm then marched through the foyer and out the front door.

Remembering the boot prints and tire tracks from earlier, Andrew followed her outside. He knelt down, his eyes moving over the imprints in the muddy snow. Xavier soon joined him. "What you got?" he asked.

"Something about those prints," Andrew said.

"What about 'em?"

"We know they end at the truck. But where do they start?"

Xavier moved back inside and scanned the hardwood. "There's one here," he said, stepping across the floor, a ring of dried mud forming a faint outline. "And another one there."

Andrew followed him as Xavier shuffled into a corner. "They end here."

"At the wall?" Everett asked.

"Seems it," Xavier said.

"But these prints are facing the front door, as if they stepped out from the wall," Andrew said.

"But that's impossible," Everett said.

"Unless…unless it's not impossible." Andrew scanned the wall, stopping at a small indent about a foot from the floor. He ran his hand over it. "It's a hinge," he said.

"A hinge for what?" Singh asked.

Andrew slid his hand further up until he found another indent. He moved his thumb over it, his nail feeling the hollows between the grooves. "Another hinge," he said. Then: "It's a door! These hinges are for a door."

"There's no door there, it's just a wall," Singh said. "Besides, where's the handle?"

Andrew rubbed along the wall until the texture changed. He pressed firmly and heard a click, like a magnetic cabinet releasing. A tiny door—no more than 4x2 feet—oscillated open.

"What the hell?" Everett said. He cracked the door open and stared upon a narrow set of stairs leading down into the earth.

"Did you know about this?" Andrew asked, turning on Wanda. "This secret entrance?"

Wanda shook her head and when she raised her eyes to meet his, he could see she was as scared as he was.

"What do you think is down there?" Singh asked.

"Probably a lot of answers," Everett said.

The front door burst open as Powell, Rachel, Juliana, and the two children bounded into the main room.

"What's everyone doing?" Alice squeaked. "Did you find any weirdos?"

"We're not entirely sure what we found," Everett said. He turned to Andrew. "What's our move?"

"I don't think we have a choice," Andrew said.

Everett exhaled through his nose and nodded. "I think you're right."

"If answers might be down there then…" Andrew trailed off, bringing the rifle close to his body.

"We're going down there?" Alice asked.

Andrew nodded then ducked, stepping through the narrow archway. He moved down the stairs, the group following behind, trekking silently into the dark.

Chapter Twenty-Nine

November 1995
Day 642 | Afternoon

With the thrum of his heart pounding in his ears, Andrew led the group down the stairs and along a lengthy hallway. Singh brought out his flashlight and flicked it on.

"Where are we going?" Alice chirped.

"You need to be quiet," Rachel whispered. "We don't know who's down here."

"Like more of those weirdo guys?"

"Yes, maybe more of them."

Alice smirked as if being let in on a secret only adults were allowed to know. "But you guys will shoot 'em, right?"

Rachel reared around to face her. "Alice, you need to keep quiet! Look at your brother, he's being quiet as a mouse."

"More like boring as a mouse," Alice mumbled.

The group crept along the corridors. As they rounded a corner, Alice piped up again. "Are we underground?"

Wanda turned to the child. "Yes, we're underground." She placed Alice's hand in hers. "But we need to be quiet down here, okay? Can you do that for me?"

Alice nodded, staring up into the woman's fierce but kind eyes.

"This chatterbox is gonna get us killed," Andrew said, shouldering up to Xavier. "Why the hell did we bring the kids?"

"In case those things came back," Xavier said.

"We could've just left them upstairs."

"If they're with me at least I know they're protected."

"Xavier, the great protector, huh?"

"Hm."

"Look how soft you've gotten. Ev's really done a number on you."

Xavier grumbled and moved past him, arriving at a damaged door. He pushed it open and the group filed in behind. Singh swung the light, the dull beam needling into the corners. Several claw marks ran down the wall, a patchwork of unfinished drywall and plywood.

"Not much here," Xavier said. But as he stepped back, something crunched under his boot.

"What was that?" Singh asked.

Xavier raised his boot as a piece of white plastic lay crushed on the floor.

Andrew bent low into the light, examining the object. "It's a plastic cap."

"From what?" Singh asked.

Andrew picked it up, inspecting it in his palm. "From a needle."

"You think he's injecting them with this new drug the branch office talked about?" Everett said.

"A new breed," Wanda said.

Xavier eyed her. "Let's keep moving," he said. "See what else we find."

The group exited the room and continued down the hall

until they came to a second door. Xavier pushed it open and everyone stepped inside.

They gathered around a closet door at the far side of the room. With revolver drawn, Powell swung it open and her breath caught. "Wh-what's all this?"

"Looks like someone was tied up," Andrew said. He squatted, examining the tangle of rope and bloodied wire bolted halfway up the wall, a trail of blood and stool smeared into the floor.

"Like a prisoner?" Powell asked.

"Could've been Mackenzie," Everett said.

"You think Simon kept him in *here*? But why?"

Andrew dropped the rope. "The bullied becomes the bully," he said.

Everett stood stoic, absorbing the scene, until the group turned and left the room. They moved further down the hall then stopped at a heavy metal door. A padlock had been drilled into it but it remained open, the shackle loose.

"Someone was in a hurry," Powell said. "Didn't even lock up."

"Are we going in there?" Singh asked.

"We don't have a choice," Everett said, gripping his revolver, an edge to his voice.

He pushed through the door and the others followed him in. Singh shone the light at the wall. He spotted a switch, and when he flicked it on, the room illuminated in front of them.

There were the high ceilings and the bowed bookcases, the centrifuge, the desk jammed into the corner, the cluttered bench.

Andrew stepped toward the desk, its surface littered with medical texts and newspaper clippings, a scatter of pencils, pens, and notes. A whiteboard above the desk contained several equations. His attention was drawn to the familiar BioHealth Pharmaceutical research documents—the menacing deer logo and 'CONFIDENTIAL' warning embossed along the top.

On the bench, he saw a mess of pipettes and stirring rods, flasks and funnels, a ring stand, a compound microscope. There was a filthy lab coat, latex gloves, a smudged pair of goggles.

He took note of a rack of test tubes, a murky liquid congealing within them. He recoiled from the stink.

He stepped toward the looming oval dome in the centre of the room. It was constructed of twelve-foot walls made of tempered glass, the space inside dark and foreboding, an underground tomb torn into the earth.

"Wh-what is this place?" Juliana said.

"Is that…is that a man?" Rachel gasped, pointing to the far side of the dome.

The group stepped closer, staring down at the naked man. He had a long torso with filthy hands and a cropped goatee. But that was all that was distinguishable.

His stomach was stretched open, organs exposed, as if a wolf had rooted down into him. Like wet sausages, his innards were in a mushy pile beside him. His feet had been severed, grey bone jutting out at the ankle. His blood was slick and glossy and spread all over his body so that it resembled a garnish, similar to how one would prepare a bird for the oven.

"My God," Powell said. She turned and buried her face in Everett's chest. "What is all this, Tom?" she said, her voice shaking.

Everett just stood and stared, his jaw moving but saying nothing. Eventually, he muttered, "I dunno…just that…just that horrible things have happened here."

Juliana gagged and held a hand to her mouth.

"You okay?" Andrew asked.

"Do you not see that guy?" Juliana said.

"Yeah, I see him."

"How can someone do that to another person?"

"I-I don't know."

"Look at him! How are you not scared?"

"Oh, I'm scared. I'm plenty scared."

She raised her eyes to meet his. "Wait, was this what it was like last winter?"

Andrew swallowed.

"You saw stuff like *that*?" Juliana asked.

Andrew nodded.

She reached for him and brought him close. "I had no idea it was this bad," she said. "I'm so sorry."

She held him and they both retreated to the corner beside the desk. Her hand brushed over the research papers. "These are just like the ones in your apartment," she said.

"Yeah," Andrew said.

"This guy has the same ones?"

"He and Rachel's sister were working on the same experiments."

"Together?"

"Separately. Apparently, she didn't know much about him until later."

"Look at this!" she said, leafing through a separate set of pages. "These are legal documents. Motions to sue."

"Really?"

"I saw a tonne of these when I worked at the firm."

"Who are they issued from?"

"All of them signed by an 'A. Pak'."

"Pertaining to what?" Andrew asked.

"An assortment of stuff," Juliana said. "'Cease and desist,' 'Failure to comply.' There has to be a dozen notices here."

"What does it mean?"

"If this Simon guy has been served with these then he's going to be locked in litigation for years."

"How's that?"

"I've seen it play out. Pharma never caves. It will be financial hell for this guy if this Mr. Pak pushes through with these."

"Pak's a ghost," Xavier said, joining them at the desk. "Everett said they've been looking for him for months."

"Why?" Juliana asked.

"His name's all over these documents. That's what triggered the initial search."

"But who is he?"

"Some investor," Andrew said. "Cops think he's a big player, but they still don't have much on him."

"Do you mind if I take these?" Juliana asked.

"Why?"

"I can make a few calls to my old firm, see if I can find something out."

Andrew glanced toward Everett standing by the dome, still holding Powell. He nodded and Juliana slid the folder underneath her jacket.

He turned back to the desk and a glint of metal caught his eye. He bent down and slid a metallic-blue briefcase out from beneath the office chair. He heaved it onto the desk, springing the latches open. Inside was a pear-shaped metal object cushioned within a bed of foam.

He removed the object, turning it over. Every few seconds a red light on the device flickered, followed by a faint beep.

"What is that thing?" Xavier asked.

Andrew studied it then looked closely at the papers strewn across the desk. He eyed the whiteboard hanging above. Scribbles filled it along with a crude drawing of the same object he held—'Prototype 19' scrawled above it.

"Whatever it is, it isn't the first one," he said.

"Meaning what?" Xavier asked.

Andrew gestured at the whiteboard. "Looks like he's been trying to develop this thing for a while."

The whiteboard contained a jumble of random chemical compositions. Andrew recognized some of them from the confidential documents, but many remained a mystery.

And then he noticed something peculiar. Each of the formulas contained a common compound: H_2O.

His attention shifted to a laminated map spread out on the wall. There were dozens of black pins affixed to it and one red one. The black pins were pushed into the names of nearby towns: Red Falls. Blackstone. Kassup. Hiltsville.

Xavier stepped toward the map. He pressed his thumb down on the single red pin. "Here's Barn Wood," he said.

Andrew leaned closer and noticed a tiny drawing of the strange object. The same drawing was repeated across the map—like a small pear beside each pin—numbered sequentially.

He turned the device over and noticed a sliver circle protruding from the top. He pulled at it and it extended into a three-foot antenna. The device beeped again, this time louder. "It's a tracker," he said.

"What do you mean?" Xavier asked.

"It's tracking others like it. Receiving a signal from other devices."

"What other devices?" Juliana asked.

Andrew returned to the map and then to the formulas. He scrunched up his face, trying to make sense of what was before him. He gasped. "He's poisoning other water sources!"

"What?" Juliana said.

"He's putting the drug in the water, in all these towns," Andrew said, the puzzle pieces locking into place. He glanced at the map and then at the device. "I think he's set these up at other sites and somehow, this one reads off the others."

"How do you know?"

He pointed to the whiteboard. "See these calculations? He's measuring something—the concentration of certain chemicals."

"The concentration of the virus?" Xavier asked.

"That, along with the concentration of the drug."

"It measures them together?"

"Looks that way. Perhaps when combined, they produce a specific reaction."

"Is that why those things stink? A mix of chemicals reacting?"

"Could be," Andrew said. "It's just a guess, but I think when another device detects a certain chemical, this main one beeps. Triggers it somehow."

"What will that do?" Juliana asked.

"I'd imagine it lets him know when there's a high concentration of people that contain those same chemicals," Andrew said.

"But how does he know where it is?"

Andrew turned the device over and noticed a small number three glowing red. "It's numbered. It must correspond to the sites on the map."

"Number three is Hiltsville," Xavier said, reading from the map.

"Okay, but once the concentration is high in that area, then what?" Juliana asked.

"Then…well," Andrew began. "Everything repeats itself."

"They'll turn into those creatures from last winter?" Xavier said. "Or maybe this new breed?"

"My guess is soon it'll be like Barn Wood," Andrew said.

He looked to the device and it beeped again, this time louder, and the red light on top flashed brighter. He flipped over a page of crossed-out formulas to find a final one. He focused on it for some time, muttering to himself, his mind weaving through a series of calculations. His face dropped as he looked to Xavier. "Or, worse, they're already turning," he said. "It's already happening."

Everett hollered from across the room. "Do you guys hear that? That humming sound?"

He waved them over then shuffled to the rear of the dome. There was a space between it and the wall, about a foot and a half wide, just large enough for a person to squeeze through. "The noise is even louder over here," Everett said.

He stepped through the narrow opening and held his breath, bringing his shirt collar over his nose. As he tucked in behind the dome, he gasped.

Laid out before him were dozens of bodies cocooned in tarps. Plastic sheeting was wrapped tight around their neck and faces, a tangle of blonde hair matted to a forehead, the shadow of scruff on another. They were haphazardly stacked and piled and the hum of hundreds of flies was almost deafening.

"My Lord," he said.

The others followed, and one by one they came to realize what the tarps contained.

Rachel reached for Joshua and Alice. "There's nothing for you here," she said, hurrying them out. "Nothing for a child to see."

Everett knelt beside one of the tarps and tore it open. He peeled away the plastic to reveal a teenager—pale and skinny—the boy's blue eyes staring back at him. Claw marks rivered down the side of his scalp and most of his hair had been ripped out. His throat was opened, the stringy muscles exposed, brown and dry.

He gagged and folded the tarp back over, then stood on unsteady legs and looked to the brothers. "What is this?"

"It's a goddamn graveyard," Xavier said.

Everett shuddered. "But why? What is it from?"

"Maybe experiments gone wrong?" Andrew said.

"This guy's completely gone over the edge. Twenty years on the force and I've never seen anything like this." Everett wiped a sleeve across his forehead then motioned for the other officers. "We'll need to check all of 'em."

"What for?" Prasad asked. "We have a pretty good idea what's in them."

"Check if any are still alive, for any clues we might have missed."

"Clues?" Prasad said. "What clues you gonna find with a bunch of corpses?"

"Just check 'em!" Everett shouted. "Someone other than that psycho ought to be the last one to look upon them!"

Prasad recoiled. "Yes, sir."

"They were people once," Everett added. "We owe them

that much."

For the next thirty minutes, the officers moved amongst the bodies, unwrapping each one then carrying them to the opposite corner. Some seemed to have been dead for months, the stink of decomposing flesh filling the room.

When it was done, Xavier guided Evelyn away, but she turned back. "My dad did this?"

"We don't know that for sure," Xavier said. "The cops will look into it and—"

"Mom…did Dad do this?" she asked, turning on Wanda.

"I don't…I don't know," Wanda muttered, eyeing the pile of bodies.

"Did he?" Evelyn yelled, her voice cracking with pain.

"I don't think he…I-I just don't think he could do this."

"Did you know? Is this what you were hiding from Damien and me?"

Wanda trembled then welled up. She turned and fled the room.

Evelyn shuddered. She stepped forward but faltered, as if a dizzying sense of panic had set in. She spun, surveying the room, until she found Andrew. She pointed at the bodies. "Is that in me?"

"No, no," Andrew said. "Listen, we're going to keep researching the virus, piece this together—"

"Not the virus! I already know the virus is in me!"

"Then what?"

"That!" she screamed. "That anger. That…that evil!"

"Absolutely not!" Xavier said.

"But I'm his daughter. What if I turn out like him?"

"You listen to me! You are nothing like that, you hear me?" Xavier boomed. "You are good and you are kind and you are brave and you're nothing like that!" Xavier grabbed the girl and brought her to him. Her knees buckled as she sobbed into his chest.

"Don't ever think that again, you hear me?" Xavier said. "Don't ever say that again!"

"I just want everything back the way it was," Evelyn cried. "I just want Damien and Maddy and my dad the way he used to be. And I want this virus to go away!"

"I know, I know," Xavier said, rubbing her back. "We all want that, Ev. And we'll figure this all out, okay?"

"How?"

"I don't know. But somehow, we'll figure this all out."

"But my dad is the only person who knows the virus inside and out."

Xavier glanced at Andrew. "Well, there is another."

Andrew grimaced at the suggestion, but knew she might be their only hope.

"Let's go home and get some rest, Ev," Xavier said. "We'll figure out the rest later, okay?"

Evelyn wiped the tears from her cheeks as Xavier guided her out from behind the dome, the others following. They were almost through the door when the pear-shaped device beeped.

Andrew tuned into the sound. The noise was different this time. There was a frenzied state about it, the beeping growing in volume and frequency, the sound piercing as the device began to jump and vibrate. The high-pitched pulse quickened until it became one long shrill.

They're already turning.

Andrew looked at the device. He thought about how the noise resembled a heart monitor hooked up to a flat-lined patient. Loved ones gathered around, shocked and scared, all at once realizing it's too late to call for help.

Chapter Thirty

**November 1995
Day 642 | Night**

Everett and his officers scoured the underground lab late into the night. Outside of Xavier and Andrew, he had sent the others home.

He ordered for the map to be pulled from the wall, rolled up, and taken with them, along with Simon's tracker and research documents. He glanced at the dome then looked away. Now that it was known what lay behind it, there was an eerie aura about it. He stepped back, keeping his distance.

"Tom, you okay?" Powell asked.

"Yeah, I'll be fine," Everett said.

"You haven't said much since Dunvey…I mean…just don't let it sit with you for too long."

"And Caldwell and Jackson and Munroe? Them too?"

"There wasn't anything you could have done," Powell said and she put her hand in his. "Don't let it eat at you."

"Yeah…Yeah."

"Tom?"

"Yeah, okay."

He forced a smile, but his eyes remained dark and hollow. He dropped her hand and moved to a metal cabinet, shifting through objects, his shoulders slumped, a look of defeat upon him.

At the desk, Andrew flipped through a folder until his eyes rested on a particular document. It was the chemical composition for the drug, Lilasvir, repeated several times over. Each entry was doctored in the margins.

"You keep coming back to this," Xavier said, peering over Andrew's shoulder.

"This is pretty advanced stuff," Andrew said.

"What's it say?"

"Not sure. Three years of university isn't gonna cut it."

"Can you make sense of any of it?"

"I think it's a cure for the virus. He seems to have tested it over and over again but with the same result."

"Wanda said he did tests on Ev and Damien. Is that what this is?"

"Maybe. You can see here in all these identical entries. Tests 1 through 21. Each time it's the same result."

"So, he *did* find something permanent?"

"I think so. But his experiments didn't stop there."

"How's that?"

"These next entries suggest he was never actually after the cure. He was after something else." Andrew's finger moved down the document. "See these notes in the margin? He was tinkering with it to make it more…"

"More what?"

"I don't know how to describe it. Instead of curing the virus he was trying to heighten it, boost it. Trying to enhance it."

"Hence the mutated breed?"

"Maybe."

Andrew stepped to the centrifuge, taking note of several identical vials. He opened the glass hatch and removed one, the initials 'E.S.' scrawled upon it. "Somehow using Ev's blood, he's tailored the drug to create creatures that are stronger and smarter."

Andrew pocketed the vial then returned to the desk. Amongst the papers lay a copy of *The Chronicle*. He flipped through it, pausing on an article buried within the back pages. "'*The Infection of Barn Wood by Brad Moseby,*'" he read aloud, holding up the newspaper.

"Moseby? That's the same reporter that's been trying to get at me," Xavier said.

"Still?"

"Yeah, and he interviewed Everett some time back as well."

"Get this," Andrew said, returning to the article. "'*The infection of Barn Wood is a shocking story of deception, lies, and greed at the highest levels of our community,* writes columnist Brad Moseby, *who has been researching this horrific saga for months.*'"

"He doesn't know the half of it," Xavier grumbled.

Andrew tossed the newspaper back on the desk. A thread of bright yellow and red dropped from it. He froze.

"It's Mom's!" Xavier said.

"You sure?" Andrew said.

"Of course it's hers! She wore it on her ankle."

"She was here? How?"

Then something else caught Andrew's attention: a ball of laundry in the corner. He picked it up and unravelled a red and black flannel shirt. He held it to his nose. "This is Joe's! Smells just like him."

"They were both here?" Xavier said.

"I don't know, I—"

"I think I've got something over here," Everett called out,

stepping away from the metal cabinet.

He was holding a camcorder and peering into the view-finder. The group huddled around him. He pressed rewind as blurred images rushed across the screen.

"What is it?" Prasad asked.

"Looks like someone was documenting something," Everett said.

"Is it recent?"

"Date-stamped four days ago," Everett said.

He pressed play and the group leaned in to see a creature, tall and lean, curled up in the corner of a room. It was breathing heavy, its face covered, only rare flashes of nails and hair. The film was of poor quality, the image black and white and distorted. Warped lines streaked across it and even the audio screeched to a halt, resuming seconds later in a mumbled gargle. A nasally voice came from behind the camera: "Alright, now that you've settled down, it's time for your medicine."

The creature's eyes shot open and it pounced up, its legs bowed, its body low to the ground. Two massive beasts entered the frame. They hesitated, but then grabbed the other one and pinned it to the wall. It released an ear-piercing shrill and Everett nearly dropped the camera.

The beasts threw the creature against the wall once again, and then to the floor, a dent in the wood where it landed. They howled at each other, banging into the walls, until a loud sucking noise could be heard.

"Enough!" the nasally voice yelled from outside the frame. "You know the drill! You've trusted me this long, why pull up short now?"

The man stepped into frame, blocking the beasts from view. He was short, wearing a ratty dress shirt with jeans too big around the waist.

"Who's that?" Everett asked.

"My guess is Simon," Andrew said.

The man dropped a plastic cap to the floor then brought his arm back, plunging something into the creature. When he jerked his arm away there was a glint across the lens, an empty needle pulling out from its spine. The creature went limp. It whimpered then looked up sorrowful, a dog who had wronged its owner.

"I hate to see you like this, I really do," the man said. "I'll give you the permanent antidote soon enough. Your wife too. But for now, I need you…well, I need you under control."

The creature sprang up and shrieked. The beasts retreated behind the camera as the voice came again.

"He's losing patience… Leave the camera, we'll get it later. We can only do this so many times before he—"

A door slammed. The creature paced back and forth, in and out of the frame. After several minutes, it tired. It thumped against the wall and slid down it, clunking onto the floor, its legs splayed out in front, its bony hands covering its face.

Then a different voice. Softer, as if coming from an adjoining room. "Hello? Are you still there?"

There was a thumping noise and then the voice again. "Are you okay? What are they doing to you?"

Andrew leaned into the view-finder. The image was so grainy he could hardly make out the creature. He saw it jerk forward, like a tremor moving through it. The shaking became violent. Its nails regressed and its limbs shortened. Its spine straightened and Andrew could see it was more man now than beast. The creature swiped at its long hair, all matted and twisted and damp. It turned to face the camera, agony behind its brown eyes.

Andrew gasped. "It's Joe!"

"You know him?" Singh asked.

"He's my step-dad," Andrew said, staring in disbelief.

Xavier leaned in, squinting. "Jesus, you're right," he said. "It's him. It's really him!"

"We found him!" Andrew said. He put his arm around Xavier.

"I can't believe he's alive," Xavier said, his words coming out in hurried sobs. "I can't believe it."

"I know, I know."

"And Simon said something about a wife," Xavier said.

"Mom! He and Mom must both still be alive!"

"But why were they here?"

A low-battery warning flashed on the camcorder and within seconds the screen went black.

"What was in that needle?" Everett asked. "He was testing different formulas on them?"

"Looks that way," Andrew said. "Maybe some to make them stronger, others to keep them docile."

"And what about the ones up in the barn?"

"A place to observe them, maybe," Andrew said. "He administers a version of his drug down here and then monitors the effects up there?"

"Alice and Joshua said their parents were among them. How did they end up there?"

"Maybe Simon saw an opportunity to capture them, do tests on them."

"If they were reverting back from the original virus then their minds wouldn't be right," Xavier said. "Would be easy pickings for Simon."

Andrew turned the camcorder over and ejected the tape. "So, the recording was from four days ago."

"And that's if they left immediately after they filmed it," Xavier said.

"The Clearwater detachment said Mackenzie came in last night," Andrew said. "They might only have a day's lead on us."

"Wait, what are you two proposing?" Everett said.

"We track them, like all the others," Andrew said.

"And then?"

"We find and inoculate them. For good this time."

"How?"

"With Ev's blood and Simon's research," Andrew said. "It's all right here. We use it to develop a cure and make sure it's permanent this time."

"But there's a lot of logistics to think through," Everett said. "I'll need to contact my supervisor, request more offi-cers—"

Andrew glared at him and Everett drew back. "I'm just sayin' we could use more help."

"Maybe Maddy's husband?" Xavier offered. "And Wanda mentioned she had a brother not far from here."

Everett squared his hat then turned to Andrew. "It's your call."

Andrew yanked his rifle strap so the gun was tight against his back. "We go now."

He looked to Xavier who nodded and adjusted the knife along his belt. Singh, Powell, and Prasad fumbled with their revolvers.

"And if there's more of those mutated ones?" Everett

asked. "The ones he controls?"

"We still go," Andrew said. "We go and we don't stop 'til we find our parents and that son-of-a-bitch who took them."

Everett squeezed the bridge of his nose and shook his head. "Ah, to hell with it," he said. "These things have taken so much from me already. Let's go get these goddamn monsters."

Andrew nodded then turned away from the domed chamber, from the centrifuge, from the cluttered desk, from the body bags. He turned away from all of it and rushed from the room. He sprinted down the corridors then tore up the stairs, bursting out the front door of the cabin.

On the driveway, he paced one way then the other, examining the tire tracks and boot prints.

"What is it?" Xavier asked.

Andrew shuffled to the edge of the property. He surveyed the trees, the snow-dusted brush and ferns, studied the frozen ground. And just like when he found that boy in the rain, he spotted prints in the dirt and snow, broken branches along a path.

"Got something?" Xavier asked.

"Some took a truck, others broke through the trees," Andrew said.

"Where are they headed?"

Andrew raised his head to the south.

"Hiltsville's that way," Xavier said.

Andrew sniffed at the crisp night air as a wry smile unfurled. He had caught something, a distant scent, the faint whiff of burning metal on the wind.

He turned and took off like a shot, Xavier close behind, just as it had always been.

Acknowledgements

For my first novel, I thanked everyone under the sun so, for this one, I'll keep it short and sweet.

To my editor and publisher, Alanna Rusnak. Who knew writing and publishing books could be so much fun? I'm honoured you dug my submission out from your slush pile those many years ago. It's been a true joy working together since.

I'd like to thank early readers of the manuscript who offered important and critical advice: Jillian Morris, Amber Kuipers, and Jan Ferrigan. Your sharp eyes and honest feedback improved early drafts immensely.

To the Canada Council for the Arts for providing financial support to assist in the completion of this novel. How exciting it is to open an email which begins: 'You've been awarded a literary grant!'

To all the bookshops and libraries who carry my novels and hosted me for book signings and author talks. Few things warm me as much as engaging with community and sharing the love of stories.

To Asia and Will, my talented kids who inspire me daily.

To my exceptional and energy-filled wife, Amy. I learn from you every day. You're my best friend.

And last, to you, the reader. Thanks for supporting Canadian Authors and Canadian Books!

With love and humility,

Ben

Watch for Book 3 in the Feral Winter Series:
ANTIDOTE – coming 2027

About the Author

Benjamin Rempel is a Canadian writer and essayist. Nominated for several literary awards including the Pushcart Prize and the Rising Spirits Writing Award, his work has appeared in *The Toronto Star, Our Canada, Streetlight, Blank Spaces,* among others. Based on the merits of his debut novel, INFECT, he was awarded a 2025 literary grant from the Canada Council for the Arts. A graduate of the University of Waterloo, Rempel lives in Collingwood, Ontario, with his family. He can be found at benjaminrempel.com.